THE SAMPAN WAR

To Jim,
For you
Service

ROBERT E. WAGNER

[signature]

PublishAmerica

Baltimore

First printing

ISBN: 1-4137-1801-9
PUBLISHED BY PUBLISHAMERICA, LLLP
www.publishamerica.com
Baltimore

Printed in the United States of America

DEDICATION

The Sampan War is dedicated to those who served on district and mobile advisory teams during the Vietnamese War. They served in the very vortex of this brutal conflict protecting the country people and fighting side by side with the local militia, the Territorial Forces. Their collective heroism has been lost to history in the depressing fog that surrounds the Viet Nam experience, a war we lost. Many of these brave soldiers never returned. They suffered the highest casualty rate in the advisory effort. The Sampan War is, in part, their story.

And to the Vietnamese Territorial soldiers who fought the war with us and lost everything. At heart I will always remain a Hoa Hao warrior.

And to Charlotte, the love of my life, who makes all that I do possible, from raising our children, maintaining our many homes, enduring numerous separations, tolerating my personality, to the publication of this book. Charlie, you make it happen for me.

TABLE OF CONTENTS

PROLOGUE

It is the year before Tet '68, the huge battle that will dramatically change the course of the Vietnam War. The Viet Cong are preparing for this campaign under the noses of the Americans and their Vietnamese allies.

While the South Vietnamese political machinations ebb and flow, as the national leadership and general officers rotate like random bullets in a game of political roulette, while the U. S. gropes for a policy, the Viet Cong build up a strong, highly motivated force. They plan to overrun Can Tho, Saigon, Hue and other major population centers in a lightning offensive.

The VC needs the Hoa Luu District in the Southern Delta as a staging area for Tet '68. The U Minh Regiment must acquire the canals and the province road, allowing their troops to deploy and move rapidly northeast to attack populated areas. Hoa Luu offers the gateway to success. A few dedicated Americans attached to a district advisory team and the Hoa Hao, fierce Delta fighters, stand in their way.

The Sampan War is a novel based on historical events and personal observation. It represents a blending of experience and fictional story and is one of the few accounts of life in a district advisory team. Commander Re, a brave Hoa Hao warrior, and Major Tho, the District Chief, are real people.

The other characters are fiction, but most of them share personalities and experiences with people I knew at the time of the story. I have taken liberties and rearranged the geography of the Delta region of Vietnam. There is no district named Hoa Luu, but there is a district with similar characteristics. The events around the story are accurate. On occasion, actual professional material is inserted to provide story context. The battle accounts and advisory techniques mostly reflect personal experience. The Hoa Hao are a real people. The "keep it quiet" advisory philosophy did plague the war effort in areas of Vietnam. The views expressed in this book by U. S. advisors were prevalent at the time of the story, particularly the criticism of General Westmoreland's strategy. I am not John Alexander Travis III, the central character, though I served as a District Senior Advisor in the Delta and share a small part of his background. His views regarding the war, however, are mine.

There are heroes and villains on both sides in this book. Some of the characters are Viet Cong. I have attempted to describe them realistically—not as the inscrutable evil personalities portrayed by some works on Vietnam, but flesh and blood people.

The Sampan War tells the story of people on both sides pulled into the vortex of a violent conflict for the Hoa Luu District in the year before Tet '68. In a wider context, the novel describes the central tragedy of the Vietnam War, the dashed hope of thousands of simple people who trusted us.

Many years have passed since the events described in this book occurred. Many American veterans think of their old enemies as friends; opposing commanders compare war stories; wounded veterans on both sides shake hands; and Vietnam is being flooded by American entrepreneurs. Vietnam is not our enemy. The cold war, after all, is over. The war on terrorism now consumes the nation. A reasonable question could be asked, "Why write or bother to read a book like this?" There is no satisfactory answer. Those who served there recall the horror and beauty of that experience. There was a time in their lives when they risked everything and endured untold hardship and danger only to suffer eventual defeat. This memory, perhaps, takes on a special poignancy for those who served on district advisory teams, where the experience with Americans and Vietnamese alike was intensely personal. Vietnam will always be remembered as the war we did not win, but as an author rationalizing this novel, it should also be remembered that we fought there a long time, and through all the vicissitudes of this conflict, great bravery and honor were not uncommon. This war will always be an extremely controversial chapter in our history, and, perhaps, we should confront this controversy so that our understanding can grow. There are lessons here that are relevant to today's war on terrorism. *The Sampan War,* I hope, will provide an understanding of an important part of the war we lost.

PHUC KICH

AMBUSH

****** 1 ******

Sergeant Truong was having a tough time placing his men in position. The sun was sinking behind him. It seemed to hang suspended in space, a defiance of nature. Time had stopped. They could be seen. The ambush site was in the open along the dusty province road elevated five feet above the rice paddies that surrounded them. You could see forever; an expanse of dark green, geometric rice paddies was broken in the distance by swaying, rounding palm trees. The paddies were crisscrossed by dark brown canals. Everything was bright, but there was a feeling of decreasing light and impending tropical darkness. Two hundred meters from their position was the District compound.

He was worried. They were violating their hard military training. He yearned for concealment, for the night that was their ally. His company commander had assured him that the daring of this operation made it safe. Intelligence was nearly perfect. Every Thursday the American Major left the compound at dusk. He traveled alone by jeep and took the single province road northwest to the province capital. For six weeks in succession the American Major had done this.

Sergeant Truong rose once again behind a large coconut palm to check his squad. His face was smooth, his black hair cropped short. He wore black pajamas, the common work uniform of the rice paddies. He looked younger than his twenty years. There was a sense of purpose and movement about Sergeant Truong, however, that belied his age. It spelled warrior. He was the oldest member of the squad, but these young men were not boys.

Six men were in position in the ditch along the side of the road. The firing positions were not good. They would have to rise to shoot, but the fire would not be returned. He wiped the stinging sweat from his eyes. Beyond these positions, at the bend in the road, two men manned the single machinegun in an area of palm trees that rose like a small island above the rice paddies. They

ROBERT E. WAGNER

had excellent enfilade fire along the road length—if the machinegun worked.

They were armed with World War II M-1 Garand rifles, and the machinegun was a much battered, U.S. made, .30 caliber M1919 of the same vintage. All their weapons had been captured over the years from the Army Republic of Vietnam, ARVN, units. His company commander had first resisted letting the squad have the precious SUNG DAI LIEN (machinegun), but Truong had prevailed. The American Major was a worthy task for the ancient weapon. Truong had even convinced his commander to allow some practice with scarce ammunition. The machinegun was key to his plans.

The squad belonged to the Hoa Luu District Battalion. Viet Cong, the Americans called them, a title that would have amazed Sergeant Truong's men. They were Viet Minh, an organization that had earned battle honors against the French, the Japanese, the French again, the Saigon based Government of Vietnam, and finally against the Americans. They had always been Viet Minh and were proud of their military heritage. They understood little about Communist philosophy. They understood everything about years of fighting against colonial powers that would not let the Vietnamese control their own destiny and country. Ho Chi Minh, General Giapp and others were not, to them, obscure personalities, but real life heroes who would lead their country to victory. These very young men fervently believed all this. They also hoped this operation would provide advancement opportunities within their battalion, perhaps even a transfer to their parent unit, the elite U Minh Regiment, which controlled all Viet Minh forces in the southern Delta.

They had moved into the area the night before, traveling by two motorized sampans from their base area thirty-five kilometers southwest of the District compound. The engines propelling these sampans had been provided by the United States Agency for International Development, USAID, via guerrilla agents in the District capital. A good reliable engine, the Johnson outboard, gave them great mobility. Each engine was decorated with the crossed flags of the United States and the Republic of Vietnam. The sampans were hidden two kilometers south of the ambush site along a mangroved tributary to a large canal and guarded by Sergeant Truong's remaining two men.

The escape plan was to exploit the confusion of the ambush and a small diversionary mortar bombardment fired by the Hoa Luu Battalion's weapons company on the District compound. Before the enemy could react, the squad should be cruising down the canal by sampan, far from the ambush site.

Sergeant Truong surveyed the compound through a pair of shattered U.S. 7x50 binoculars. Only the left lens was clear; the other was cracked and full of water. No activity. The compound looked deserted. The sun, a big red ball, was slowly being eclipsed behind a horizon of distant palm trees. A light wind rose, cooling his flushed face. Weakening light ricocheted off the rice paddies down the road toward the District compound. The American Major would have the sun on his face. It was quiet, hushed; everything waited for the night and the end of another sultry day in the southern delta region of Vietnam. Children laughed in the distance.

There was movement in the compound a quarter of a mile away. They heard grating American voices. Suddenly a green jeep crossed the small bridge coming from the compound and turned left. The machinegunner whispered to his leader. Truong violently gestured silence. The jeep accelerated. Truong raised his hand to touch the gunner, which was the signal to fire. "Be calm, calm!" he shouted inwardly. His chest was exploding. Fire discipline was a key element of his tactical training. The time and place to fire were the responsibility of the leader. He must lead and accomplish the mission. His raised hand trembled.

He touched the gunner. There was a loud metallic click. Misfire! The gunner struggled with the charging handle of the old machinegun. Then the jeep came to a violent stop, skidding sideways on the slippery road surface. It disappeared in a cloud of dust. Strange music came from the jeep. Seconds before the misfire, the American Major had been tuning his Japanese radio that was perched on the right seat. The tuner had slipped off Armed Forces Network. Suddenly, Barbra Streisand singing "What's It All About, Alfie?" plaintively interrupted the sunset quiet. The Major looked quickly up and was blinded by the sun. He jammed on the brakes, halted, and fished a pair of aviator sunglasses from his breast pocket. He briefly looked to his right and left, placed the jeep back in gear and moved down the road.

Spurts of dust erupted in front of the jeep; it was the Major's last look at the world. The fourth round disintegrated the windshield, shattered the right lens of the aviator sunglasses, squashed his eye and exploded the back of his head in a pink shower of bone and brain fragments. The jeep careened to the right into the ditch. The rest of the squad found the target and opened up; there was a crescendo of fire, whining bullets and metallic thuds. The firing stopped. The radio continued to play. "What's It All About, Alfie?"

PART ONE – HOA LUU

JULY THROUGH NOVEMBER 1966

****** 1 ******

He was dreaming. Her hair smelled like sweet perfume. She squirmed desperately beneath him, but he could feel her legs open. She really wanted it. They all wanted it. She rose up to stop him. He hit her hard on the mouth. Blood. He put his mouth to hers and tasted it, salty and exciting.

Somebody was shaking his shoulder. He came out of the dream like surfacing from a pool of warm oil. Master Sergeant Luke Hartwell, Hoa Luu District Team Sergeant, was awakened by Specialist 4th Class Billy Turner, the District radio telephone operator.

The Sergeant did not feel well and was still slightly drunk. His temples hammered, sweat poured off his body, and his mouth tasted like stagnant rice paddy water.

"Sarge, get up. Province wants you on the radio."

"God damn it, Billy, I've told you a million times, Province doesn't mean shit to me. Who at Province wants me? Who are you talking to?"

Billy Turner was not to be deterred. "I think it's Major Dugan, the Province S-3, something about a replacement for Major Cottril."

This fired the Sergeant out of his bunk like a shot. Cottril had been dead for two weeks. His replacement? Another fucked up field grade officer, probably a non-combat type like Cottril. He strode to the radio set up on a field table in a corner of the team hut and grabbed the handset. "PAPA BRAVO, THIS IS DELTA ALPHA FIVE, OVER." No answer. He turned the radio squelch switch to the "off" position to increase the range; there was a loud rushing sound. He repeated the call. This time, a response.

"THIS IS PAPA THREE. YOUR NEW SIX WILL ARRIVE AT 0900 HOURS BY PROVINCE CHOPPER. MAKE SURE YOU MARK THE LIMA ZULU. THE LAST TIME WE ALMOST LANDED IN A MINEFIELD. OVER."

"ROGER, OVER."

"NEGATIVE FURTHER—OUT."

The Sergeant glanced at his watch, 0737 hours. Nothing much to do. There were no operations today. He said nothing to the team. Turner would tell them about their new leader. Sergeant Minh, the team interpreter, would give the briefing. He walked outside the hut to a small shower stall to wash

17

off the beer smell. The new SIX (commander) might not approve of his affection for Ba Moui Ba, Vietnamese beer, which he had enjoyed liberally since they took Cottril away in a body bag. The shower consisted of a 55 gallon drum mounted on a wooden scaffold. A chain was pulled and the bather was doused with canal water. After a good soaping, the Sergeant felt clean.

Master Sergeant Luke Hartwell was from Tennessee. He spoke with a drawling Southern accent and often slurred his words to the point that he was difficult to understand. The drawl and a lanky, loose appearance concealed a violent temper and belied a very different personality. Hartwell had been in charge of the District Team for the past two weeks.

0900 hours. Hartwell stood on the very same road where Cottril had been killed. Turner stood beside him with the PRC-25 radio to talk the chopper down. No landing in a mine-field this time. The Sergeant had elected to direct the chopper down right on the province road.

WHOP! WHOP! WHOP! The sound gradually grew louder. Children crowded the roadway to see the great show of a landing helicopter. Hartwell and Turner picked up a black spot in the sky flying southeast above the province road toward the compound. The helicopter maintained a comfortable fifteen hundred feet altitude because that was the burn out point for enemy tracer fire and this was Indian country.

A disembodied voice came over the radio. "DELTA ALPHA BRAVO, THIS IS PAPA HOTEL ONE, HAVE A VISUAL ON THE COMPOUND, REQUEST SMOKE."

Hartwell grabbed the handset from Turner. "THIS IS DELTA ALPHA FIVE. SET DOWN ON THE ROAD, SMOKE IS YELLOW." He threw the smoke grenade to the side of the road.

Turner was having a hard time pushing the kids off the road. They were yelling, "OK Sa-lem, OK Number One."

"The hell with them," yelled Hartwell. He stood in the middle of the road with both arms raised.

"DELTA ALPHA FIVE, I RECOGNIZE YELLOW SMOKE." With that transmission the helicopter plummeted from the sky. The pilot was anxious to avoid the hostile airspace between fifteen hundred feet and ground zero. The air crew was blinded by billowing dust sucked up by the main rotor blade. The pilot, an experienced Delta hand, pressed down evenly on the collective and set the machine down fast. He maintained ground reference with the line of trees to his left, above the dust. The helicopter landed with a bump on the skids.

At the last minute Hartwell and Turner turned away from the landing. They didn't face the aircraft until the rotor pitch had changed, settling the dust. The helicopter continued to tick over. The pilot wasn't about to shut down here where that Major had been zapped two weeks ago.

Sergeant Hartwell approached the helicopter's right door. A duffel bag flew out and landed on the road followed by a rucksack. Then a lithe, athletic figure dressed in faded jungle fatigues and carrying an M-2 carbine leaped onto the roadbed. Sergeant Hartwell immediately noticed the Infantry insignia, the Master Jumper Wings and the Ranger Tab. No Combat Infantry Badge, which indicated no combat experience—still the Sergeant quickly reflected, this man was combat arms, no pussy.

"I'm your new District Senior Advisor, Sergeant Hartwell," said a baritone voice with a slight Southern accent. The Sergeant looked over the new Major: six feet tall, ramrod straight, about 180 pounds, corded arm muscles, black hair, and dark blue eyes. *A fucking aristocrat*, Hartwell thought.

Major John Alexander Travis III had arrived in Hoa Luu District. He was 30 years old and from Norfolk, Virginia, a member of an old family. He had attended the Virginia Military Institute where generations of his family had graduated. Korea had been his last duty tour where he had spent one year near the Demilitarized Zone as a company commander and a battalion training officer. He had recently been promoted to Major ahead of his contemporaries, a member of the new breed the Army was sending to district teams to boost the advisory effort.

Major John Alexander Travis III subscribed to mid-nineteenth century values. He believed in his heritage and destiny. He knew that his ancestors, including many dead Confederate officers, were looking down at him with the expectation that he would conduct himself in this combat situation with the gallantry and honor demanded of a Virginian and a VMI graduate. He was convinced that these qualities and a strong belief in Episcopal Christianity would pull him through. He would do his duty or die on the field of honor. All of this had yet to be tested.

Suddenly, with a roar of rotors, the helicopter unceremoniously lifted off. The pilot said to his crew, "We're getting out of Dodge." Travis, Hartwell, Turner and numerous cowering Vietnamese kids were smothered in choking dust on the province road.

Travis slapped the dust from his duffel bag and rucksack and hefted them to his shoulders. He looked at Hartwell and Turner who rapidly looked the other way. Neither had offered to help him with his gear or show the way to the District compound.

"Lead on, Sergeant Hartwell."

Hartwell led the way into the District compound. They left the road and crossed a small wooden bridge barely strong enough to hold a jeep. Travis paused on top of the bridge. He could see most of the District compound. A parade square of packed earth in front of a large yellow stucco building with "QUAN HOA LUU" printed in peeling black paint on the front wall faced him. A red and yellow Vietnamese flag hung limply from a flagpole in the middle of the square. On his left was a long building constructed of corrugated aluminum which glinted in the sun. Beyond this building and the mud fortifications of the compound was the village of Hoa Luu, not much more than jammed together thatched structures spread out along the Hoa Luu Canal, the main waterway in the area. On his right, paradoxically, was another compound with its own parade square, headquarters building and fortifications. Above the headquarters building was a bright sign printed neatly in black and yellow paint. It read "DAI DOI 122" (the 122 Company); below that was "The Delta Tigers" in English and under the printing, a good likeness of a tiger's head.

There was little activity. Two military personnel— they looked like officers—were talking in front of the District Headquarters. A woman dressed in black pajamas was hanging up laundry at the near end of the corrugated building. Two armed soldiers guarded the gate of the Delta Tigers' compound.

Travis said nothing, but his practiced military eye noticed that the mud walls surrounding the District compound were eroding, and many of the firing positions had no overhead cover and were filled with water. The fort within the fort, however, appeared immaculate, with firmly constructed walls, overhead cover for fire positions, a well painted sign, and a military looking guard detail.

They walked diagonally left across the parade square. Travis noticed that the walls of the large yellow building were crisscrossed with small white patches, battle scars from past attacks. Hartwell led him to the gap between the corrugated building and the District Headquarters. As he walked between the buildings, he saw a green rectangular hut with a screened opening between the plywood walls and the corrugated metal roof. Sandbags lined the walls at waist level. Above the sandbags the walls were perforated with many black holes as if someone had haphazardly fired a shotgun at the hut. At the left end of the hut, covered with decomposing sandbags, was the team bunker which abutted the flank mud wall of the District compound. Beyond the wall huddled the family structures of Hoa Luu Town. *Dangerous*, Travis thought.

"Your new home, Major," Sergeant Hartwell drawled. They waded through the debris of broken sandbags and entered the hut through the small opening between the bunker and the hut. It was divided into two areas: a sleeping area of bunks covered with mosquito netting and an open area which tripled as a common room, kitchen and operations center. An arms rack loaded with a variety of weapons separated these areas. The hut had no electricity. There was a kerosene cooking stove and a butane refrigerator. Gas lanterns were spaced throughout the hut. A slight smell of rotten meat permeated the air.

The five man team gathered in the middle of the common room. They looked at Travis. Nobody spoke.

Travis waited for a few seconds then broke the silence. "I'm Travis, your new DSA. I want to meet you guys."

He smiled openly but his blue eyes remained serious. He thrust out his hand to a stocky, dark-haired man with a carefully trimmed black mustache who looked at him steadily.

"Welcome, Major," a firm handclasp, "I'm Sergeant Hector Gonzales, your BAC-SI, your medic." Gonzales was a Staff Sergeant, a career medic, from El Paso, Texas. His accent was part Texan, part Mexican. Travis had great confidence in senior Army medics.

"Nothing is more important than medical services for the entire district, Doc. I need a review of the medical situation soon."

Billy Turner was next. He shuffled, looked at his feet, then, with obvious courageous effort, looked straight at Travis. "I'm Billy Turner, radio telephone operator, the RTO. I run your radios." Turner was a large, beefy, twenty-year-old kid from St. Louis, Missouri.

"You're an important man, Billy. That radio is our lifeline."

He looked strong enough to hump the radio on the rice paddies.

A small, slight man, a Vietnamese, moved around Turner. "Sir, I am Sergeant Minh. I am honored to be your interpreter." Minh had a thin face and an intense squinting expression. He spoke English with clipped, educated precision. Sergeant Minh had been a medical student in Saigon. His wife and daughter had been killed two years ago by the Viet Cong. Unable to continue his education or to get a commission, Sergeant Minh had joined the Army to kill the enemy. A fighting job had always eluded him because the army took advantage of his language skills.

"Sergeant Minh, I was damn near a dropout at language school. You're going to have to keep me honest."

Sergeant Hartwell stood aside, viewing these proceedings with a bored expression. Travis sensed tension here, a strange attitude. The senior NCO had ability, if his stripes were any indication, but was reluctant to bring his new leader on board or show him basic hospitality.

Travis said a few introductory words. "I'm not going to give you guys some kind of pep talk. You've been here; I'm a rear echelon puke. I'm sorry about Major Cottril, and I expect you to tell me how he operated. I understand Cottril had his style and I have mine, so there will be some changes. Be flexible.

"I'm going to need some help, and I expect you to give it to me. Get me up to speed ASAP because right now I'm probably pretty dangerous." He grinned at this point, and they all half smiled with him, all except Hartwell. There was a sense of relief in the room.

"There are a few things we need to do. I need a team district briefing at 1300, followed by a security walk through the District compound." He looked at Sergeant Hartwell. "And I need to meet the District Chief and the staff. Sergeant Minh, that's probably your department."

"Yes, Sir."

"Within the next few days I want to tour the entire district. We'll play the exact time for this by ear." He paused, looking hard at each man. "One thing I want you all to understand: I believe in this war. We all must believe in this war. Communism must be stopped. The Vietnamese people need democracy. We, as a team, are not going to just put in our time and go native. We're gonna knock the shit out of the Viet Cong. We're gonna win."

There was an audible sigh from Sergeant Hartwell which Travis, after a brief glance, ignored.

"One other thing: get rid of the rotten meat smell. Where do I bunk?" he asked to no one in particular.

Sergeant Hartwell and Sergeant Minh stood in front of a large acetate covered map of the Hoa Luu District. Next to the map was a chart titled "Briefing Sequence" which indicated the order of the briefing. Both Hartwell and Minh were fidgeting and uncomfortable.

"Major, I don't do no briefing. Major Cottril and Sergeant Minh always

HOA LUU COMPOUND

HOSPITAL

PROVINCE ROAD

CANAL

BRIDGE

PF OUTPOST

500 M

HOA LUU CANAL

SCALE

100 M

0

BREAK IN SCALE

RICE PADDIES

HUTS

FORTIFIED

TREES

©1981 Owen Lock

PARADE GROUND

OFFICES

TIGER COMPOUND

DISTRICT HQ

DISTRICT BUNKER

TEAM HUT

BUNKER

MORTAR PIT

FLYING SHIT HOUSE

QUARTERS

300 M

PF OUTPOST

N

did that," Sergeant Hartwell drawled, his eyes pinned to the floor.

Travis raised his eyebrows. "Sergeant Minh, can you handle the whole briefing?"

"Yes, Sir."

Travis sat down and said, "Let's have it." He looked at Minh. Hartwell slouched in a corner. Minh pulled a small silver pointer from his breast pocket and started in his precise English.

"Sir, the briefing will consist of these parts." He pointed to these on the chart: General Area Orientation, District Description, Enemy Forces, Friendly Forces, and Civilian and Pacification Situation. He paused; Travis nodded.

"Hoa Luu District is part of the Ngoc Hoa Province. It is located in the Southern Delta Region. We are 200 kilometers southwest of Saigon. This district is a major communications center." Minh tapped his pointer for emphasis. "If we do not control this area, the entire defense of the Southern Delta could be jeopardized. Look at the major enemy base areas. Binh Xuyan Province to the south, the U Minh Forest, a heavily mangroved area, to the west, and the Vinh Cheo Triangle in the southwest part of the district. Enemy forces must use the roads and waterways in this district if they are to stage any offensive operation from these base areas toward the more populated areas of Can Tho and Saigon to the northeast. Hoa Luu District would be the crossroads, the tactical staging area for these operations." Sergeant Minh made this point with something of a flourish by outlining the roads and canals throughout the district, showing their convergence and northeast orientation.

Travis saw this immediately. He interrupted, "Surely the VC are not capable of that kind of operation, to overrun major population areas in the Delta."

Hartwell spoke up, "Major, this is one of Cottril's ideas. He was a Mil..." He almost said Military Intelligence puke. "He and Minh were big brain buddies. They came up with this idea, and I think it's a bunch of crap." Sergeant Minh looked carefully at Travis and continued.

"Sir, there are rumors the Viet Gong are building up strength, preparing for something. I think you will come to believe this. I believe it should provide a framework for our entire advisory effort." Hoa Luu was a major enemy offensive staging area, a part of the 'Minh theory.' Travis filed this for future reference.

"Sir, Hoa Luu District encompasses 1200 square kilometers. The population is approximately 40,000 and is broken down into the typical delta religious divisions: Catholic, Cao Dai, Buddhists and an important other belief." Here Minh paused.

"We have a significant Hoa Hao population. They represent 30% of the population, but occupy the majority of the important military and civil positions."

Travis interrupted, "Hoa Hao." He drew it out like a war cry, Whaaa Haowww. "Never heard of them."

Hartwell drawled from his corner, "You will or..." His voice trailed off.

Minh continued, "The Hoa Hao hate the VC, but there are..." he stumbled "... other things." He hesitated and returned to his briefing. Travis was intensely curious, but let Minh continue. "The people live generally along the major canal areas in close proximity to outpost security. There are ten villages in the district, each with a village government. These are not effective. District keeps an iron hand on the villages. There are only two population centers that could be considered towns, Hoa Luu Town where we sit and Vinh Thanh Town ten kilometers west of here. Both have a population of approximately 5000. They are located at the confluence of the province road and a major canal. Huong Tho, the province capital, is fifteen kilometers west of Vinh Thanh.

"Roads and canals, as I mentioned before, Sir, are key to the delta. The only road that will hold vehicular traffic is the province road which enters the west central boundary, traverses the district east-northeast, and crosses the northeastern boundary. As you can see, our area is crisscrossed with numerous small canals. There are two major water routes which dominate the district. The Vinh Thanh Canal, which bisects the western part of the district southwest to northeast, and the Hoa Luu Canal, which moves in the same direction in the eastern part of the district. Again, the town of Vinh Thanh sits at the confluence of the Vinh Thanh Canal and province road, and we in Hoa Luu sit at the confluence of the Hoa Luu Canal and the province road. You will notice that these lines of communications are all oriented northeast towards major population centers and are easily accessible from major Viet Cong base areas." Sergeant Minh again emphasized the 'Minh theory.' Travis quickly nodded. This briefing had his attention. He was sitting on the edge of his chair taking notes in a spiral notebook.

"Sir, the enemy. I will not cover the overall VC organization under the Central Office South Vietnam (COSVN), which you know. All enemy forces in the Southern Delta are under the command of the U Minh Regiment, which is based in the U Minh Forest. This organization is the umbrella for all enemy activities and is almost division size. I emphasize all enemy organizations: the local guerrillas, the agents, the Viet Cong village government, the district battalions, and, of course, the organic regimental fighting battalions. Nobody knows for certain how many battalions are organic to the U Minh Regiment, but at least two, the 309th and the 310th, often operate in Hoa Luu. These battalions operate at approximately three hundred rifle strength in the field. Regimental heavy weapon capability is limited, though there are reports they are building up with North Vietnamese support. They have many 81mm mortars. Most small arms are World War II vintage.

"In the district there are approximately 300 local guerillas organized into platoon groups. Many of them are armed with old German Mausers. They operate generally along the periphery of population areas, and most are part-time formers. Their training level is poor, often the Mausers misfire. These guerillas operate very loosely under the VC village governments, which also control numerous agents. Eight VC villages are in Hoa Luu. We have no clear idea of the boundaries, and the village headquarters are not fixed. These elements—the village government, the agents, and the guerillas—are named collectively the Viet Cong infrastructure, the VCI.

"The major Viet Cong base area is in the southwest part of the district, an area named the Vinh Cheo Triangle." Sergeant Minh gestured to the map. "Here they occupy areas outside of the pacified zone but astride both the Vinh Thanh and Hoa Luu Canals, which gives the enemy ready access to our pacified areas.

"Vinh Cheo is the home of the Hoa Luu District Battalion which controls all enemy forces, to include the VCI, in the district. The battalion comes directly under the control of the U Minh Regiment. You might say the Hoa Luu Battalion performs the same functions at district as the U Minh Regiment performs in the entire Southern Delta region. The Hoa Luu Battalion is a complicated organization. The headquarters is divided into two sections: military and political. There are three rifle companies of about a hundred and fifty rifle strength each, a heavy weapons company, mostly 81mm mortars, and a large political action section to control the Viet Cong Infrastructure. The companies normally operate separately all over the district, often in conjunction with the U Minh Regiment."

"That's a confusing set up," Travis observed. "How in the hell do they make it work?"

"It works," Hartwell observed. "That's how Cottril got wasted."

Minh replied, "Here is an example. The VCI collect intelligence. They spot a target in the pacified area and pass this information back to the Hoa Luu District Battalion. The Battalion either disapproves the concept or asks the U Minh Regiment for permission to execute. In this case let's say the target is large, a company sized outpost. The VCI have observed weak security and reported this vulnerability to the Hoa Luu District Battalion. The Hoa Luu District Battalion checks with the U Minh Regiment and secures permission and the services of the U Minh's 310th Battalion. The operational forces, consisting of the Viet Cong Infrastructure in the immediate target area, two companies of the Hoa Luu District Battalion, and the 310th Battalion, U Minh Regiment, plan exhaustively. They are employed as a task force under the operational control of the Hoa Luu District Battalion Commander. The assault forces consist of two Hoa Luu companies and the 310th Battalion. The VCI provides the guides and the coordination for these assault forces to hit the objective which is well inside the pacified area. They have an intimate knowledge of the terrain and the local security situation. The task force executes; the intelligence is reliable; the operation is almost perfect. They often succeed. You see here the cooperation of the VCI gathering intelligence and providing the conduit for main forces to hit an objective in the pacified area. The Hoa Luu District Battalion acted as a planning and execution catalyst for the entire operation."

"Put another way," interrupts Travis, "you take out the VCI and sever the link between the fighting units and an objective in the pacified area. Or, you jump on the fighting units in the base areas to destroy their combat power to hit population centers."

Minh looked at Travis with growing respect.

"The problem is," Hartwell drawled, "the VCI are like a shadow. I sometimes think all these slopes are Viet Cong." Sergeant Minh visibly stiffened.

"Last year," Minh said, "we conducted a four company operation, all the District Regional Force companies, into the Vinh Cheo. The first day we surprised elements of the Hoa Luu District Battalion and inflicted many casualties. That night the U Minh Regiment reinforced the area with two battalions. There was a fierce battle, and we lost almost one third of our force. Air support, gun ships, and artillery were all requested through Province— and we got nothing. The Province Chief would not approve the support. We have never returned to the Vinh Cheo Triangle since." Sergeant Minh stopped here, bitter, remembering.

"What was wrong with the Province Chief? How could he pass up such an opportunity?" Travis asked.

"All the unit leaders were Hoa Hao. Many of them were killed. The Province Chief would not respond. He was not Hoa Hao."

"Goddamn it!" Travis raised his voice. "Is that the kind of Vietnamese leadership we have to deal with?"

"We now have a new acting Province Chief," Minh replied.

"What happened to the last one?" Travis asked.

Hartwell interjected, "The Goddamn Hoa Hao assassinated him, blew his shit away right in his own fart sack."

Travis was quiet at this. Minh continued the briefing.

"Sir, friendly forces. You know the basic Government of Vietnam (GVN) and the Military Assistance Command Vietnam (MACV) military advisory structures. There are forty-four provinces in Vietnam. They are similar to states in your country. Each province consists of four to six districts similar in organization to US counties, except, of course, American counties do not include armed forces. Each province in Vietnam is counterparted by a large MACV advisory team commanded by a Lieutenant Colonel. The district advisory teams are subordinate to the province teams and are led by majors. The Ngoc Hoa Province team is under command of the 64th ARVN Division Senior Advisor, a full colonel, along with all other province teams in the Division sector. You know the organization of the 64th Division. They seldom operate in this district. They have all the heavy combat assets, however. The V Corps Senior Advisor, a brigadier general, commands all advisory operations to include division and province U.S. advisory teams in the Southern Delta."

Minh paused and fingered his silver pointer. The heat was a growing physical presence in the small hut. Travis's shirt was black with sweat, but he was oblivious to the wet hotness. This briefing wiped out all physical discomfort.

Minh continued, "There are 1,250 Territorial Force soldiers located at 29 outposts in Hoa Luu. You know that the Territorial Forces are divided into two categories: the Popular Forces and the Regional Forces. The PF are rice farmers mostly and part time soldiers with local security duties; the RF are full time soldiers and comprise the mobile forces in the district. The PF are organized into 26 platoons of approximately 30 to 35 men. Each platoon guards an outpost." Minh referred to the map. "The three RF companies are the 122nd here in Hoa Luu, the 125th in Vinh Thanh, the two major towns, and the 123rd, which is positioned 27 kilometers south of here at the apex of

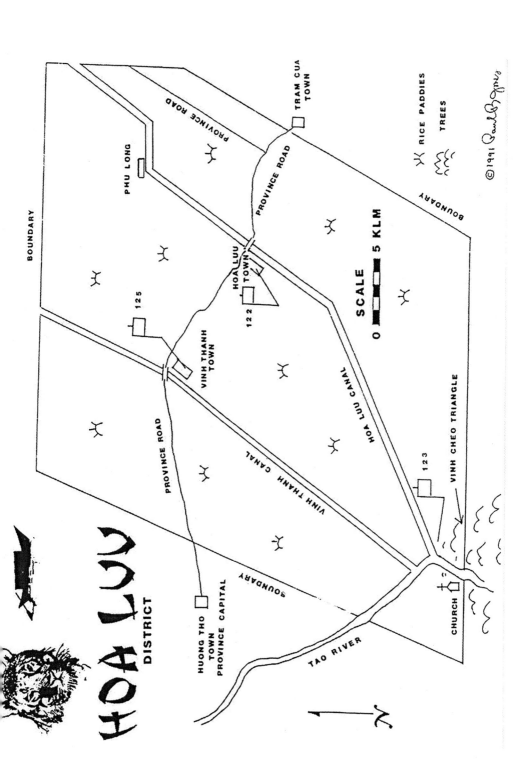

HOA LUU DISTRICT

BOUNDARY

PROVINCE ROAD

PHU LONG

TRAM CUA TOWN

RICE PADDIES

TREES

©1991

BOUNDARY

125

HOA LUU TOWN

122

PROVINCE ROAD

VINH THANH TOWN

SCALE

0   5 KLM

HOA LUU CANAL

VINH CHEO TRIANGLE

PROVINCE ROAD

VINH THANH CANAL

123

HUONG THO TOWN
PROVINCE CAPITAL

BOUNDARY

CHURCH

TAO RIVER

N

the Vinh Cheo Triangle. This company secures the approach between Vinh Cheo and the district capital. Each RF company fields approximately 130 rifles. They are armed with US World War II weapons to include 60mm mortars. There is no artillery garrisoned in the district."

"I thought we had four RF companies." Travis said

"The losses suffered at the Vinh Cheo battle were never replaced. We lost an RF company forever."

"This was never briefed to me at Province. They still carry four RF company flags for Hoa Luu. Why?"

Hartwell shrugged. "The advisors at Province never get out to know the goddamned difference, and the pay for every swinging dick killed at Vinh Cheo goes into the Province Chief's pocket. On the books they're still alive."

Travis blinked at this. "How is their morale? Can they fight?"

Minh answered, "The PF are bad; they are very poorly trained. The RF are good. The Delta Tigers, the 122nd right here, are the best fighters in the Southern Delta. All of the Tigers are Hoa Hao."

"They guard District Headquarters?"

"The Tigers are a mobile force and normally do not conduct garrison security operations for the district."

That explains the compound within the compound, Travis thought.

"Shit," Hartwell said. "Mostly they just guard the chief Hoa Hao around here, Commander Re and Major Tho, the District Chief. The VC will never get those bastards."

Sergeant Minh continued the briefing. He mentioned the rice economy, the Chinese owned rice lands and rice mill, the school system, medical services, and the national police. He addressed the entire fabric of the little world that was Hoa Luu District. Travis was quiet, letting Sergeant Minh finish. He reflected that he had been talking to Sergeant Minh as an officer. This Vietnamese Sergeant was a rare asset. The briefing troubled him. He must know more about the Hoa Hao. The bottom line seemed to be that it was a small team of Americans and the Hoa Hao against the world, with no coordination and no integration of outside support. And what about the 'Minh theory?' Could the VC attack in strength? Something was wrong here. It wasn't... what? The world here wasn't neat and was not susceptible to military school solutions.

That night, lying on his damp cot, Travis remembered the summer of 1954 when he decided to be a soldier. He had just graduated from Granby High School and was a lifeguard at Virginia Beach. The University of Virginia,

William and Mary, and the Virginia Military Institute were pursuing him because of his outstanding academic and athletic record. His father kept pressing him for a choice. "It's decision time, Jack. You have a good high school record behind you and now's the time to select the right school, one which will give you flexibility after graduation."

The father looked hard at his son. The elder Travis wanted to force a decision. He had attended the University of Virginia and had gone on to graduate from the University of Virginia Law School. He had then joined the family law firm and eventually became a senior partner. He had a wish, not a secret to his son, that Jack join the firm after attending U. VA. for undergraduate and law degrees. 'Flexibility' was emphasized during these discussions. Young Travis had not decided what he wanted to do after college. These discussions embarrassed him, and he felt as if he were letting his father down. Though his father was never explicit, his ambitions for his son floated like a cloud between them. "Go to U.VA., get a law degree, and join the family law practice." The son sensed that somehow his father saw this life plan as his son's duty, but he had another calling. Young Travis wanted to march to the sound of the drums.

The military had always fascinated him. His ancestors had fought in the Revolution and the Civil War. An uncle, a VMI graduate and professional soldier, had been killed at Anzio. He had been very close to his uncle as a young boy. Military history consumed him, particularly the works of Douglas Southall Freeman. The Tidewater area in southeast Virginia was steeped in ancient conflicts, including the Battles of Yorktown and the Civil War campaigns staging out of Fort Monroe on the southern tip of the Virginia peninsula towards Richmond.

Courage under fire and personal combat gripped his imagination. One of his favorite books was *The Red Badge of Courage*. He loved words like duty, gallantry, and battle. He was an Eagle Scout and believed that the uniform highlighted a certain elan of scouting activities. "A serious boy," his coaches, teachers, and Scout leaders would say, "with a clear sense of direction. Jack Travis will amount to something." And young Travis believed all this. He believed in his destiny which had suddenly become obscured that summer. Earlier that year he had wanted to apply for an appointment to West Point, but his father had vetoed that idea, again applying the 'flexibility' argument. West Point is too final, with too much obligation after graduation which would delay 'other things.' Law was always implicit in these 'other things.' VMI would give him the flexibility to follow numerous careers but not the preparation U.VA. would give him for law school. U.VA. and William and Mary had the lead for law school preparation. And so young Travis hesitated, violating the credo of decisiveness he had acquired in the twilight of his teenage years.

The day of decision was hot and cloudless with no breeze. Before him were the blazing white beach and the blue-green of the Atlantic glistening at him. The beach was almost deserted, a welcome change from Memorial Day weekend. A few family groups lay about listlessly on beach towels, slowly soaking up the sun through thick layers of coconut oil. Three small girls around ten years old were playing near the water's edge, laughing and kicking water at each other, having a grand time but reluctant to enter the water because they were probably poor swimmers. One had a yellow float and was urging the others to go in deeper. Young Travis noted this and other things; a low shiny swell was breaking over the barnacle-encrusted jetty with a tired swishing noise; the barnacles appearing and disappearing as if the jetty was smiling at him. The torpedo buoy, with line neatly coiled, was planted in front of the lifeguard stand. This was the lifeguard's most important item of equipment. The buoy was hauled through the water and pushed toward the victim who, hopefully, would grab hold and be towed to shore. This rescue technique required strong swimming, but was more effective than a body contact attempt such as the cross chest carry. "Never, never attempt a body contact rescue unless it is a last resort. The result is often a double drowning," the Red Cross told you.

Young Travis, sitting on his lifeguard stand under a faded blue umbrella, was not worried about all this. Lifeguards sit endlessly in the sun, almost reflexively reviewing the beach situation while contemplating other things, particularly if that lifeguard is John Alexander Travis III during the summer of 1954.

He was not only thinking about his college decision, but other subjects, life subjects. He squinted out of his sweat stinging eyes and recalled a recent conversation with some of his football teammates, buddies who did not have three colleges clamoring after them. "Jack, you're too serious; you need to loosen up; you study too hard; if you weren't such a gutsy ballplayer, people would think you're a goddamn creep; you need to make it with girls; you're probably the only cherry on the team; you're just a fucking Eagle Scout" and on and on. He would listen to this advice from his buddies, and they were his buddies, friendships forged on many football fields, double dates, some teenage hell raising and serious beer drinking where Jack was present but not quite participating. Young Travis firmly believed he had a secret; he possessed something they did not, a family heritage and a destiny, a destiny of obscure military glory, a dream now threatened by indecision.

It was hot on the lifeguard stand; sweat ran off him and the wood under the faded umbrella burned his skin. Even his girl Mary agreed with the guys, except when it came to sex and their future as a couple. "Don't take life so seriously. Remember, we have a long time together." Young Travis wasn't so sure. They had known each other forever. Their families were friends, and he crewed on her father's racing yacht. In a few years she would come out, and he had already been selected as her escort. Life stretched out, comfortable family life, marriage at the Episcopal Church, Norfolk Yacht Club parties, babies—God! He was only eighteen. What would this future do to his thing, his destiny? And sex? Last week he had been all over her as his buddies would say, bare tits, lying on top of her on the back seat, her dress up, feeling her hips thrust up to him, but when he reached down "there," she turned off like a light bulb.

"We have a life together, Jack. Wait until we're married." Wait until marriage! An event beyond college, the far future. He would be a cherry forever!

He had told her about his love for the military, for honor and glory. She was appalled. "You would leave this?" "This" meaning the way she measured life, the whole Tidewater scene. He would go on to explain about history, his ancestors in American wars, about his uncle who was killed in World War II, his military heritage, his responsibility.

"That's not a heritage. Your heritage is here with me, working with your father, and all the things we love together." The damn law firm again.

It was middle afternoon. Heat and light ricocheted off the sand. The sun bounced off the water like an intermittent searchlight. A high pitched scream tore through the heavy air, charging the sweltering beach with danger. Young Travis sat bolt upright, scanned the water and saw nothing. Two little girls were running from the water's edge toward the lifeguard stand, pointing to the water. "She went under! She went under!" one yelled over and over. The other was crying hysterically.

Something cold gripped his chest, his heart thudded in his chest. THIS IS A REAL EMERGENCY! The cold feeling increased, almost immobilizing him. "Where is she?" he choked out.

"There! There!" The one who had been yelling pointed to the jetty swishing in the low swells and smiling with barnacled teeth. Young Travis grabbed a pair of battered binoculars and searched the length of the jetty. He saw a small yellow float half way out. *Have to move, must save this girl.* He galvanized himself for action.

The coldness began to evaporate. He blasted off the lifeguard chair, hit the beach at a dead run, scooped up the torpedo buoy, sprinted and entered the water in a hard flat dive. He had practiced this often. His arms flew in a strong crawl motion. He couldn't see the yellow float from the water but had picked out a jetty piling in the vicinity. Fifty yards to the jetty. He had swum about twenty-five against the tide and was beginning to tire. Heart pounding, he remembered his Red Cross instructions. "Don't exhaust yourself before a water rescue. Again, avoid at all costs a double drowning."

He slowed and began the breaststroke. He saw her. The girl was clinging to the slippery boards below the piling. He closed. There was blood in the water. The barnacles were lacerating her arms and hands every time she tried for a hold. In spite of the pain she held on. Wide, blue, terrified eyes were looking at him just above the water line. The water rose. Her head disappeared, arms and hands flailed at the barnacle encrusted boards. The water foamed red around her. The swell receded, her head reappeared, and the left side of her face was a mass of blood.

"Grab hold," he shouted above the water noise and pushed the buoy toward her. She slipped down the boards, her hands leaving streaks of blood. He shoved the board into her chest, but no response. Suddenly she slipped beneath the water. He took a deep breath and dove. With a sharp pain across his chest, he was pulled up short by the torpedo buoy line. He surfaced, frantically threw the line off his body, and dove again. The water was a murky green. He saw nothing. The surf banged him against the jetty; there was a short tearing pain in his right leg. He went deeper; the murky green water turned black. Desperation, a terrible feeling of claustrophobia, he forgot the girl, must get to the surface! He clawed his way up the jetty with bloody hands, broke the surface and gasped for air. He looked wildly around him, then dove again.

Something white loomed up through the green. He grabbed her around the chest and clawed up the jetty with his one free arm. She was inert, dead like in his arms. They broke the surface. He looked for the torpedo buoy, but it had drifted away. Ignoring the pain, he pushed off the jetty toward the shore. Explosively, she became a wildcat in his arms. Turning with amazing strength, she wrapped her bloody arms around his neck. Surprised, he went under, choking salt water. He pushed her away. Abruptly, the fight went out of her. Again he attempted the cross chest carry; he could feel her gasping breathing under his arm. Slowly he started a laborious sidestroke toward the shore.

"Take it easy. It's you and me together; we're a team. We're almost there," he gasped between strokes. Her breathing slowed and incredibly, she answered him with a high but controlled voice. "It's okay." *A gutsy kid,* he thought.

He carried her through the shallow water to the beach. A small crowd had gathered. A tall man came running up to him, tears streaming down his face, yelling, "She's my daughter! She's my daughter!" He laid her down on a beach towel. She half sat up, but he gently put her down, his arm behind her back. The girl looked up at him, half smiled through her bloody face and said again, "I'm okay." Somebody handed young Travis his first aid kit. An ambulance was on the way he was told.

He often thought about the rescue. It was all there: duty, gallantry, action, perhaps similar to battle. That wonderful, brave little girl, he had saved her life! He fought against arrogance, against a swelled head as his father always advised him, but knew he had done well. His long dead uncle at Anzio would have been proud. That day of the rescue John Alexander Travis III knew it would be VMI and the Army.

Later, disoriented, mixing up thoughts and dreams of home and Hoa Luu, he woke up shaking, covered with sweat. His head hit the mosquito netting as he sat up. It was black and moist. The blackness had a tangible quality, like hot steam. A soft snore in the corner. Had he heard something? There was a far off crumping sound, like thunder echoing through the wet tropical night. Something was out there beyond the hut, beyond the District compound. Something different, formless, lurking. Something inscrutable and ultimately terrible. Travis lay back on the wet sheets, a small icicle melting in his chest. He shut his eyes and tried to sleep.

****

Major Travis walked into the District Chief's office, halted and stood at attention before the large desk. A brawny figure was hunched over the desk studying a map. The room was filled with choking cigar smoke. "THIEU TA, TRAN HUU THO DISTRICT CHIEF" was engraved on a brass nameplate positioned on the desk. There were oriental dragons on each side of the letters.

"Sir, Major John Alexander Travis reporting for duty," he boomed in his best VMI voice. There was no answer. The silence grew longer. The District

Chief looked at the map and Travis continued to stand at attention. He had been in Hoa Luu District three weeks and had almost given up seeing the District Chief. The district orientation tour and the district staff briefing had been completed the week before.

Major Tho looked up and stared at him. He had a wide, beefy face with large, intelligent almond eyes.

"Can you get?" He tapped his cigar. "I am out. Major Cottril gave me cigars. Good man, Cottril." He had a deep gravelly voice, guttural but understandable English. He peered through the smoke, his eyes quizzically asking if Travis was a good man, too.

"What is the brand, Sir?" asked Travis, continuing to stand at attention.

"Dutch Master Panatellas," the gravelly voice responded. A wide smile showed gleaming gold capped teeth. "Sit down, Major."

Travis walked up to the desk and offered his hand. "Sir, I'm Major Travis and I'm proud to serve with you in this war that's so important to both our countries." He had rehearsed this greeting.

Major Tho raised his head quickly at this, surprised. He stood, or rather lurched, up. His barrel chest strained the buttons of his fatigue shirt. His arms were massive. Even though he stood five inches below Travis, he emanated a sense of strength, power. Travis thought, *brutality.* Travis's hand was grasped in an iron grip, and then he was propelled downward into the chair beside the desk. Major Tho was in his mid-forties but still physical.

Unlike his other Vietnamese briefings, Travis was offered no tea. Major Tho looked at him intently, squinting slightly. "Well, Major Travis, what you think? You been here long time—tell me."

Travis thought rapidly. He half suspected the only reason he was here was to correct Tho's cigar problem. He knew the first encounter was important. He also knew that Tho had a reputation for riding roughshod over his American advisors. Travis looked at the District Chief and pulled a spiral notebook from his breast pocket. On this first visit, he had decided to take a hard line, to make a good, tough first impression.

"I think we have a very complex situation here, Sir. There is much to learn. I do have some early observations." He looked at his notebook and thought back to Sergeant Minh's briefing. "Hoa Luu is a major crossroads in the Southern Delta. Do you think the district could become an enemy staging area if the Viet Cong attacked in force, particularly to the northeast towards Saigon and Can Tho?"

Major Tho's voice was even more gravelly. "I do not know." Silence. No explanations.

"Sir," changing the subject, "I visited all the significant outposts in the district and spent some time with the units garrisoned along the Vinh Thanh and Hoa Luu canals. Some of these PF platoons are in bad shape. Morale appears low; their families are extremely poor; there are health problems; the mud fortifications are falling apart; weapons are dirty; positions are full of water." Travis reported a litany of problems he had observed.

Major Tho listened impassively. "What about Regional Forces companies?"

"I was very impressed with these units. They appear to be tough fighting formations."

"They are Hoa Hao. The PF," he snapped his fingers, "they are like chaff of rice. The Regional Forces will fight. They are warriors."

"Sir, the PF are our soldiers, too. They secure many critical areas in the district. We must take better care of these units."

This was interrupted with the wave of a meaty hand. "They my men—not yours. Remember, I command." There was a note of menace in the deep voice.

Travis shrank somewhat. The hard line approach was not working. He was silent, trying to think of a friendlier subject.

Then Major Tho winked, actually winked, at Travis and smiled slightly. "How were staff briefings?" he asked. The question sent Travis back to his notebook.

Travis turned to the intelligence briefing notes, the S-2. At this point he decided to be more indirect. "Sir, the S-2 appears competent. He did not know much about the activities of the U Minh Regiment."

"Tell me activities of U Minh. Share with me this secret."

"No great secret, Sir. You know the importance of the Regiment. They control all enemy activities in the Southern Delta. There are rumors they are rebuilding their forces throughout the Delta, recruiting, intensive training, reequipping with new weapons coming down from the North to include the AK47 assault rifle, new mortars and anti-tank weapons."

Tho shook his head. "My S-2 not worry about U Minh. Province, Division and Corps worry about U Minh. We worry about the Hoa Luu District Battalion, local guerrillas, enemy agents, enemy village chiefs, what you call Viet Cong Infrastructure, the VCI. They are enemy."

"Sir, the U Minh Regiment coordinates all activities in this area. Information dealing with their capability, their equipment, and their future operations is fundamental to our security."

"Major Travis, you speak like book, like school boy. You learn about Vietnam in days. You are expert. Do not talk to me about U Minh. I fought with them and against them. Anything else on, how you say it—intelligence?"

Travis winced and then reflected on Captain Giao, the S-2, a small, stooped, reptilian man with a heavily pockmarked face. Sergeant Minh had informed him that he had tortured many VC. He was a killer. Travis decided not to share these views with Major Tho.

"How about Operations—the S-3?" Major Tho prompted.

Travis thought the S-3, Captain Luom, was a clean-cut, straightforward soldier. He was a graduate of the Vietnamese Military Academy, their version of West Point. He appeared to be professional. Luom shared Travis's concern about the sorry state of the PF units. Travis did not touch on this subject again, but voiced some other problems.

"I don't believe we conduct enough operations in the district. We have to enter some of these base areas, particularly in the southwest part of the district in the Vinh Cheo Triangle. Also, there are no night patrols even here at the District compound. We need patrol training. The enemy could attack undetected." Major Cottril's death often came to mind when Travis thought about security—death in the afternoon within sight of the District compound.

Major Tho nodded and asked, "Have you met Commander Re?" Re was the commanding officer of the 122nd RF Company garrisoned in the District. He also appeared to have special status among the Hoa Hao. Sergeant Minh had told him Re had studied in France.

"Not yet, Sir, though I have visited the Delta Tigers, a great outfit."

"Commander Re very important, a warrior. You must talk to him."

Major Tho was obviously growing restless. He started glancing at his map again. They had yet to talk about the civil aspect of Hoa Luu District, particularly civilian medical support which concerned Travis. The district medical section was almost non-existent. They had been short a medical officer for over a year. Sergeant Gonzales wanted him to bring this up. That afternoon the team was going up the canal on a medical support trip. Travis decided not to push any more problems and lapsed into silence.

The District Chief stubbed his cigar out like it was an enemy. Smoke and ashes puffed around the desk in a minor explosion. He stood up. "Good luck, Major Travis. I enjoy conversation. Don't forget cigars." He opened his desk drawer and handed Travis an empty cigar box. "And," he looked hard at

Travis, winked again and flashed his gold capped teeth, "see Commander Re."

Travis jumped to attention, saluted, and exited the office into the blinding, mid-afternoon sunlight.

* * * * * * * * * * * *

The sampan moved through the chocolate brown water of the Hoa Luu canal. The entire team was on board. They moved under swaying coconut palms, alternating with wide open rice paddies. The team passed through hamlet areas, clusters of small wooden structures thatched with paddy grass and built on stilts over the canal. People waved. Many were fishing, throwing circular fish nets gracefully onto the surface of the water. The children shouted, "Okay Salem" and "Okay Number One" from the bank. A pacified area.

The sampan was the cavalry mount of the Delta. This graceful craft powered by a US supplied Johnson outboard could cruise at 15 mph and provided both sides with tremendous mobility. The VC exploited this capability far more than the Government forces. They would attack an objective 50 kilometers from their base area one night, redeploy and hit another target 35 kilometers from the original objective two nights later. The Government never designed a system to match this capability.

The team was going to the northern edge of Vi Loi Village six kilometers northeast of Hoa Luu District town to conduct a Medical Care Assistance Program visit, termed MEDCAP by the team. Beyond this northern village boundary was Indian country.

Their lives were measured out in these MEDCAPs, Travis thought. A MEDCAP consisted of a village sick call. Sergeant Gonzales would set up a small aid station, and the Vietnamese would queue up for treatment. The treatment was very basic, and Gonzales seldom administered anything more sophisticated than aspirin, APCs and various salves for the many tropical baby rashes. It generated tremendous good will from the people, however. If someone was seriously ill, and this was often the case, Gonzales would report the patient and the particulars to the District Medical Detachment, usually without results. Frequently, they would return from a MEDCAP with a mother and very sick baby and transport them to the province hospital in Huong Tho.

The sampan motored smoothly up the middle of the canal. Travis thought not for the first time, that Hoa Luu District was beautiful. Colors were deeper here, a vivid Technicolor land.

The team landed at a small wharf and was immediately inundated with shouting children. They pulled at trousers, reached into pockets. The team had brought rock candy, which they threw over the heads of the children to disperse them.

Sergeant Minh forged ahead to a small open marketplace. He explained to the village elders about the MEDCAP. One spry, toothless, wizened man moved to the middle of the marketplace. "BAG SI, BAG SI, medic," he shouted. People came running, mostly young mothers with babies and a few old people, too. The old man, with visible self-importance, put them all in line.

Sergeant Gonzales went to work. Travis watched. The medic was very compassionate in his treatment. He cared. Sergeant Minh handled the translation between patient and "doctor." There was closeness between these two men. Sergeant Gonzales did not hesitate to take babies into his arms, or to salve the most virulent tropical rashes. Sergeant Minh looked on approvingly.

The old man motioned the rest of the team into a small hut. It was very dark, but once his eyes were accustomed to the dimness, Travis noticed the Buddhist altar to the family ancestors on the far wall. They sat around a small, scarred table. A toothless woman, appearing even older than the man, served tea in tiny porcelain cups which the Americans had trouble holding in their large hands. Talking was difficult, but clearly the old couple was enjoying this encounter. They kept bowing to Travis, the Co Van My, the American Advisor of Hoa Luu District.

After a time of silent tea sipping and bowing, Hartwell put his cup down on the table with a bang. He looked at Billy Turner. "Billy, go outside and have a commo check with province. I hope this time you remembered your two niner two antenna." He referred to a longer antenna which gave the radio greater range.

"Okay, Sarge." Billy moved out.

Travis looked at Hartwell. "Look, Major, I don't want to get wasted out here while Gonzales is feeding fucking pills to these slopes. They ain't worth it."

Travis looked quickly at the Vietnamese couple. They continued to smile.

"These dinks don't understand a goddamn thing we're saying," Hartwell said.

"In that case," Travis smiled, but his eyes flashed, "I want you to understand some rules. The words slopes and dinks will never be used by this team. Part of our job here is to make life better for these people."

"Shit, Major." Hartwell stood, bowed with exaggerated formality to the Vietnamese couple and stalked from the hut. The Vietnamese returned the bow.

Hartwell walked through the crowd of mothers, babies, and old people to the canal's edge. He stared hard at the flowing brown water as if to pierce the surface and escape to another world where wimps and especially dinks were not allowed. He felt a growing anger, a desire to kill someone. "Must get control." he visibly shook himself. A calming memory came to him, the battle of Barnsley.

Hartwell had entered the Army through the West Virginia National Guard in the early fifties. He had escaped from the cold hollows in West Virginia and a scratched out life consisting of an alcoholic mother, who often could barely recognize him, a small army of grimy, fat brothers and sisters, all sired by different men, and a vicious stepfather whose favorite sport was to beat his pugnacious stepson near to death at every opportunity.

He took easily to Army life, the drill, the structured routine, marksmanship, inspections, field exercises, but he remained aloof to his fellow soldiers. Often on exercises he demonstrated a cool leadership over his squad members, a leadership which was devoid of camaraderie and affection. He simply enjoyed control over other men.

Early in his first enlistment, his unit had been mobilized by the Governor to quell a coal miner's labor dispute. The miners had taken over Barnsley, a small town deep in a wooded hollow. The mayor, the police force, even the volunteer fire department had ceased to function. The miners ruled the small community and had closed the local mines. They demonstrated in the small town square, demanding higher wages and health benefits. Hartwell remembered the briefing his Platoon Sergeant had given him.

"These goddamn miners are crazy! They're boozed up and armed. Our job is to clean them out!" Here the sergeant paused and looked at some notes on a soiled white paper. He continued, looking them all in the eye, "We will carry ammunition, but under no circumstances will we shoot to kill unless our lives are endangered." He referred to his notes again. "The police call this deadly force or some fucking thing. Anyway, we can't shoot at them, but we can shoot over their heads to scare the shit out of these stupid hillbillies."

Hartwell had to grimace at this. They were all hillbillies. The sergeant went on to cover the details of movement and deployment in the town.

It took three hours to get to Barnsley. It was springtime in West Virginia, and the low tired mountains were colored light green, sprinkled with the bright colors of redbud and dogwood. The scenery was lost to the other soldiers, who were nervous. What was waiting for them in Barnsley? They tinkered with their weapons and equipment. Not Hartwell. He looked at the spring beauty with barely controlled anticipation. It heightened his awareness of the situation. They were going to hunt—men. The spring colors intensified the experience.

The convoy stopped outside the town. The soldiers dismounted and were formed up. After much grumbling, they were allowed to break formation and go into the woods and take a leak. Later they reformed and were ordered to fix bayonets, lock and load, and place their weapons on safe. Instructions about firing over the miners' heads were repeated. The soldiers fumbled with their weapons. Hartwell caressed his M-1 rifle almost lovingly. They marched down the road into Barnsley to the town square. The town center shone with civic pride and glory of spring. Tall, nearly green, elms surrounded the square, which was edged with tulips and daffodils in different colors. A pure white church tower rose from the other side of the square, glistening in the spring sun. There was a scent of damp earth in the air.

The miners, men dressed in denim coveralls, let out a ragged shout when they saw the soldiers coming. They formed a circle around the square, shoulder to shoulder. The soldiers took up positions across the street from the miners. Each man held his weapon in the high port position. A nervous Captain strode to the middle of the street and ordered the miners to disperse with a high shaky voice. Hartwell paid no attention to him. His eyes were riveted on a balding, heavyset man twenty-five yards in front of him.

Suddenly a shot rang out from somewhere behind the miners. The Captain ran back to the soldiers' side of the road. "Prepare to fire a volley over their heads," he screamed. Hartwell took up a perfect standing position. His trigger finger flipped off the safety. The stock of the M-1 rifle felt warm to his cheek. A sensual excitement came over him. There was a passion to this. The weapon lowered to the middle of the heavy man's broad forehead just above the eyes. Holding his breath, he gently applied pressure to his trigger finger. He did not hear or feel the weapon fire. The broad forehead in his sight picture simply disappeared.

Pandemonium! All the soldiers were shooting in the air. The miners held their ranks for a few minutes then broke and ran. The soldiers were ordered to advance at high port. Hartwell stepped over the man he had shot. He lay face down in a carefully tended bed of tulips. No wound was visual but there was a growing pool of bright red blood around his head. It mingled beautifully with the colors of the tulips.

The memory stopped. Hartwell returned to Hoa Luu. He smiled as he looked at the flowing brown canal. He was content.

The MEDCAP was completed. "Two hundred people," Sergeant Gonzales reported with pride. A crowd followed them to the wharf. Now, young men who had returned from the fields were in the group. You did not often see young men in Indian country villages. These men came up and shook Travis' hand. They embraced Gonzales, who appeared to be a kind of saint along the Hoa Luu canal. The old man gave them each a coconut with the top cut off. Hartwell fired up the engine, opened the throttle to medium speed, and they moved to the middle of the canal.

The sun shone almost parallel to the paddies, throwing dark shadows mixed with light beams across the cut of the canal. A breeze rippled the surface of the water. Travis took a swig of the sweet coconut milk. *My God, this is like Lord Jim,* he thought. A kind of Eden. He felt content, almost lethargic. He dozed in the moving sampan.

There was a high zipping sound, like letting air out of a tire, followed by a CRACK! Another. This time, the water erupted in a small geyser fifteen feet in front of the sampan. Hartwell went full throttle and violently turned the sampan 90 degrees right toward the bank. Travis snapped the safety off his M2 carbine and half stood up. The sampan rocked dangerously and almost capsized. Water came over the gunwales.

"Down, goddamn it!" Hartwell shouted. The men crouched in the sampan like they were protected by bulletproof armor. Hartwell piloted the craft at 15 knots almost right into the bank, swung to the left at the last possible minute and continued up the canal. Travis experienced an urge to jump into the water, to hide, to have the canal protect him.

"Give me the handset!" Travis yelled to Turner. His hands were shaking so much he had to hold the handset with both hands.

"PAPA BRAVO: THIS IS DELTA ALPHA SIX." His voice was uneven. No answer. He called again. The rushing sound from the radio remained unbroken. He looked ahead along the canal bank at the tops of the palm trees. Nothing. Hartwell had the engine wide open. It had developed a whining high and low sound. One klick to go before the next hamlet. Travis thought, *If we break down here, we're dead.* He checked his carbine again, making sure he had a round chambered and the clip firmly inserted in the receiver.

Hartwell throttled back the engine. The Johnson resumed an even tempo. "You can't reach Province from here, Major, because of the river bank," he

43

said, very calm. Travis turned to look at Hartwell. The sergeant smiled at him. "That's VC Charlie. I reckon he's paid about five piasters to fire two rounds a month. You got to hug the bank in this situation. Old Charlie did manage to hit the canal; he must be practicing." Hartwell laughed loudly; the American members of the team smiled weakly and looked at each other. Sergeant Minh's face was expressionless.

Travis had that cold feeling in his chest again. He switched off the safety and leaned his carbine against the gunwale. His hands continued to shake, and he held them together hoping nobody would notice.

The light dimmed as the sun sank behind the palm trees. To the west, heavy cumulus clouds towering thousands of feet took on a pinkish hue. The sampan entered the next hamlet. People waved. Smiling children shouted their usual greetings. There was the smell of cooking fish. *A dangerous Eden,* thought Travis.

****** 2 ******

Someone was knocking authoritatively on the rear door of the team hut. It was just dark. The team had spent the day up the Vinh Thanh canal, inspecting outposts with the District Operations Officer, the S-3. They had finished dinner and cleaned up. No one answered the door. This time of day, they had little contact with the Vietnamese. Hartwell was reading a nearly memorized dog eared paperback about the incredible sexual exploits of a World War II paratrooper. Billy Turner, earplugs on, was listening to his small Japanese radio, tapping his feet to some esoteric rock beat only he could hear. Minh was, as always, studying a map of the Southern Delta and making little tick marks with a red grease pencil as he studied the intelligence log. Gonzales was inspecting his medical supplies and meticulously recording his needs in a notebook. Travis was writing a training program to improve what he judged to be the sad state of Popular Forces combat readiness. His judgment had been reinforced by the recent inspection trips. The common room of the hut was lit by kerosene lamps.

The knocking continued, now louder. Sergeant Minh opened the door. Outside stood a soldier of the Delta Tigers, the 122nd RF Company. He wore the bush hat and the green neck scarf that were the special insignia of the Tigers. The soldier strode past Sergeant Minh and entered the hut uninvited. He looked carefully at each team member until he identified Travis.

"Commander Re see you now!" he said in a high, loud voice. He left the hut.

Travis looked at Minh. "It is very unusual," Minh observed. "I've been here for two years, and the Commander has never had a visit with an American at this time."

Travis was elated. He had been trying to see Commander Re for weeks, though he had seen the District Chief on numerous occasions, probably because he had provided him with a new box of Panatellas. Re had remained elusive.

"Sergeant Minh, should you go with me?"

"No, Sir, the Commander speaks excellent English. I suspect he wants a private meeting."

Travis walked across the compound and entered the special Delta Tiger enclosure. A crisp present arms with Ml rifles nearly as tall as they were was executed by two sentries at the entrance. The precision would have done credit to a VMI color guard. An escort led him to a building in the middle of the Tiger compound constructed of white painted cinder blocks and fronted by a large porch.

"Go," his escort grunted. He went up on the porch and lifted his hand to knock on the door. The door opened. John Travis looked straight into the eyes of Commander Re. Both stood six feet tall.

"Come in, Major," he said in a steady, authoritative voice with a slight French accent. Travis' quick eye scoped the room; it was symmetrical, orderly and yet graceful: a Chinese carpet covered the entire floor; the walls were covered by off-white wallpaper; a picture of a brightly colored Delta sunset hung on each wall; rattan easy chairs were positioned in every corner and flanked by black lacquered tables. The room was gently lit by a large brass kerosene lamp suspended from the ceiling. A large circular low table was in the center of the room with a stuffed tiger's head in the middle. The tiger seemed to be staring at Travis.

The Commander motioned him to a chair. Commander Re remained standing. He wore dark gray slacks and a pale blue Philippine barong sport shirt. A white silk ascot was knotted at his throat. His face was strongly featured with a firm jaw and dark, round, almost European eyes. A dark ridged scar ran down his left cheek and pulled down the left corner of his mouth, which gave him a slightly sinister look.

"I thought we should have a short visit this evening. You have impressed Major Tho, the District Chief." Re sat down on one of the rattan chairs and elegantly crossed his legs, revealing black loafers and dark blue socks. "He has been impressed over the last month with your activity, your many—how do you say it?—MEDCAPS and visits to district units. You have much energy and initiative." He smiled, revealing even white teeth. "The people and the soldiers like you. Unlike past advisors, they believe you care. Of course, they love Sergeant Gonzales, the great healer of Hoa Luu. Major Tho appreciates that you go everywhere in the district, by foot, by jeep, and, of course, by sampan, even to the dangerous areas. I am aware of the sniping incident at Vi Loi. Be careful. The District Chief and I also believe in your efforts to upgrade the Popular Forces."

Travis was amazed. He had thought he was going nowhere in Hoa Luu. His experience in the rat line as a freshman at VMI, as well as his military training, had been essential over the last month. You went forward. You did your best.

"Major, you must understand we are not open with Americans. We do not trust Americans. Most of our advisors in the past simply did their time until they left the country. You appear to be different. I am going to tell you something about the Hoa Hao. I agree with you that the Viet Minh are preparing something big, perhaps a major offensive. We will face major security problems in the months ahead, and you must understand my people.

"A simple man named Huynh Thu So founded the Hoa Hao faith in the late 30's. He has been called a faith healer, but he was more than that. He believed that man could improve his life through four precepts: adhere to Buddhism but have deep commitment to living a life of good works on Earth; honor your parents; respect your fellow man; and revere your country. We Hoa Hao depart somewhat from other Buddhists in Vietnam in our belief in the individual, the importance of life on Earth, and our dedication to nationhood."

Here Commander Re paused and looked hard at Travis. Travis was sitting bolt upright, transfixed. The lamplight flickered in the room; the stuffed tiger glared at him. The glare said pay attention. Re continued, "The late 30's was a time of great trouble. We lived under the colonial foot of the French, and the Japanese were threatening all of Southeast Asia. Hoa Hao was a religion which gave the common man individual pride and a belief in Vietnamese nationhood. The Hoa Hao faith spread throughout the Delta. The new faith frightened the French. Looking in the face of Japanese expansionism, the last thing they wanted was a national movement in their most important colony. They jailed So. He later escaped and joined forces with the Viet Minh in their fight against the French and later the Japanese.

"The Viet Minh were uncomfortable with So. The Hoa Hao movement continued to grow, and the Viet Minh did not doctrinally recognize any established religion. But beyond religion, So was a political and military leader. He established a Hoa Hao military and political infrastructure throughout the Delta that threatened the Viet Minh, even though they shared the same military goals. So was murdered by the Viet Minh in 1947, and the Hoa Hao were persecuted.

"For this outrage, we Hoa Hao hate the Viet Minh and will destroy this abomination to our people and our nation if it takes forever." Here Commander Re's voice rose. He leaned forward in his chair, a man of passion and revengeful force. Travis recoiled slightly on the other side of the room.

"We eventually allied ourselves with the Government, an uneasy truce.

The only link which holds us together is our common enemy, the Viet Minh. This link is often close to breaking because we believe the Government is a corrupt, venal organization, dedicated to looting the country for the benefit of its leadership. You can see this, Major Travis, in Ngoc Hoa Province." Jack nodded before he could catch himself. His job was to support the Government.

"Now we both fight the Viet Minh. Hopefully, the Government will purge itself in this war and become the strong national force Vietnam must have. The Hoa Hao must be a part of this government because of our strong moral dedication to individual and nation." He paused, looking at the tiger's head with reverence as if it were a source of spiritual strength.

"Major Travis, this is our creed. We are united in thought to be Buddhists; to be Vietnamese individuals who believe in the worth of life on this Earth; to assist in the construction of an upright nation; and to fight communism and destroy the Viet Minh."

The Commander had finished. He looked at Travis, expecting some response.

Who is this man? he thought. He said lamely, "Commander Re, that was a fascinating talk, but…" He stumbled, unsure how to ask the question. "Sir, I can't ask you any other way. What is your job? Your rank?"

Re laughed. He again became the debonair host. "This will sound typically inscrutable to you. I have no real job, other than direct command of the 122nd RF Company, yet I am involved in all things. The Hoa Hao have no established hierarchy such as pagodas, temples, or priesthood solely dedicated to religious matters. I am…" he reflected. "You would call me a warrior priest. What you must understand is I command all military training and operations here in Hoa Luu. The Regional Force companies work directly for me. The Popular Force platoons work through the S-3, though the important decisions are mine."

"So, you are the military deputy to the District Chief?"

"Deputy?" Re smiled again. "You can call me a deputy, but understand, I am not a soldier. I have no military rank. I am simply 'The Commander'." He said this with dignity. Travis was frowning, perplexed. Hoa Luu violated his sense of military order.

Re stood and rang a bell. A servant entered wearing a white mess jacket over jungle fatigues. He carried a bottle of cognac and two small glasses on a lacquered tray.

"We drink." Re handed a glass to Travis. The Commander proposed the toast. "To brave men and to victory." The two men drank. Travis felt the brandy's warmth, a strange sensation in the tropics.

"In one week the Tigers will go on a short operation. You will be with us." Commander Re smiled. "Good evening, Major Travis."

That night there was a sharp banging explosion! The first 81mm mortar round exploded twenty feet behind the team hut. The second sprayed the left wall with hot metal fragments which splintered the plywood and whizzed through the interior of the hut. A part of the corrugated metal roof blew off the plywood walls with a tearing sound and crashed metallically back.

The team scrambled for the bunker. Travis stood up, fumbling in the arms rack for his carbine. "Mortar attack!" he screamed. "Get to the bunker!" The others were already there.

"Get the District bunker by wire, raise Province on the radio, we need Spooky," Travis shouted, too loud for the closeness of the bunker. Spooky was a converted C-47 transport aircraft packed with mini-guns and phosphorous flares.

Hartwell spoke evenly, calmly, to Province. "PAPA BRAVO: THIS IS DELTA ALPHA FIVE. WE ARE UNDER MORTAR ATTACK. REQUEST SPOOKY."

"THIS IS PAPA BRAVO. CONFIRM MORTAR ATTACK. HOW MANY ROUNDS HAVE YOU RECEIVED? ALL SPOOKIES ARE COMMITTED TONIGHT."

"THIS IS DELTA ALPHA FIVE. MY SIX WANTS SPOOKIES. WE HAVE RECEIVED TWO ROUNDS. OVER."

Province answered, "WAIT. OUT."

Travis stood in a shadowy corner of the bunker, shaking, fighting for control. Billy Turner turned to Travis. "I have the District compound on the field line. The S-3 wants to talk to you, Sir."

Travis grabbed the field phone with both hands.

It was Captain Luom. "Major Travis, everything is quiet in the district. We have received only two rounds in the compound, and the Tigers have reinforced the Popular Forces on the walls. Major Tho believes this is only a harassing attack. We will remain on alert for two hours. Major Tho does not want Spooky at this time, but he wants you to maintain radio contact with Province. Do you have contact?"

"Yes, we will stand by," Travis's cracked voice answered. He struggled to keep his voice even, calm. Take command! "Go back to the hut and get your weapons!" he ordered the team. Hartwell remained with the radio.

"Do you want Spooky or not?" he demanded.

"Tell them our counterparts want to stand by. They think this is a harassing attack." His voice was smoothing out.

"Of course it's a harassing attack. Two fucking rounds!" Hartwell muttered.

Travis listened to Hartwell's return transmission and then walked outside the bunker. It was black, a dark suffocating velvet black, no moon. The stars glimmered closely but without light. Travis felt a stillness, as if something were holding its breath for the next explosion. There was a sense of some primordial existence beyond the tropical night. He felt a growing coldness.

* * * * * * * * * * * *

A graying darkness promised the new day. The 122nd Regional Force Company moved liked tigers. Only the occasional click of military equipment marked their passage. Commander Re was satisfied. He had a hundred and thirty rifles on the ground. They were moving in a column of three platoons. The 60MM mortar section was to the rear in sampans. The leading platoon moved on two parallel rice paddy dikes to watch for ambush. Re and the American advisors were co-located with the lead platoon headquarters. It was cool, a good moving time. They had been moving for hours in the darkness. It would be difficult for the Americans when the sun came up. Re looked at Travis and the rest of the American team. He approved of their equipment.

"Always remember, LIGHT, LIGHT, LIGHT," he told Travis. "You Americans load yourselves up like water buffaloes pulling a cart of tin plates. The enemy can hear you across the entire Delta. Weapons and ammunition are important. Anything else is extra. Your survival in a fire fight depends on weapon firing, your fitness to move quickly and your fighting spirit. If you load yourself down, this can happen: you will tire, the enemy will hear you and know where you are, and you will be ambushed and killed. Here there is no overwhelming fire support to save you like the American units have up north. There you can make enemy contact, take cover behind a paddy dike, and wipe out the entire countryside with incredible fire power. In the Southern Delta, you must fight like a light infantry warrior."

Re had persuaded Travis to leave the team's steel helmets and bulletproof vests behind, to exchange their heavy jungle boots with their metal insoles for black canvas sneakers, and to leave their rucksacks containing an extra pair of jungle fatigues, boots, socks and a bedroll back with the sampans. Travis

50

looked like a Delta Tiger: a brown bush hat to keep the sun off his face and neck, a dark green scarf around his neck to prevent bugs and the dreaded red ants from falling under his fatigue collar, his load bearing equipment (LBE), and a harness for carrying military equipment hung from his shoulders. The lower ends of the shoulder straps hooked to his pistol belt. A first aid packet was clipped high on his left shoulder strap. Beneath the packet was a six inch knife honed to a razor's edge in a leather sheath secured to the harness with green tape; a yellow smoke grenade was taped to the right shoulder strap. The pistol belt was worn low on the hips for comfort. Attached to the pistol belt were ammunition pouches, two baseball-like anti-personnel grenades, two canteens with water purification tablets, and a compass. Two carbine banana clips taped together for quick reversal were inserted into his M2 carbine.

The entire team was equipped like their leader with a few exceptions: Hartwell carried an M79 grenade launcher, a shotgun-like weapon that fired a 40MM anti-personnel grenade, Turner humped the PRC25 radio, and Gonzales carried his medical bag. Sergeant Minh was a mirror image of his leader.

All of them, Commander Re thought. *Vietnamese and American alike, looked like brothers.* He was armed with a pearl handled Browning automatic pistol. Most of his soldiers were armed with Ml rifles. They carried their ammunition in cloth bandoliers carefully secured to their LBE harnesses to prevent rattles. The Tiger infantryman carried no canteens, smoke grenades or compasses.

Re reflected briefly on the company organization. Each platoon had two rifle squads and a machinegun squad of two .30 caliber M1919 machineguns identical to the one that had killed Manor Cotril. This was double the machinegun strength of the other District RF companies. Communications were key. The platoon leaders had contact with Commander Re via the PRC25 radio net. Re had two radios in his command group, one for the company command net to the platoons, and one for District Headquarters where they monitored the company's progress. The American team maintained contact with Province at Hung Tho with their PRC25. This radio link was critical for air, artillery, and MEDEVAC support, although these assets were seldom available for territorial operations.

It was brighter. Light was flowing over the coconut palm trees on the right. The Tigers still remained in the gray morning gloom on the rice paddy dikes beneath the palm trees.

Travis began to worry. Their objective, a small thatched farm building, was two kilometers to the north over broken rice paddies. Once the sun rose above the palm trees, they could be seen.

He caught up with the Commander. "Should we tell the lead platoon to pick up the pace?" he whispered.

"Not yet, they might see us."

Travis fell back and considered the plan. It all sounded very shaky to him. They had been informed by a defector that a small group of Viet Cong young men frequently visited this small farm and spent the night. They had family in the area. The defector had indicated this very night for a visit. Travis thought the intelligence was soft, but Sergeant Minh told him defector information was usually very good. If the Territorial Forces were misled, the defector back in the district was usually shot.

Captain Giao, the District S-2, was the instigator of this operation. He was with them and would interrogate the prisoners. Travis knew this hunched, ugly man had a killer reputation. He ran the District prison cage and tortured prisoners. Sergeant Minh had told him that in this war, such men were needed. Giao obtained vital enemy information.

Travis continued to brood. They had too many soldiers for this mission; the chance of discovery was high. Re had responded that they were operating almost 10 kilometers north of Hoa Luu, not Indian country but almost. The Vietnamese also used the term Indian country, borrowed from a previous American advisor. There was a dangerous chance that elements of the Hoa Luu Battalion would trap them out here. Division was always reluctant to support Territorial Forces. They could easily be isolated and destroyed.

The gray was changing to the soft light of early dawn. Solid black shadows showed above the rice paddies. The Tigers could now be seen.

The lead platoon stopped. Lying on the muddy rice paddies, the entire company went to ground. Re tried to raise the platoon leader on the radio, but no answer. A runner appeared in the early light and spoke in whispers to Re.

Suddenly many shots, M1's, underscored by short automatic bursts of machinegun fire. Re was up and sprinting forward. Travis followed with the team. Re ran on the slippery top of the rice paddy dikes like an Olympic competitor. Travis slipped and crashed down into the rice paddy and got up covered by black mud. Gasping for breath, he remounted the paddy wall and continued at a dead run.

At the edge of a small tree line Travis stopped. Re was lying flat on the ground beside his lead platoon leader. Beyond them, in a small clearing, was a single thatched farm building under small arms attack. Sergeant Hartwell slipped the safety off his M79 grenade launcher and opened fire. A hollow metallic sound, a small spherical black baseball arced through the air and exploded just in front of the farmhouse.

"No!" Re shouted at Hartwell. He stood up and shouted, "NGUNG BAN. Cease Fire!" The platoon leader blew on a whistle and immediately all firing stopped. The roof of the building had started to burn. A single dark figure ran out of the front entrance headed directly for their position. Crack. An Ml rifle. The figure dropped to the ground.

Re shouted to the farm building, "RA DAY VOI HAI TAY DUA LEN. Come out with your hands up. MAY THAY RO CHUYEN GI DA XAY RA CHO BAN MAY CHUA! You saw what happened to your friend!" There was silence broken only by the sound of flames. Then two youths wearing black pajamas emerged from the building. They slowly approached the Tiger position with their hands up. Many soldiers were standing now with weapons leveled at the two Viet Cong. Suddenly, there was a movement on the opposite side of the building. Two slim figures were running for cover on the other side of the clearing. The Tigers, for an instant, were distracted, securing the prisoners and also trying to draw a bead on the fleeing figures. They escaped. "Lie on the ground!" The two prisoners fell on the ground with their faces in the dirt.

The platoon leader ordered the lead squad to search the farmhouse. They returned with a body, which they dumped in front of the prisoners. A girl flung on her back, her young face gazing at the dawning day with sightless eyes. Her blouse was partially open, revealing a small white breast. A sharp intake of breath, one of the prisoners started to rise and was kicked to the ground. Travis looked the other way.

"Well, fuck me, we caught these goddamn dinks with their pants down," Hartwell laughed.

The Americans and Commander Re were drinking tea in what was left of the farmhouse. Travis was nervous. The prisoners had been hustled away right after their capture. Was he participating in some sort of atrocity? He had talked to Commander Re, who was not reassuring. "There are things here you do not understand. This is war. A terrible civil war. We must have the information."

Captain Giao conducted the interrogation. One VC prisoner sat beside a stagnant green pond guarded by two soldiers. His left arm was in a sling. Sergeant Gonzales had treated him. The other prisoner sat in the pond, the water lapping at his neck. His arms were tied behind him and his legs were bound together. Two soldiers held him down. Captain Giao, the S-2, faced him, a short hoe handle in his right hand. He shot questions at the prisoner. "DON VI CUA MAY GA GI? What is your unit? CO BAO LON? What is its size? BO CHI HUY CUA MAY NAM O DAU? Where is your command post? AI LA NGUOI CHI HUY CUA MAY? Who is your commander?" The young man stared impassively beyond his interrogator into some place which gave him sanctuary. After every three or four questions, the two soldiers pushed the prisoner's head under water but with no success.

The S-2 grew more excited with every unanswered question. His voice rose to a scream. This was, after all, an intelligence gathering operation and he was receiving no information. He gestured violently to the soldiers. "TRAN NUOC NO. Down with his head! Keep it down this time!"

The young prisoner thrashed violently. He half stood, but the guards knocked his bound feet out from under him and he fell forward in a great splash. They grabbed his hair and forced his head under. Bubbles foamed up around his head; the thrashing weakened, then stopped. The guards yanked the head above the surface. Eyes tightly closed, it lolled on the shoulders. They threw the prisoner up on the bank. He was still breathing, a labored watery sound. A paroxysm of coughing, he threw up. His eyes opened and fixed on Captain Giao, who asked another question. The response was carefully aimed spittle which hit the S-2 full in the face. Captain Giao grunted in anger and hit the prisoner on the side of the head with the hoe handle. The young man fell back unconscious, the side of his face covered in blood. Captain Giao drew a large Bowie knife and ripped open the prisoner's pants. He grabbed the man's penis and severed it from the body with one swift stroke. Bright red blood pumped out between the prisoner's legs. The S-2 stuck the penis deep into the prisoner's mouth. A gasping, gurgling sound was heard; the prisoner jerked convulsively. The captain watched the twitching figure on the ground drown in his own blood and body parts. He turned and beckoned for the remaining prisoner. The young man was trembling. One of the guards grabbed his wounded left arm. He screamed a shriek from hell.

Sergeant Gonzales, a hundred yards away, heard the cry. He came at a dead run, followed by Travis. The soldiers were forcing the remaining prisoner into the water. Gonzales readied his weapon. "No, he is my patient!" The soldiers looked at him in amazement. He fired a round which splashed between the prisoner and Captain Giao. "Goddamn it, give him to me." He jumped into the pond and dragged the young man up on the bank. Travis joined him and readied his weapon. The soldiers looked at the Americans, confused. Commander Re arrived on the bank above the pond area. Fingering his holstered pistol, Captain Giao remained, glaring malevolently at Travis and Gonzales.

Travis looked at the body, at the horribly swollen, mutilated face with red blood coursing out of the mouth. He turned and retched.

A long line of sampans motored down the canal towards Hoa Luu Town. The Americans were near the front of the column just behind Commander Re's craft. A nautical sight, the canal lined with palms, the column of low slung, graceful sampans loaded with green-clad warriors and weapons. The Hoa Hao Navy. *This was a sea battle as much as a land battle,* Travis reflected as he conned the team sampan. Hartwell sat just in front of him. Turner in the bow manned the radio, and Gonzales and Sergeant Minh were amidships with the prisoner.

Gonzales examined the prisoner's left forearm. The wound was clean, with little swelling. Gonzales applied a fresh, sulfur impregnated compression bandage. He attempted to talk with the prisoner through Sergeant Minh. The young man swallowed frequently; tears rolled down his cheeks, he trembled uncontrollably. But, he was silent.

"He will not talk," Sergeant Minh said. "The defectors told us before the operation that these young men were probably from the Hoa Luu District Battalion. They are young but have reached full manhood. Their training and discipline are very tough. Soon these two would have been recruited into the U Minh Regiment."

"This is a brave man," Gonzales gestured to his patient, "and so was his buddy. The guy they killed by the pond."

The prisoner was very important to Hector Gonzales. He had "treated him." This placed the young VC soldier in a very special category, as if he had undergone a form of baptism. Gonzales had always been a healer, a helper of hurt people. Even as a kid growing up poor in the dusty barrios of El Paso, he took care of stray cats and dogs. Denied a formal medical education, he found his place as an Army medic. The District had greatly expanded his healer role. He was virtually the resident physician serving thousands of people. He was a legend in Hoa Luu. His attachment to his patients was close to spiritual. A devout Catholic, Gonzales believed that healers had a special responsibility to God. The barbarity of Hoa Luu would never change this responsibility. It was a fact which daily reaffirmed his faith.

Travis, too, thought of these young men. He felt unclean, dirty because of what had happened—disgusting, indescribable barbarity. But he still had respect for Commander Re and the Tigers. It was Captain Giao who had committed the atrocity. Or was it that simple?

Hartwell brooded. They should have squeezed this prisoner. Look at the sniveling fucker. Captain Giao would have had him singing like a bird. This entire walk in the rice paddies and sampan ride for nothing—not a goddamn thing. Fucking Gonzales and all his patient bullshit. And Travis was another God squader. All his outside toughness was bullshit, Travis was a wimp underneath. He'd almost puked back there. Hartwell understood war, total war. There was no room for anything else.

The line of sampans cruised around the bend in the canal like a large, jointed serpent. Suddenly, with a violent rocking of the sampan, the prisoner lunged up over the left gunwale. Hartwell snapped off the carbine safety; the little son-of-a-bitch has got to come up somewhere. The prisoner surfaced ten feet off the left side, struggling with his arm sling. As Hartwell snapped a bead, Travis pushed him face down into the sampan. Sergeant Minh fired into the air, alerting the forward parts of the flotilla. Eyes scanned the water, ready for a quick shot. Nothing, just smooth running current. The lead sampans circled back to the left, searching the bank.

Suddenly, a splashing, the prisoner surfaced and began to scramble up the steep bank. He was half-way up. Gonzales thought, prayed, that he would make it. Fire erupted from the sampans. The young man stood slowly erect, arched his back, raised both arms and slowly toppled backward into the canal. The firing stopped.

Hartwell looked at Travis. "You will die in this war, Major," he said softly.

****** 3 ******

The traveling team had just returned to the compound from another outpost trip. Gonzales met Travis at the door, visibly excited. He talked to him as he took off his gear.

"Sir, we finally have a District Medical Officer. Now we can get the hospital in high gear and start that inoculation program we talked about. Your talks to Major Tho must have done some good."

"I'm amazed, Doc. All I've heard is that Vietnam is out of doctors. They don't have enough to staff Army requirements much less Territorial Forces." Travis laid out his LBE to dry and started to strip his weapon.

"Uhhh," Gonzales looked down at his feet. "He's not a doctor actually; he's a nurse. She's a nurse. A Government nurse who will fill the position."

Travis thought this over. "That's going to be tough, Doc. How do you think she'll fit in? Will the people respect her?"

Gonzales was thoughtful. "I think so. You know midwifery is a big thing around here. They deliver all the babies, and they are all women."

Luke Hartwell had been listening. "I've met the new nurse," he said, rolling his eyes. "I know she's good for one thing. She's got the body to keep this soldier happy, great tits."

Gonzales looked murderously at Hartwell. "You touch Co Linh and I'll blow your balls off."

"Take it easy," Travis broke in. Hartwell laughed loudly and left the room.

Gonzales was quiet, gaining control. "Sir, I've done something I'm not sure you will approve."

Silence. "Well, what?"

"I've invited Co Linh to dinner tomorrow night."

"To dinner? For God's sake, Doc, what do you think we're running around here? A restaurant? If she ate with this gross bunch, we'd turn Vietnamese medical support back a generation." He thought of their eating habits: C rations in the field or whatever the Vietnamese could dig up, cold stale cereal and coffee for breakfast, bread brought from the local bakery and cold cuts for lunch, and dinner, interminable meals of fried foods. They had a cook duty roster and each team member served as "cook of the week." Now a dinner party!

57

"Doc, who shall we invite? The Province Chief? Commander Re? General Westmoreland?" he asked.

Doc winced, and Travis realized how serious he was. He backed off.

"How are we going to do it?"

"Sir, I would like to prepare a Mexican meal in her honor. I got the supplies on our last trip to Province. We must persuade her that we are on her side to fix the medical situation here. I believe medical services to the people are a large part of this war." Gonzales, as usual, was right.

"Okay, tomorrow your single duty will be chef. The rest of us will clean the hut. We were going to be here tomorrow anyway. What's her name? Co Linh will have a feast in the company of some of the most scintillating men in the Delta."

The day, a garrison day Travis called it, had been plotted out. Hector Gonzales, the grand Mexican chef, was preparing the meal for Co Linh; Billy Turner had the hut cleaning duty and after he completed that, he was to assist in the bunker construction detail; Travis, Hartwell and Minh were rebuilding the bunker, a dirty, never ending task.

The bunker detail was filling sandbags. A few weeks before Travis has discovered that the old wooden framework of the bunker was rotten. They had been piling sandbags on rotten wood. The team and some soldiers provided by Commander Re had recently completed a new cinder block structure. The men worked quietly. An athlete, but not familiar with manual labor, Travis was awkward. Minh worked efficiently, no wasted movements. Hartwell attacked the sandbags with a vengeance, another enemy. They hoped to finish the job in a week.

Travis had many plans to improve the hut complex. He had personally financed the construction costs for a rear screened-in porch with louvered wood walls which would be the team recreation room. His big plan was to construct a new latrine, an improvement over the two-holer in back of the hut. *The idea*, he thought, *was to live here in some style. Keep up our own standards and set an example for the Vietnamese.*

The men stopped work early. Travis inspected his little estate. Billy had done a super cleaning job, and Gonzales was working like a house afire in the kitchen area. The construction crew had covered the bunker with a single layer of spanking new sandbags. They were ready for a guest.

All five men were excited, even Hartwell. Travis enjoyed their high spirits, their first dinner party.

The hut had never been so clean. The spicy smell of enchiladas filled the air. Showered, shaved, and doused with various brands of aftershave lotion, the team was ready. All wore clean jungle fatigues, and they had actually dug out their U.S. issue jungle boots and shined them. Travis borrowed a table from Commander Re and had covered it with a clean camouflage poncho. Two candles placed in shined brass candle holders were at each end of the table. The table was set with GI utensils. Canteen cups were placed at each setting. Commander Re had provided them with French wine. Soft music played from their best Japanese radio.

Sergeant Minh had been dispatched as a guide to escort Co Linh to the hut. She lived in a small cottage adjoining the hospital, just on the other side of the canal outside the district compound. They waited nervously. Sergeant Hartwell was gulping down another Ba Muoi Ba. Travis looked at him.

"Take it easy, Luke," Hartwell grunted.

A knock on the door and Sergeant Minh entered with the new District Medical Officer, Co Nguyen Thi Thuy Linh. She wore a light blue ao dai, a close fitting bodice with a skirt split on both sides over white silk pants. This traditional dress accentuated her firm breasts and rounded hips. Her face was slightly elongated with high cheekbones. Dark curved eyebrows set off her wide set almond eyes. Her lips were full, almost petulant. Shimmering coal black hair was cut short over her forehead. A clean smell of soap surrounded her. *An absolutely gorgeous woman*, Travis thought.

The team stood stock still, hypnotized. Travis stepped awkwardly forward and offered his hand.

"Welcome, Co Linh, we're delighted to have you here for dinner."

She took his hand and shook it with surprising pressure. Her hand was strong. Sergeant Minh introduced her to every member of the team. Billy Turner stammered a greeting. A trifle unsteady, Hartwell leered, looking at her breasts. Hector Gonzales actually bowed. Her voice was low and clear, with a singsong quality. She carried herself with poise, but also with a sense of strength. Travis offered her some wine. She declined. She looked around at all the team directly with confidence, as if they were in this together, as if they were buddies.

"How do you find the district hospital?" Travis asked.

"It is not very good. The building is very dirty, and we have little medicine. Doctor Gonzales will help." She smiled revealing even white teeth. Gonzales blinked.

"Believe me, Co Linh," Travis said, "we are very glad to have you in the

District. I know, working together, we can put together an excellent program."
He knew this sounded stiff.

"I know we can." And she laughed a hearty, loud laugh. The whole team, except Hartwell, relaxed.

They sat down to dinner. Gonzales seated Co Linh. He then served the enchiladas he had prepared accompanied by Spanish rice and refried beans. He had even managed a small bowl of salad.

Travis invited Co Linh to begin. She took the first bite. "Delicious," she said, obviously savoring the food, and immediately went for a second forkful. They all dug in. At first there was just eating. The Mexican meal was delicious, a great culinary departure from their usual fare. They came up for air. Co Linh looked brightly around the table, expecting some conversation. All, except Hartwell, studiously looked at their plates. Hartwell continued to look at her breasts. She looked quickly away.

"Tell me about the team. What do all of you do?"

Billy Turner, his face flushed, jumped in with "I'm the radio telephone operator." She looked at him. He continued bravely, "You know, ma'am, radio here is important. What did you say it was, Major? Oh yeah, our lifeline." Co Linh nodded as if asking for more information. Billy looked back at his plate and audibly sighed. He had done his duty.

Gonzales spoke up. "You know, Co Linh, medical services is a large part of our program." He explained how they inspected outposts in conjunction with medical support. "We show the territorials we're not only interested in them for..." He stalled. He looked for help from Travis.

"We demonstrate to the Territorial Forces that we care not only about their combat readiness, but their physical well-being as well, especially their families." Travis came to the rescue.

"How are you doing?" *She looked at him directly, challenging, like a man,* Travis thought. He outlined his programs with emphasis on medical support. She visibly warmed to this. "So, you are doing well, you are winning." This stopped Travis.

"Winning?" Travis frowned. "Not many people talk about winning around here, especially the Americans."

"But we must win. Someone must win to stop all this suffering."

"Not someone. We must win," Sergeant Minh broke in. He emphasized the 'we.' "The enemy is barbaric. they kill families, women and civilians."

"It is on both sides, this brutality."

"They killed my wife and child."

"And they killed my husband, a Ranger Captain." Her eyes glistened in the candlelight; she appeared softer. Silence at the table. Sergeant Minh was angry. He didn't know why. Was it because of this beautiful intruder? These were his Americans, not hers. Or was it her lack of focus? *Our side must win.*

Travis broke the silence. "Doc, time for dessert." Gonzales jumped up and served vanilla ice cream, a real treat for a district team. They polished off this delicacy in a feeding frenzy, even Co Linh.

She looked up after finishing her ice cream, putting her GI spoon down with determination. She glanced briefly around the table, then again at Travis.

"I'm glad you are doing well here," she said. Travis felt good, expansive, almost happy.

"Yes, things are going well. As I told you, our programs are working. VC attacks are falling off." And at that time, all this was true.

"Would you like more ice cream?" Travis asked. She shook her head and stood up as if she had abruptly decided these proceedings were over.

"No, I must go." With difficulty, Travis swallowed his disappointment. This woman made up her mind fast.

Gonzales stepped in. "Co Linh, you can't go yet. You must have a cup of our special French coffee. I brewed it especially for this occasion."

"Yes, you must stay," Travis desperately reinforced Gonzales.

Thinking this over, she wrinkled up her forehead slightly which made her even more beautiful, Travis thought.

"All right, but only one cup." She sat down, and all the team sat down with her except Hartwell, who was slouched deep in his chair in a Ba Muoi Ba stupor.

Gonzales served the coffee in canteen cups. Co Linh eyed the cup handle doubtfully. Jack unfolded the handle. She murmured a thank you to him. Travis' heart stopped.

There was a pause in the conversation. Co Linh appeared preoccupied. The team looked at their cups. *Have to crank this up again,* Travis thought, searching for a subject. "How is the coffee?" he asked lamely.

"It is fine." Travis noticed she was drinking rapidly. He tasted the coffee—lukewarm. Damn! She was drinking it like water. The coffee should have been scalding hot to slow down her intake, to keep her here longer,

With another try, he asked, "Where are you from?" He wanted to return to the early evening's warmth.

"I am from the Delta. I was born in Can Tho, the region capital north of here." A long swallow of coffee, it was going down fast. Soon the evening would be over.

"How did you get into medicine?"

"My father was a doctor. He died a few years ago. My mother still lives in Can Thos and is a nurse." STOP—end of answer. Since she had decided to leave the dinner after ice cream, she appeared to be mildly irritated over the coffee interlude. She was interested in making conversation. The coffee was somehow a diversion to keep her from other duties. Travis thought she was a strong woman who did not like her plans changed, especially after finishing delicious ice cream and then having lukewarm coffee thrust on her.

"Finished." She placed her canteen cup down with a decided bang and looked at Travis with a half smile that said, "I'm not angry, but do not interrupt my plans again." She stood up, looking at her watch. She shook every team member's hand with her strong grip. Travis was the last.

"Thank you, Major Travis, for your hospitality. I will remember this evening. All of us," she looked around, "will work well together." Her warmth returned, like turning a bright light on in the room. "Sergeant Minh, will you, please, take me back to my cottage?"

"I'll take you, Co Linh," Travis said, a stroke of genius. She looked up, surprised but faintly pleased. Jack held open the door to the porch.

She was a fast walker. Travis tried to slow her down, but she forged ahead. They walked across the parade ground, crossed the bridge and continued on to her small cottage next to the hospital. He had a barely controllable urge to hold her hand, to put his arm around her, but he restrained himself. He did place his arm around her as they crossed the bridge. He could feel her firm body under the ao dai. He was enveloped in her scent, a clean, soapy aroma. Would she ask him in? He got his answer, another firm handshake.

"Goodnight, Major Travis. I cannot remember a more enjoyable evening. You, Doctor Gonzales, and I will accomplish much to help the people at Hoa Luu." She shut the cottage door softly behind her. He looked at the closed door for a moment. What a woman! Beauty, dedication, and purpose. She did like to get her way. Hoa Luu District looked good to Travis that night.

Except for rudimentary furniture, Co Linh's cottage was bare. The only item that had a personal meaning was a large photograph of a Vietnamese Ranger Captain on the back wall. Beneath the picture was a small mantelpiece with a bowl of incense sticks on it. She stopped before the picture and looked into the eyes of the captain. She spoke to him. She spoke to him every night. There was a small catch in her voice.

"Ky, you have been dead two years, and I still miss you terribly. This war has robbed us of our love, cheated us of having a family. You are with me every day." She concentrated on the face in the picture, her eyes wrinkling in the corners, willing the captain to come alive, aching to have him take her in his arms. But the picture remained still and flat.

"I am glad to be here in Hoa Luu," she continued. "It is what you and my father would have wanted. Here, I will serve the people. There is much to do; nothing will be allowed to get in my way. Perhaps, dear Ky, in a small way, I can live up to your terrible sacrifice. Maybe I can give meaning to your tragic death. I have always known that beneath your brave uniform was a poet, a sensitive man who had a deep feeling for the people. You yearned for the war to end so you could teach. As you told me before you left that last time, when you were sick of the killing, the people, the simple Delta people, are the terrible losers in this war. They suffer the most. You said your heart was with them. Ky, I share your sympathy. I do not take sides in this war. Only the people matter. Perhaps, in a small way, I can relieve their suffering in Hoa Luu."

Tears blotted out the picture. She bent over, sobbing. A grief engulfed her over her friend, her lover, an irreconcilable loss which had maimed her young life forever.

Abruptly she stood up. Her full lips tightened with determination. She sat down at a small writing desk and removed a folder from a stack of papers. She reviewed her notes for the District midwife training program. Death during childbirth and infection afterward was a serious problem in Hoa Luu District. Her thoughts wandered. She couldn't concentrate. Was she losing her will, what Ky called her inner steel? He had always joked about her determination. Sometimes they had argued about her abrupt mood changes from frivolous things to what she called her medical duties. Back to her notes. Her eyes again slipped off the page. She thought of the dinner that night, of the tall American major, his dark hair, his even blue eyes, his strong arm when they crossed the bridge. Co Linh thought young woman's thoughts. Never again! Back to the midwife program.

* * * * * * * * * * * *

"DELTA ALPHA BRAVO: THIS IS PAPA THREE."

"THIS IS DELTA ALPHA SIX, OVER." Travis answered the Province call.

"THIS IS PAPA THREE, PAPA SIX WANTS TO SEE YOU THIS LOCATION TOMORROW TEN HUNDRED HOURS REFERENCE

BRIEFING YOU GAVE ME LAST WEEK. OVER."

"ROGER, OVER." The Province S-3 was on the radio. Travis had briefed him the week before on his advisory programs.

"NEGATIVE FURTHER, OUT."

Travis had been in Hoa Luu District for three months. He had never met his commanding officer, who had been on R and R in early July when he first arrived. Since that time, according to military etiquette, he had tried unsuccessfully to set up an appointment. The Province Senior Advisor returned from R and R, attended numerous meetings with the Division advisory staff at the 64th Division Headquarters and frequently went to Saigon and Can Tho to participate in pacification conferences. On these trips he always kept the Province's helicopter with him which deprived the entire Province team of this important asset. During the past three months Travis's only contact with the Province advisory team had been a few supply trips and daily radio checks.

This bothered him and he continued to badger Province for a meeting, if not with the Province Senior Advisor, then at least with some of the principal staff. Last week Major Bill Dugan, the Province S-3, had finally visited Hoa Luu by helicopter. Dugan had been in Ngoc Hoa Province for six months and had yet to visit any location except by helicopter. Sampan or jeep travel on the single province road was too time consuming according to him. He had never spent the night with a district team.

Travis was exploding with ideas, particularly a concept he called activating staff channels. He wanted to bounce them off other Americans, his commanding officer, the province staff, and his fellow District Senior Advisors.

The meeting with Dugan hadn't been a success. Travis and Sergeant Minh had briefed him in the hut common room. It was stiflingly hot. They offered Dugan an iced Coke. He had taken a quick gulp and then spit it out on the floor when informed, with some pride, that the ice was from the local Vietnamese ice plant. The ice was, in fact, frozen canal water. Then, in the middle of Travis's briefing, he had begun to doze. He explained later that the heat was getting to him. They had air conditioning at Province Headquarters. The briefing ended; Dugan drew Travis aside. They had been classmates a few years before in the Career Course at Fort Benning.

"Look, Jack, I know you're a below-the-zone fast mover, but out here you have to learn how to play the game; you need to understand the Vietnamese, the Hoa Hao, and all that shit. And above all else, you have to understand

Potty's advisory policy." Potty referred to Lieutenant Colonel Vernon E. Potts, air defense artillery, the Province Senior Advisor.

"What is his philosophy?" Travis had asked.

"He will tell you. But one thing, knock off all this "win the war" crap. My objectives are simple: to survive, stay out of trouble, get my ticket punched, and be selected for the Command and General Staff College."

"Good luck," Travis said. And that ended his single meeting with a member of the Province Headquarters in three months.

Early the next morning they prepared for the thirty kilometer jeep ride to Huong Tho, the province capital. Travis had established many operational procedures during the past three months. Battle drills he called them. Everything was treated like a military operation: if mortared at night, you rolled off your bunk, gathered your weapons and military equipment stowed under your bunk for quick retrieval and crawled to the bunker; weapons were cleaned at least once daily; the radio and wire communications from the bunker were checked every day; a comprehensive pre-combat equipment check was conducted before each operation in the field, right down to water purification tablets; the radio communications link with Province was maintained at all times, and every night a duty roster radio watch was stood to monitor the Province net.

Today Hartwell and Turner would remain at District to man the radio and continue work on the team bunker. The traveling squad consisted of Travis, Gonzales and Minh. The jeep was thoroughly checked to include the sandbags on the floorboards for protection against mines. The men carried all their combat gear as if they were on a Delta Tiger operation. The PRC 25 radio was hung on the back of the right seat.

Travis drove fast and skillfully. Sampan seamanship and driving jeeps hell-for-leather down marginal roads were two key Delta survival skills. VC Charlie was always around taking his weekly potshots, and, although he was a notoriously bad shot, Travis was not going to give him a stationary target.

As the jeep careened down the dusty road, Travis thought of the team. For the most part they were pulling together.

Minh was far more than an interpreter, he was an excellent staff officer. Travis was beginning to buy into his VC attack theory, that the enemy must control Hoa Luu to launch offensive operations. There was a morbid, brooding quality about Minh, however, which bothered Travis. He lived with a tragedy that slowly gnawed his soul. Minh had no joy. He hated. Travis did not understand people who hated - not yet.

Gonzales, the healer of Hoa Luu District. A quiet, dedicated man who had real empathy for the Vietnamese, especially the children. Gonzales and the MEDCAP program had established more team rapport with the Vietnamese than any other activity.

His thoughts turned to Co Linh. He was thinking about her far too often. This was no place to become involved with a woman. Since the dinner, she had never been far from his mind. He couldn't believe that in all the death and squalor which comprised Hoa Luu District, there was also a Co Linh. He would have to see more of her. Maybe the dinner could become a weekly affair. He thought of the other team members.

Billy Turner, a good kid who missed girls, cars, rock music and the Cardinals. Not a genius, but he could hump that radio and was good in a scrap.

And then there was Luke Hartwell. Hartwell, Travis had to admit, had some good points. He was an outstanding fighter, a good shot, fit, had excellent field skills, and remained cool under stress and fire. He was also a complete bastard, a killer, and a racist. He hated the Vietnamese and many of them sensed this. This hurt their advisory efforts. Everybody on the team feared him. Travis knew there had been a drunken incident in the period between Cottril's death and his arrival. Minh had been forced to leave the hut one night when Hartwell, high on Ba Muoi Ba beer and God knows what else, had said he would not live with a fucking slope and threatened to blow Minh's head off.

Commander Re had warned him about Hartwell at one of their weekly evening meetings which had become a ritual. "He is a fighter, a killer, which is good in war if he is on your side. I am not sure which side he is on. Hartwell seems to fight many wars and you, Major, and I, might someday be his target. You, because you are an officer and I, because I am Vietnamese, a slope, a dink. If you Americans were not so important to this war I would shoot him." Travis looked sharply at the commander over his brandy glass at these words. Hartwell was one of his biggest problems, both with the team and with the Vietnamese. But he needed him, desperately needed him in a way Travis found hard to face.

Life in Hoa Luu had improved. He was developing a close relationship with Commander Re. Four times since the interrogation incident he had been on operations with the Delta Tigers. They had experienced small arms fire, but no serious contact.

His relationship with Major Tho had strengthened. Travis persuaded him to have morning staff briefings where there was a valuable exchange of information between staff sections. They had started to have coffee together each morning before these briefings. There Tho would light his first Panatella of the day, amply supplied by his senior advisor. Captain Luom, the S-3, had proven to be a strong professional compatriot. They had made a strong start on improving outpost fortifications and training programs for the Territorial Forces.

Ever since the interrogation incident, Captain Giao, the S-2, remained an implacable enemy. Commander Re had warned him to watch this man. Travis did not like to think about the incident. He had forced it into a small corner of his mind.

And yet, in spite of success, Travis was not comfortable: the Hoa Hao thing, the absence of guidance, the apparent lack of interest by the Province Senior Advisor and his staff, and the total insufficiency of combat support for the Territorial Forces, when clearly they had the potential to fight a large part of this war. There was no defined focus to win the war in the Southern Delta. Who was in charge? Where were they going?

What concerned Major John Alexander Travis III the most was his own problem which lurked just beneath the surface. His own unique little hell in this war: the nightly sweats, the cold feeling in the chest, the disorientation he experienced in many combat situations. His heritage, his training, his God must pull him through. Some of these values didn't seem to sync with the barbarity and casual death of the Hoa Luu war.

The briefing room was cold, noisy and breezy. The air conditioners rattled in the windows and above that was the muffled roar of a generator somewhere outside. A fan slowly rotated on the ceiling. The room felt like it was about to take off, to go airborne. Travis shivered as he reported to Lieutenant Colonel Vernon E. Potts, the Province Senior Advisor of Ngoc Hoa Province. Potts sat behind a long wooden desk which looked out over a large room painted battleship gray. At the end of the room, facing the desk, was a map of the province. Arranged in front of the map were four rows of folding chairs. The room served as the Colonel's office and the team briefing room.

Potts rose, medium height, small growing paunch, bald with a frieze of mousy blond hair, a round red face with veined cheeks, and small, round eyes, which, this morning, were bloodshot. Potts was 45 years old. He had not commanded soldiers for fifteen years, and had recently been passed over for full colonel. The United States Army had selected him to command the American presence in Ngoc Hoa Province. In this capacity, he commanded two hundred American advisors, implemented advisory policy for a province of 6000 square kilometers and a population of 250,000 Vietnamese, advised a military structure of 7200 Territorial Forces, watched over the plans to improve the primitive rice economy, monitored all district and village governmental functions, and distributed millions of dollars worth of United States Agency for International Development, U.S.A.I.D., building materials and food to the Vietnamese. To prepare him for this responsibility, he had attended a four week course at Fort Bragg which was mostly lecture and little application, even in military security operations.

Lieutenant Colonel Vernon E. Potts was the senior U.S. representative in one of only forty-four provinces during a counterinsurgency war which targeted the people and the economy in a hotly contested part of Vietnam— the Southern Delta, often called the bread basket of Vietnam.

Potts held out his hand. "Glad to see you, Travis. Sorry it took so long, but you know how busy we are." He gestured expansively around the battleship gray room. The voice was high pitched and hoarse. He motioned Travis to a seat beside the desk. "Bill Dugan told me you had some hot shot advisory ideas." Hot shot was emphasized. "It's great to have this new young crop of District Senior Advisors come in—the cream of the Army. You're going to save us here in the Delta. Bill tells me in three months you've developed some incredible advisory programs." Potts lit up a cigarette and brushed away some ashes from the top of his desk. "Tell me, what are you guys doing over there in Hoa Luu, starting a revolution?"

Travis shifted uncomfortably in his chair. "Nothing like that, Sir. I just wanted to cover some things with you to make sure we're on the right track."

"Well, have at it." Potts pushed back in his folding desk chair and folded his hands over his paunch.

"Sir, I would like to brief you off the map." He pointed to the far side of the room.

"Okay, shoot." Potts did not budge from his desk, and Travis was forced to brief across the long gray room above the noise of the air conditioner and the generator. He walked to the other end of the room, stood before the map and fumbled with his written brief. At first he had planned to speak off notes, but had decided to read most of the briefing to insure nothing was left out. He wanted to impress Potts with meticulous staff work and the importance of his message. His plan was to pause from time to time in the briefing, establish eye contact, and emphasize key points. The Command and General Staff College would have been proud.

Standing at the end of that long, noisy room with his boss ensconced half a basketball court away, Travis realized his plan was a mistake. Potts couldn't see the map detail, and he would be forced to read his presentation in a loud voice similar to giving commands on a parade ground. To add to his difficulties, there was no lectern for his briefing which would make it difficult to find his place after map references. Travis filled his lungs with the frigid air conditioned air and shouted, "Sir, you know our mission, to advise and assist the District Chief and his staff in the overall conduct of counterinsurgency." At the first explosive impact of Travis' VMI trained voice, Potts almost bolted from his chair. He then slouched down into an almost fetal position.

Travis was fond of his words. "This mission can be distilled into more basic language," the parade ground voice continued, "To create a district headquarters through professional advice, example, and sincerity. To accomplish this, my team has designed an advisory technique we call 'activating staff channels.' As you know, staff channels comprise the major functional areas of District activity such as intelligence, military operations, civil affairs, and medical services. The central theme is to initiate a simple program in each staff channel. The magnitude of the program is predicated on the training level of the district staff and the importance of the initiative. If the program is too ambitious, it will fail. Consequently, it is better to start at a very basic level to avoid discouraging counterparts. Once a staff section has initiated its own program in its functional area of responsibility, or in the language of this briefing, "activated its staff channel,' the main barrier to creating a vital district headquarters will have been surmounted—the district staff will be thinking for itself. There will be initiative at the District level— not just the reaction mode we see today."

"Wow! I'll tell you, Travis, this stuff is hot shit. Real original. I can see the Army sent me a good man," Potts injected.

Undeterred and even louder, Travis continued. "Naturally, security-related programs take precedence. This morning I will concentrate on the training programs we have started for the Territorial Forces. Before I do this, however, I would like to give you an overview of the district's characteristics." At this point, frequently referring to the map, Travis went over the key data pertaining to Hoa Luu District. There were several awkward pauses as he searched for his place between map references.

From his seat across the room Potts couldn't see the details on the map. He smirked at Travis' awkwardness with the briefing papers and then stretched out of his fetal position and looked at the ceiling, fascinated by the rotating blades of the fan.

Travis left the map and clumsily scooped up his briefing papers from a nearby chair. After a hesitation hugely enjoyed by Potts, he found his place and plunged into the heart of his advisory program: intelligence collection, the Sgt. Minh theory, the VC buildup in the Vinh Cheo Triangle area and the U Minh Forest, training and support programs for territorial forces, integrated staff procedures, the establishment of District operations procedures, improved relations with Vietnamese counterparts, the strong fighting qualities of the Hoa Hao, current and future operations, and finally, he recommended operations into the Vinh Cheo Triangle area.

Potts had reacted twice during the briefing, "The Hoa Hao are bloody assassins who only care about themselves." and "Stay out of the fucking Vinh Cheo Triangle—keep it quiet!" The remainder of the time the colonel was preoccupied with alternately studying the ceiling fan, which appeared to hypnotize him, or assembling and disassembling his ballpoint pen.

"Sir, in closing, I believe great strides have been made in improving district security. I would like to have an opportunity to exchange these ideas with the other district senior advisors, so that we can work together, work in concert. Perhaps you could establish some sort of monthly meeting." Travis stopped here. Potts was back to studying the ceiling fan. Travis almost shouted, "I would like to discuss some serious problems with you." More silence. Travis looked across the large room at Potts, who had returned to his IN box. Travis raised his pointer and hit the briefing map with a loud wham which reverberated through the room like a gunshot. Potts jerked erect.

"You're finished?" he asked, more a command than a question. "Come over here and sit down."

Time for Potty's advisory philosophy, Travis thought. "Sir, I said I have some problems," Travis repeated. He sat down beside the desk.

"Shoot." Potts leaned back in his chair with an air of great impatience.

"We need better intelligence, especially about the U Minh Regiment. What are their activities? Do they plan any major offensive operations? You know this is a very strategic location."

"Don't worry about the U Minh Regiment. Didn't they teach you anything at Fort Bragg? We have specific force missions here. The Territorials, the RF and the PF take care of the local guerrillas. The district VC battalions, that's our job; ARVN fights the main VC units such as the U Minh Regiment; and the US Forces up north are primarily targeted against the North Vietnamese Army, the NVA. Remember, what the U Minh Regiment does is 64th ARVN

Division's concern, not yours. Perhaps I can set up an appointment with General Westmoreland if you disagree with the strategy because he designed it."

That's a very tidy way to fight a war if the enemy cooperates, Travis thought.

"What other problems?" Potts asked.

"Sir, we desperately need more combat support. If we could get air and gunship support, and maybe some artillery, I know we could persuade Tho to enter the Vinh Cheo Triangle. Perhaps we could start an entire Province operation."

"Are you out of your goddamn mind? I told you before, we're not going to stir up that hornet's nest. Everything is quiet now, and we're going to keep it that way. As far as combat support is concerned, that's the 64th ARVN Division's business and that's the way it will remain. Anything else?"

Travis had planned to re-address the Hoa Hao situation but let it drop. "No, Sir."

"You know, Major Travis, we're delighted that the Army is sending us fast movers like you to win the war. You've figured it all out in a remarkably short time. In fact, I'm going to call you 'Hot Shot.' Now, Hot Shot, I want you to listen to my advisory philosophy, and listen hard.

"One. Don't rock the boat, particularly with all these crazy ideas you've got.

"Two. Get along with the Vietnamese and do what they want to do. Stop putting pressure on them. They've been here a bit longer than you have; they know the score.

"Three. Watch out for the Hoa Hao. They hate some people in this province more than they hate the VC. They're good fighters, but also a bunch of murdering bastards."

Travis started to interrupt but Potts waved him down.

"Four. This is related to my first point. Survive. Think of your future. You've done well so far; don't screw up here. Get your ticket punched and leave in one piece."

Travis thought, *This is war; we are committed. Does anybody want to win?*

"Anything else?"

"No, Sir, thank you for your time." He rose, saluted, and walked out of the cold gray room into the brightness and stifling heat of midday in the southern Delta.

The traveling squad spent the day and that night at Province. Minh received a complete intelligence update, Gonzales replenished his medical supplies, and Travis made a round of the Vietnamese and American staff sections, obtaining all the information he could. There wasn't much. The Vietnamese were not communicating. Minh told him the team was tainted because they came from a Hoa Hao district. The Americans here seemed more interested in the daily volleyball game than prosecuting the war.

Two new members reported to the Province Team that day, Major Philip Cochran, the new Army aviation officer, and Major Robert Harris, the new District Senior Advisor of Tram Cua District, the district just south of Hoa Luu.

That night most of the Province Team sat under the stars and watched a movie. The projector started chattering and then abruptly stopped half-way through *IN HARM'S WAY* starring John Wayne. After many catcalls, the operator gave up. It could not be repaired. Travis retired to the team club, an air-conditioned Quonset hut with a long bar and a loud jukebox. Tables and chairs were strewn haphazardly around the single room in the club. The two newcomers were drinking beer at a table in the corner. The club was filling up because of the movie breakdown.

Travis sat down with them and introduced himself. They were talking and bitching about the war. They hated being assigned to this sleepy hollow called the Delta. The real war was up north, fighting with an American unit. Out in the Central Highlands where men were men and you fought real soldiers and didn't screw around with all this advisory bullshit and Vietnamese civilians.

Travis took a long pull of his very cold Budweiser. He listened to this tirade for a while, then broke in.

"I used to think that three months ago, sometimes I still do. But mostly, I think the real war is here in the Delta." He paused. "But we don't know it yet. Maybe we will never understand."

"How can you say that?" Cochran asked. "God, man, have you met Potty? Don't stir up the enemy; don't rock the boat; get your ticket punched." Bob Harris nodded in agreement.

"I think Potts is dangerously wrong." It surprised Travis that he said this. "Look at the nature of this war. They tell us this is an insurgency, whatever that means. The population and the economy are the objectives in an insurgency. The Delta is the rice bowl of Vietnam and the most densely populated area in the country. By definition this is an important place. The enemy is trying to coerce the population, and most of that population and agricultural wealth is right here where we sit drinking beer. In fact, you can argue that in an insurgency; if you are fighting for or securing an area with no economy, no people, you're fucked up." Travis didn't usually say things like 'fucked up.' "The question is, what are we doing about it? Our troops and combat assets are up north. U.S. units never operate south of Can Tho. ARVN controls all the combat support allocated to this area, but from what I see, theirs is a search and avoid game. They carefully avoid VC base areas. Our war, which I have come to call the Territorial War, fought with Regional Forces and Popular Forces, forces of the people, much like the militia in our own Revolution, receives no support, yet this is the part of the war which defends the population. Hell, we're operating down here with equipment frozen in time. We are literally a live, walking goddamned World War II military museum. You'd think it was 1944, and it's 1966."

"But," Bob Harris interrupted, "there isn't much enemy around here. The Province S-2 painted a very quiet picture."

"That's bullshit. There's a lot of enemy down here. They're quiet because ARVN and the Territorial Forces leave them alone. Hell, Potty doesn't want me to enter the Vinh Cheo Triangle. There are many reports the VC are using this relatively quiet time to build up new equipment, training, that sort of thing. And we ain't doing a damn thing about it. We're looking the other way. The point is, what are they up to?"

"But," Cochran chimed in, "our forces are fighting like hell up north. We're taking some casualties and pasting the shit out of the North Vietnamese Army, the NVA."

"Remember what I said. If you fight where the people ain't, you ain't right. Maybe what the enemy is trying to do is suck American forces away from the populated areas."

The conversation swirled on. They ordered a few more rounds of beer. After five beers, Travis was feeling expansive and a bit giddy. He looked at his new friends. Flip Cochran, short, muscular, reddish hair and a line of freckles over a nose which had been flattened in many barroom fights. He was a loud, fiery, hell for leather Army aviator, an OCS product from Pittsburgh, Pennsylvania. The Army had been his life since he left home at seventeen. He was 31. Bob Harris, 30 years old, was tall, taller than Travis, dark haired and somber looking. He was thoughtful, quiet and spoke slowly with a distinct New England twang. Harris wore glasses and looked like a young bespectacled Abraham Lincoln.

He had received his commission through ROTC at the University of Vermont.

Travis told them about his advisory programs and his problems. He described his successes and urged that at least, between Hoa Luu and Tram Cua Districts, they should share ideas. Bob Harris emphatically agreed. "After all, Jack, we're neighbors. I could drive up there every day."

"Be careful," Travis replied, splashing some of his beer on the table. "That's how my predecessor got it."

Travis asked Flip Cochran about his air section. What in the hell did they do? In three months he had never seen an airplane, except an occasional Province chopper flying over his district.

They hunched over the table to talk. Somebody broke a glass. The jukebox was blaring out "A Hard Day's Night" by the Beatles.

"Well, I've got one Bird Dog. I have a crew chief and a small maintenance section. My job is to fly surveillance missions, act as a radio relay on operations, adjust artillery, and put in air strikes."

"You mean you have only two jobs. There ain't any artillery and I've yet to see a gun ship or a fast mover."

"I heard your lecture, Jack. Goddamn it, you sound like a professor. I think I can square some of that away. There are some Army buddies at Division who will help us with gun ships, and I know the Air Force liaison officer. I also have another idea." Flip grinned, giving his face a puckish expression. "We're going to load up the Bird Dog with 2.75 high explosive rockets as well as white phosphorous (WP) smoke markers. Hell, we never get any air support anyway. This mad Irishman is going to be Ngoc Hoa Province's first fighter bomber pilot."

"Well, flip my stick!" Travis cried and the three of them broke up with laughter. Thereafter Philip Cochran became known as Flipstick. The nickname even became his radio call sign.

More beer. The conversation charged on about sports, women, R and R and more women. Harris was married. Cochran and Travis were bachelors. "I'm new here, but the real question is, where to go on R and R. The deciding factor there is women," Cochran said solemnly. Harris and Travis nodded.

"You know, maybe we should all three go together," Harris said. They enthusiastically agreed.

Finally, Travis rose unsteadily to his feet and raised his glass. "To us, to victory." They clashed their glasses together.

"An old, very old, hoary Hoa Luu District tradition." He crashed his glass to the floor. The others followed. Nobody noticed. Unsteadily the three of them wove their way out of the club. An alliance had been formed.

✱✱✱✱✱✱✱✱✱✱✱✱

ZIP! He jumped! His left leg slipped between the slippery logs of the monkey bridge up to his knee. ZING! VC Charlie fired again. He scrambled to release his leg, another shot, his body tipped over the bridge, a terrible strain on the ligaments of his knee, the bridge swayed to the right. *Christ*, he thought rapidly, *either the bridge breaks, my leg breaks, I get shot, or all three.* A coconut log broke and Travis pitched into the canal with a heavy splash. Suddenly he was submerged, flat on his back in the oozing mud, looking up through eight feet of murky brown water. Travis struggled to his feet and extended his legs to rise. His feet buried in the soft mud. His combat gear was a dead weight. He struggled with the straps but nothing budged. His weapon sank to the bottom. With difficulty he unhooked his pistol belt and wriggled out of his LBE and radio harness. They sank in the muddy canal bottom. Travis lunged, broke surface, and gulped for air.

PF soldiers lining the bank were watching all this with great amusement. There was a large cheer when he broke the surface of the canal. *This is the only goddamned place in the world where you can be shot in one second and drowned the next,* Travis thought. VC Charlie, the ubiquitous sniper had struck again.

Captain Luom, Travis and Sergeant Hartwell had been training three RF platoons on bridge security and night stakeout operations. Luom had selected the bridge. Travis had thought it was a very doubtful structure. A typical Vietnamese monkey bridge: a trestle of four sets of x'd coconut palm logs stuck in the mud and connected with two horizontal logs upon which the crosser balanced himself precariously. Bridge classification: 135 pounds; Travis weighed considerably more. This was not his first encounter with a monkey bridge, which he was convinced was a VC invention. It plagued every fighting man in the Delta who weighed over 135 pounds.

That night the training objective was to deploy the three platoons for training on night stakeout operations. In many areas of the district the "night belonged to Charlie." The PF would snuggle into their coconut log fortifications and nothing could pry them loose from their security blanket. The VC were allowed to roam at will. Travis and Luom were determined to correct this situation which threatened security throughout Hoa Luu.

It was a tough training challenge. The Viet Minh had a supernatural reputation for night fighting. Lurking menacingly beyond the log fortifications, the VC threatened death in the night to any who ventured outside. This bogeyman notoriety had to be destroyed. The night must become a friend, not an ally to the enemy.

The first efforts at night training failed abysmally. The training load of twenty-six platoons was daunting. Travis, Luom and Hartwell conducted night basic training during daylight hours in training groups of three platoons. The platoons were then handed over to RF training teams who conducted the night application phase. These teams had previously been trained on actual night ambushes as part of the Regional Forces Ranger Program. However, the nighttime phase deteriorated to a mere walk in the woods. The RF didn't like night operations any more than the PF, and the ambush patrol proved to be too difficult a tactic. Basically, if the Americans were not present, there were no ambush patrols.

Travis and Luom had decided to restructure the training program. The ambush patrols were eliminated. The PF learned how to establish security stakeouts, positions at night to block enemy avenues of approach into the PF outpost positions. The PF related to this mission because it was defensive. Ambushes had frightened them because the positions were farther from the outpost complex, and the operation entailed closing with the enemy and fighting. Travis thought this was too fine a distinction, but Luom had explained, "The PF must think of security stakeouts as an extension of their outpost facilities. Nightly stakeouts make their position safer."

They believed the training was taking effect. Proper reports were coming into the TOC, and the nighttime enemy activity had decreased throughout the District. Sergeant Hartwell didn't agree. "It works now because the VC ain't doing shit. When they stir up, these PF slopes will run like a bunch of quail and hide behind their logs."

That night, the three PF platoons with their RF training teams moved out of the outpost just before sunset. Travis, Luom and Hartwell each accompanied a platoon. The first phase was a walkthrough of possible stakeout sites for terrain familiarization. It always amazed Travis how different things appeared in the dark. There was a lot of talking and chatter during this period. The RF training teams kept up a running harangue with their PF charges.

Next, Travis' platoon broke down to squads, conducted a short tactical movement and occupied squad perimeter positions. They remained in these positions for two hours and then began movement to their night stakeout positions. Travis was with the first squad. They got lost. He could hear muffled voices, then loud splashing. The lead fire team was floundering in the water. He half ran to the head of the column, stumbling over PF soldiers, and went down on one knee as they had been trained. Suddenly the ground beneath him gave away; he was falling into a pit. His breath stopped. All he felt was sharp fear, as he imagined the razor-sharp punji stakes smeared with buffalo excrement emasculating him. He landed, feet spread wide. No pain. In the gloom, he could see the punji stakes between his legs.

Crack! Wham! Suddenly they were under fire, grenades and small arms to the front. Travis scrambled out of the pit. They were 150 meters from the PF outpost. No enemy could be this close. He reached the lead fire team, who were stumbling around in the waist deep water. Bullets were cutting through the foliage. He tried his school Vietnamese on the soldiers. "KE DICH 0 DAU." Where is the enemy? They responded, "KHONG BIET." I don't know. Then shots went off behind him, bullets zipping over their heads. His squad was returning the fire. Travis had no radio and marginal Vietnamese— big trouble. The lead fire team sank up to its neck in the water for protection. Travis felt that familiar cold disorientation about to engulf him. His mouth was dry. Must think through this! No automatic fire, all rifle fire. An inspiration, he shouted out in English, "Who's there?" A laconic reply, "It's me, Hartwell." Very close. "We thought you were a bunch of fucking VC." The Vietnamese shouted to each other "NGUNG BAN, Cease fire!" After a few scattered shots, the firing stopped. Jack's cold fear turned to anger against Sergeant Hartwell.

The platoon returned to the outpost complex. Travis and Luom conducted a detailed review of the exercise. Land navigation, friendly recognition procedures, and security were chief points.

The PF were very excited. They talked about their friendly fire fight as if it were an actual enemy contact. "Like a bunch of goddamn kids playing guns," Hartwell said. Travis felt the training was a success in spite of the friendly battle. At this point they had trained over half the District's platoons and these units reflected a better readiness, a sort of rustic elan. They were proud of their colors, the guidon, they received at the graduation ceremony.

After the review, Travis drew Hartwell aside. You could have killed us out there, Luke."

"You look awfully healthy to me, Major."

"This is no joke. You knew there were other squads in the area and made no effort to challenge us. There was no fire control. You just opened up."

"You need more points to earn your Combat Infantry Badge, Major, but

I'm not sure friendly fire counts."

"Don't you understand our job out here, Sgt. Hartwell? We've got to get the PF's out in the dark."

"I don't understand any of this training bullshit. You couldn't train most of these dinks to take a shit."

"Why do you think we're doing all this? What's the point? You're a senior NCO, give me an answer." His voice rose.

"You want an answer, Major? The whole program beats the hell out of this hillbilly. Maybe you want to get some sort of officer brownie points with higher headquarters."

Travis glared at Hartwell's smirking face. He could imagine his bare knuckles crunching through his cheekbone. His right fist trembled with anticipation.

"You could have killed me out there." He stepped forward.

"Listen to me. The next time you pull a stunt like this, I'll have you up for charges." Hartwell backed up a step.

"You listen to me, Major. You need me in this fucking war because you don't like to fight. You ain't got it. You're afraid of something."

Travis approached Hartwell again; his right arm drew back. The sergeant turned on his heel and walked off into the night.

Somehow, some way I've got to make this work with Hartwell, Travis thought, fighting his anger. He had another deeply disturbing thought, perhaps Hartwell was right. He didn't have "it."

****

He followed at a distance. The compound was not well lit. Crossing the bridge was the hardest part. He waited until they were out of sight before crossing. The hospital was on the other side of the road, her cottage beyond. He slid into the ditch beside the road and waited. Sweat poured off him; his hands shook. Sergeant Minh, his escort duties over, walked by on the road, returning to the compound. He crept around the hospital to the cottage. The door was open! She sat in front of a small mirror combing her short black hair.

He looked at her: the swell of her breasts which pushed tightly against the ao dai, the outline of her bra strap, the trace of her panties under the tight white pants. He crept behind her. She started to rise. He gripped her from the rear, one hand squeezing her breast and ripping open the ao dai, the other over her mouth. She bit his hand and drew blood. He grunted and tried to throw her to the floor. She was strong and struggled furiously. He finally tripped her. On the way down she kneed him in the groin. She screamed "GIUP, help!" Her voice carried like a bell in the night.

A fully armed soldier from the Delta Tigers ran into the room. He pulled him off Co Linh. He stood up, confused, looking at the soldier in amazement. The soldier motioned him with his rifle toward the door. He left.

He was breathing hard. Had to get control! There would be bad trouble if Travis found out. The attack had sobered him.

Standing in the middle of the bridge was a shadowy figure. A white ascot stood out in the night. The man held a Browning automatic pistol loosely, almost casually, in his right hand.

"Sergeant Hartwell, you have done a terrible thing, and I am going to kill you painfully," a deadly calm voice said. The automatic rose slowly and fired. There was a searing, terrible pain in his left kneecap. The automatic fired quickly again, blowing his right kneecap apart. Hartwell stumbled and dropped to his shattered knees. He screamed in agony and fell on his face. The man kicked him over onto his back. Another shot, this time in the groin. His hips jerked with the shock. Hartwell was losing consciousness. The pain was impossible, stupefying. His sight was dimming in a darkening red haze. He saw the muzzle of the automatic come slowly down. It caressed his lips and then with great force shattered his front teeth. The man was kneeling beside him. They looked at each other. "You will live in Hell forever. For you there is no other life." A shot, the report muffled inside his exploding head. Immediate blackness.

Travis heard the shots. Hartwell was missing. He jumped up, left the hut and started running toward the bridge.

Commander Re stopped him in the middle of the parade ground.

"What happened? Where is Hartwell?"

"I'm afraid VC Charlie had a lucky shot. The Sergeant was killed crossing the bridge. We are trying to recover his body, but the current is swift."

"How do you know he was killed? I heard a scream. What the hell is going on?"

"My friend, it is best in Hoa Luu District not to know too much. Now, Major Travis, you must talk to Co Linh. She is very distressed."

****** 4 ******

At fifteen hundred feet, safe flying altitude in Vietnam, the significance of
the Vinh Cheo Triangle and the Vinh Thanh and Hoa Luu Canals can readily
be seen. Running southwest to northeast, the two major canals angle out of
the Tao River in the southwest quadrant of the district. The confluence of
these waterways marked the general apex of the Vinh Cheo base area which
stretched in a widening triangle for twenty kilometers to the south. The VC
had to control both canals to stage operations to the northeast from Vinh
Cheo. The Tao River, three hundred meters wide, meanders west, southwest,
to the deeply mangroved U Minh Forest, the home of the U Minh Regiment,
fifty kilometers beyond.

The Hoa Luu Battalion trained, maintained, and recruited in the Vinh
Cheo Triangle, and staged occasional successful operations into Hoa Luu's
pacified areas. The U Minh Regiment accomplished the same throughout the
Southern Delta from the U Minh Forest. The Government forces knew these
forces were there and the Viet Cong command knew they knew. This was
wartime accommodation at the highest level. "If you do not attack me
seriously in the base areas, I will launch only sporadic operations into
Government pacified areas."

In Hoa Luu this accommodation translated into low level guerrilla activity
such as VC Charlie, the occasional mortar bombardment of an outpost, and
from time to time an assassination similar to the killing of Major Cottril. On
the Government side, the tactics of accommodation meant an emphasis on
installation security, operations in areas within the district but outside the
enemy base areas, and constant surveillance of the northern apex of the Vinh
Cheo Triangle. No penetration into Vinh Cheo was allowed or supported.
Flip Cochran in his illegal fighter-bomber was not even permitted to fly over
the Triangle.

This accommodation on a strategic level had existed for some years
throughout the country. There were many Vinh Cheos and U Minh Forests in
Vietnam.

In the Southern Delta, the VC needed Hoa Luu District. They had received
a warning order to prepare for future offensive operations against population
centers to the north. The U Minh Regiment required the canals and the

80

province road which would allow their troops to deploy and rapidly move northeast toward Can Tho and Saigon. Hoa Luu provided the gateway for success.

Most of the Vinh Cheo was uninhabited, deserted rice paddies pock-marked by water-filled shell holes. The area had been fought over for years. Paradoxically, just south of the confluence of the Hoa Luu Canal and the Tao River, there was a Catholic church located on the west bank of the Tao, a relic of the French colonial era. Not a scar marred the surface of the church. A trimmed green lawn flowed down to the river bank. There were brick walkways lined with tropical flowers. The church was light blue with white external facings. The building was fronted with a large portico of three adjoining arches. A cross soared above the portico, like a beacon sending out a Christian message to a world that no longer existed, a lighthouse overlooking a long evaporated sea.

Major Nguyen Van Tong, the Hoa Luu District Battalion Commander, sat on the porch sipping tea with the Mother Superior, Mother Maria. Mother Maria, along with three nuns, was in charge of the church. The VC had run the priests out long ago. The Sisters held services every Sunday and a few old women would attend. The service was not a real mass because there was no priest, but the old women didn't mind. Often, young men of the Hoa Luu Battalion would drop by to talk with Mother Maria, not because they were Catholics, but because they liked the old lady.

Mother Maria was a Viet Cong. She lived in their territory, the sisters nursed their sick families, she gave them some spiritual support, and, most seriously, she allowed the Hoa Luu Battalion to use the church facilities as a forward command post. None of this bothered Mother Maria. She had lived here most of her life. She loved people, the Delta people, and she loved God. Many in the Hoa Luu Battalion revered this old nun attired in her black habit with white bib. There was something timeless about her, her thin but erect figure, her slightly wizened face with its perpetual smile, something unchanging in a simple rural world gone crazy. Mother Maria was a talisman for the commander of the Hoa Luu Battalion. She had been a mother to him as long as he could remember, since he was orphaned in a war long ago.

She looked at Major Tong. He was dressed in the usual black pajamas of the Delta farmer—but there were differences. A pistol belt curled on the table before him with a bolstered Chinese Communist automatic, and there was a thick, scarred leather briefcase filled with maps and papers. He didn't wear sandals, but the same black sneakers the Delta Tigers wore on operations. He kept crossing and uncrossing these sneakers. Major Tong's lean, narrow face looked tired and nervous. He had a tic in his left eye. She knew he was waiting for his superior, Colonel Le Trung Truc, the commander of the U Minh Regiment. There would be a meeting tonight. It happened once a month.

"It will be all right," she counseled.

"I don't know. It is not going well in Hoa Luu," he said in a worried voice.

"But you have done your best."

"Yes, I think so," he replied slowly. "but…" He lapsed into silence. She respected his silence. Together they waited for Colonel Truc and drank their tea.

Major Tong and Colonel Truc had been talking for hours. They were located in an inconspicuous building hidden in a row of coconut palms on the church grounds. The building was crammed with maps, charts, and radios. A small generator whirred in the background. The room was lit by small, naked electric lights. The forward command post of the Hoa Luu District Battalion, unlike the American Hoa Luu District hut, had electricity.

"Look, Chau," Colonel Truc said, calling Major Tong by his familiar family name. They had fought and bled together for years and were related. "You must face realities. Hoa Luu District is not the Hoa Luu District of old. Look at the intelligence. The PF train constantly, the platoons have those stupid flags, the fortifications have improved, bridges and installations are actually guarded, and now, the most dangerous, the three regional force companies have completed some sort of elite infantry commando course and are conducting operations closer and closer to this base area. My God, they are acting like Viet Minh! Last month you fought a battle not four kilometers from here, and you were screaming on the radio for another battalion."

Major Tong broke in, "I do not scream like a woman, Colonel Truc. I requested the battalion based on my military judgment. They had the capability to break into the Vinh Cheo."

There was a brief silence. Colonel Truc had a large head paradoxically connected to a thin body, as if the war had starved everything but his brain. He scowled, which creased his forehead and gave his heavy face an even meaner look. He looked menacing, even sitting in a chair. Truc looked at the ceiling, then reached for the bottle of Ba Si De, a fiery Vietnamese whiskey they had been drinking sparingly. He unscrewed the cap and filled his glass, then screwed the cap back on.

"Listen, Chau," he said intently. "Hoa Luu is the cap on this bottle. If the cap cannot be pried off, the fiery fluid will not be allowed to burst forth and liberate our country. You must understand that the Vinh Thanh and Hoa Luu Canals and the province road must be under our control, or we will lose access to our objectives. You know we have received a warning order from the North to prepare for offensive operations. We have talked for hours, but I have heard nothing of your plans. What are you going to do?"

Major Tong looked down at his hands folded on the table, then reached for the whiskey bottle. This man was his leader, his kinsman, his friend. He was not going to be intimidated, however. He might be nervous about the situation, he persuaded himself, but not about his commander's visit. Actually, it was a little of both. Truc had never talked to him so directly, so authoritatively.

"We should not have killed the American Major," Tong muttered.

"My God, that is the only operation which went well in five months. Why?"

"The Major we killed was weak. He was replaced by a strong officer who has strengthened the district. You know, comrade, you have counseled me many times about killing American advisors. You have said that a weak American advisor is a strong ally of the Viet Minh."

"Ahhh, Chau, Chau, don't throw my words back at me. You know the assassination was ordered from above. They wanted a dead American officer, and you gave them one. Incidentally, what have you done with that outstanding young man who commanded the ambush; what is his name? Sergeant Truong. I want him in the Regiment."

"He is now a platoon sergeant in the same company, and I need him. Comrade, you put pressure on me with new missions and then threaten to take my best soldiers."

Colonel Truc smiled at this and looked at his kinsman with affection. "Understand, little brother, you are the only one in the Delta who can talk to me like this. But, now, tell me, what are you going to do?"

But Tong would not be specific. "Then there are the Hoa Hao. They are more militant than ever before. They are recruiting and converting all over the district. I tell you, this Commander Re person is a real villain, a warrior priest. Even some of our own soldiers say he has good Karma. Men on both sides value his reputation." Colonel True flinched. Tong knew he was a Buddhist.

"And Major Tho," Tong continued, "another conniving Hoa Hao, almost as bad as Re. We must wipe out these Hoa Hao, or the 'cap,' as you call it, will never come off."

Colonel Truc was losing his patience. He banged on the table with an open hand. "Stop telling me the obvious. What are you going to do? Am I to do your job?" Tong started to interrupt. "No, you listen to me. I am going to give you specific guidance for this mission." He stood up next to the district map on the wall. "Get your operations officer. Both of you take notes. This must be understood!" A young officer came running up, paper and pencil in hand.

The commander continued. "The objective is to neutralize Hoa Luu District so that in one year's time, they will not have the combat power or the desire to interdict our attacks north. This objective," he looked hard at Tong, "is subtle, like silk over sharp steel." He paused. "We will call the operation "CHIEN DICH LUA BOG SAT," Silk over Steel. If we attack the district like a bunch of rampaging elephants, the chances are they will attack Vinh Cheo or worse, bring in the Americans. That would be a disaster for the future offensive. No, we must start slowly, then grow relentless. We will impose our will on the enemy. Many Government soldiers will survive this operation; many outposts will remain intact. We do not want to destroy them all. That would raise a storm against us. But the soldiers who remain will cower behind their coconut logs when we attack, fearing the fighting spirit of the Viet Minh.

"You will start with a major attack on Hoa Luu Town." He punched the Hoa Luu location on the map with his finger. "I want you to overrun the district capital. Do not hold it, but destroy it completely. Pick a time when you can kill the traitors Tho, Re, and the American advisor. The programs that are hurting us start there. We will cut off the head, then overrun the outpost just north of Vinh Cheo, destroy the 123rd RF Company and hold the surrounding countryside." He pointed to the outpost on the map, four kilometers north of where they were meeting. "That will eliminate their security operations in the vicinity of the confluence of the Tao River and the Hoa Luu and Vinh Thanh Canals. I don't want them to conduct any operations into the Vinh Cheo base area. Do the same at Vinh Thanh. I want the province road permanently interdicted at Vinh Thanh. Then hit these outposts, but do not destroy them." He gestured to numerous outposts throughout the district. "It is November; I want these operations completed by spring. You have five months. After these attacks we will maintain a steel grip on the district, but not through open combat, through terrorism. We cannot have heavy fighting here just before the offensive. We would lose the element of surprise for our large offensive. I also want you to step up your terror campaign throughout the district. You know what I mean: assassinations, minings, make it difficult to travel in Hoa Luu." He paused, looking fiercely at Tong. "Any questions?"

"What about Huong Tho, the province capital?"

Truc grinned. "I will take care of that."

"What casualty status should we inflict? I am against the policy of GIET SACH, no survivors, not because I am soft, but because it turns the population against us."

Colonel Truc's grin disappeared. "You are soft, Tong, and I know why."

Tong looked away from his commander's eyes.

"There can be no mercy in this war. You and I have lost our families. Chau, you were brought up here as an orphan in this church. The people who live in the Government area, if they accept the handouts of the Americans, they can expect death. Anything else?" But he had not directly answered Tong's question about GIET SACH.

"What forces are available to me?"

"You are over strength. We are all bulging with men and equipment."

"Not for this mission. I need more mortars. I must be fully supplied with the new rifle we have been training with, the AK47."

"No AK47s, but continue to train with them. They are our surprise for later. I will give you additional mortars, but be careful of wasting ammunition. The Hoa Luu Battalion uses more ammunition than any other district battalion in my command." Major Tong frowned.

"The 309th Battalion will be under your operational control for designated operations." Tong raised his hand. "And that is final, no more, I have no more!"

Tong knew this was not true. He had seen thousands of soldiers training with new equipment in the U Minh Forest. He resented that the U Minh battalions were better equipped than his district battalion. Most had new clothing, a fine pith helmet with a red star on the front, and a new pistol belt. They also had liberal amounts of ammunition and were allowed to practice far more than his soldiers. All for the big plan, the huge offensive. Meanwhile, his battalion was on line, fighting the enemy every day attired in ragged black pajamas and armed with ancient weapons. There was no appreciation that he had political responsibilities as well, not shared by his fellow battalion commanders in the Regiment. Tong looked at his commander and said, "I understand your guidance, comrade."

"Let me repeat the key points of the mission: subtlety, silk over steel, first smash the District Headquarters, next Vinh Cheo and Vinh Thanh, then attack the other outposts I designated. All this hard fighting must be completed by April, but it also must be phased. You know, one at a time. We don't want to attract attention. After April, keep the district in a grip of steel."

"Comrade, the Hoa Luu Battalion will do its duty," Tong said in a firm, hard voice. Colonel Truc laughed heartily, reassured for the first time in the conference.

"I trust you, little brother."

Mother Maria held both of Tong's hands and looked up at him in the early morning darkness. They were standing on the small landing in front of the church. The Regimental Commander had left the night before. A sampan with engine running was secured at the end of the dock. A soldier manned the engine; another, fully armed, stood on the dock holding the mooring line. Except for the low cough of the engine, everything was quiet. A white mist hung over the river's surface.

"Do not lose your love for the people, my son. The Viet Minh, the Government, the Hoa Hao are all people of the Delta, all God's people. GIET SACK, no survivors, is a terrible thing, a crime against God."

"I will not, MA." He used the word for maternal mother, not the religious title. But Tong was already thinking hard about his new mission. "Do you still wear it?" she asked, hanging onto him, not wanting him to go.

"Yes, always." The silver cross around his neck had been worn in hundreds of battles.

Tong hugged her hard and was gone, his sampan disappearing in the river mist. Mother Maria stood a long time on the landing. Tears ran down her weathered cheeks.

****

There was a roar over the district town. The team raced outside and looked up. The 0-1 Bird Dog pulled up, banked right and returned on another gun run right on the rice paddies. The aircraft almost knocked over the radio antenna on top of the bunker.

The radio crackled, "GOOD MORNING, DELTA ALPHA, ARE YOU GUYS AWAKE DOWN THERE? THIS IS YOUR GOOD BUDDY FLIPSTICK."

Travis answered more formally. "FLIPSTICK, THIS IS DELTA ALPHA SIX. AFFIRMATIVE. WHAT'S GOING ON IN THIS PART OF THE WORLD?"

"NOTHING MUCH. TALKED TO OUR GOOD BUDDY BOB HARRIS, CORRECTION, CORRECTION, DELTA BRAVO SIX. SAYS

HE ENJOYED HIS VISIT WITH YOU AND WILL TALK TO YOU LATER IN THE DAY ON THE RADIO. VERY LITTLE BANDIT ACTIVITY. ANYTHING YOU WANT ME TO CHECK? OVER." Cochran was frequently counseled on his terrible radio procedure, but with no apparent effect.

"ROGER, MAKE YOUR USUAL RECCY OVER SECTOR DELTA [the Vinh Cheo area]. ALSO WE'VE RECEIVED SOME REPORTS OF ENEMY SAMPAN ACTIVITY IN THE NORTHEAST SECTOR OF SECTOR ALPHA [northeast Vinh Thanh Canal area], TAKE A LOOK. OVER." Travis had divided the district into surveillance sectors for security purposes and to facilitate communications with Flipstick.

"ROGER, ANYTHING ELSE?"

"NEGATIVE, NEED TO TALK TO YOU MORE ABOUT FIREFLY MISSIONS. GOOD HUNTING, OUT."

Cochran performed this mission for all six district teams every day. He was also laboring hard for more air support. The Bird Dog he flew was literally a fighter bomber armed with eight 2.75 HE rockets hung on the wings. He now landed his Bird Dog on the province road outside the compound. Flip would zoom over the road on a reccy run to insure no water buffalo or kids had wandered onto his landing strip. He would then bank the airplane around and set it down in an explosion of dust. That part of the province road became known as the Hoa Luu International Airport.

He and Travis were developing a Firefly mission request. The objective of Firefly operations was to interdict VC night movement along the canals. The operation consisted of one helicopter equipped with search lights to light up the canal, followed by two gun ships to destroy illuminated targets. Travis believed the enemy moved with impunity at night, particularly in the Vinh Cheo Triangle. They had good targets and needed air assets. It was the old question of support for Territorial Forces again.

Flip Cochran: A poor orphaned kid brought up in South Boston by an indifferent aunt; flunked out of Boston U after two years and was drafted; surprisingly, he was accepted for OCS but he barely survived because of a near fist fight with a TAC officer; flight school at Fort Rucker where he excelled and qualified both in fixed and rotary wing aircraft; his many successes and near disasters as a small unit commander where he was effective, in spite of a hot temper, a hatred for arrogant commanders and all things chicken shit. Flipstick possessed a huge secret which only those who were close to him knew. Behind the cocky exterior, the constant hassle with his military superiors, he loved the Army. He was a skilled pilot and strong commander. Flip Cochran was a helluva soldier.

That day he was having the time of his life. Flip was finally doing some real soldiering as he flew the tiny O-1 Bird Dog above Hoa Luu District. He owned everything in view 2000 feet below. They were his mangrove swamps, his rice paddies, and his canals. The little dots working on the rice paddies and gathered around the open markets were his people. Huddled somewhere in the mangrove swamps lurked the VC, his enemy, and Cochran was going to do his damnedest to destroy them and protect his people and his land. He headed the little airplane southwest down the Hoa Luu canal toward the Vinh Cheo Triangle. The 360 horsepower engine didn't miss a beat.

Later that morning, Major Tho conducted a medical military visit at the Vinh Cheo outpost complex, the home of the 123rd RF Company and three PF platoons. The District Chief, his military inspection team, Co Linh, a medical orderly, a Province official with two sampan loads of bulgur wheat, cooking oil and aluminum roofing, and the American team comprised the medical military effort.

Medical military visits, or MEDMILS in Travis language, consisted of inspecting all outposts at least once a month, and in conjunction with these inspections, to distribute commodities, building materials, and medical aid to military families. MEDMIL's central theme, as Travis often briefed, "... is to improve the Territorial Force soldier by demonstrating that District is not only concerned with his military proficiency, but the welfare of his family as well. The family is what motivates these men to fight. Remember, the Territorial Force soldier in Hoa Luu is not merely a part of our security here, he is our security. He is the unsung hero in the war."

Vinh Cheo was the last outpost complex in the southwest corner of Hoa Luu District and guarded against VC encroachments from the Vinh Cheo Triangle. It had been earmarked for destruction by Colonel Truc, the U Minh Regimental Commander. Vinh Cheo was the typical mud fort of the delta, a square brown structure made of mud and rice grass. The walls were constantly eroding and requiring repair. A two story machinegun emplacement stood at each corner. Along the walls, two-man foxholes were constructed at spaced intervals. Just outside the square were minefields and long fields of fire which were constantly groomed to permit maximum machinegun grazing fire. Inside the square was a small, bricked parade ground, living quarters for soldiers and families who lived in the fort in time of emergency, and a fortified command bunker. The red and yellow

Government flag hung limply from a flagpole in the center of the parade ground.

This ugly, mud brown fortification with the red and yellow flag overhead was the symbol of the Government of Vietnam for much of the Delta. Travis thought these forts looked like a rerun of a bad, French Foreign Legion film, yet another image which added to the impression of the Delta War as frozen in history.

Major Tho was all business. His inspectors had detailed checklists covering their areas of responsibility. First, they inspected a formation of soldiers and all their individual weapons. Then they branched out and looked at supplies, ammunition storage, and minefields just beyond the perimeter. The district was short of mines, but they put "Beware of Mines" signs out anyway, hoping to scare the VC away. Fortifications received the most attention. Were the walls intact and smooth with no evidence of erosion? Were the firing positions clean and dry, with overhead cover, each equipped with a grenade hole? Later that day, the entire inspection process would be repeated at each of the PF outposts.

As the inspection was conducted, Co Linh, Sergeant Gonzales and Sergeant Minh set up their medical aid station in the local hamlet. Women, children, and old people lined up for treatment. There was much jostling around in line and loud singsong conversation. A happy scene.

Co Linh was a thorough, tough inspector. Often, she provided the fireworks for the visit. She would raise hell over unsanitary instruments or a dirty dispensary. She required a detailed inventory of all medicines, and if the local medic or midwife could not account for every pill and bottle, they were berated in a style which would have given credit to Major Tho on one of his bad days. Travis would wander around during the MEDMILS, looking into nearly everything. These visits, the PF training program, the RF ranger training, and weekly overnight operations with the Delta Tigers added up to life in Hoa Luu. All of these programs were having a positive effect. *There was a sense of purpose about Hoa Luu District*, Travis thought, *a feeling of winning*.

Later, after a rousing speech which praised the Government, but mostly praised the Hoa Hao, Major Tho would hand out the foodstuffs and building materials to the people. There were always evangelical overtones to the District Chief's talks. Tho enjoyed this role and always had a Dutchmaster Panatella stuck firmly in his teeth, like a ward politician.

Much of what Travis had accomplished in Hoa Luu was mirrored in Tram

Cua District to the south. Major Bob Harris agreed with Travis' programs and was having some success. Tram Cua, however, was not a Hoa Hao district. It did not have the leadership of the Hoa Hao and was far more closely controlled by Province than Hoa Luu, which was allowed to go its own way. *This cut both ways*, Travis thought. *They were left alone but received little support.*

The other district teams in Ngoc Hoa Province did not have similar programs. Jack Travis and Bob Harris became professional compadres because they could visit each other by sampan and jeep. The other districts might as well have been on the surface of the moon. The Province chopper was never available for District use, and Lieutenant Colonel Potts never conducted district advisor meetings to share information or ideas.

The Unholy Alliance, as Travis, Harris, Cochran called themselves, met frequently. They had some war winning ideas and were looking for someone to listen. The Firefly mission was one of their initiatives. Cochran was trying to activate some of his aviator buddies at Division for support. Travis was dubious about receiving the aviation assets.

Co Linh had jumped right in and organized medical services in the district. She and Doc Gonzales were a medical legend.

Travis treasured his time with Co Linh. Her energy and unconscious sensuality fascinated him. Even her frequent anger on inspection trips had a cleansing quality. He would stare at her as she sat in the sampan, the wind blowing her coal black hair, eyes dancing with sheer delight at the beauty of the trip, and the infectious excitement that they were doing good for the people. She had suffered in the war and yet she possessed a spirit, an indomitable enthusiastic strength that could not be destroyed. Travis loved her. She was becoming a symbol, a being who kept an upside down world on its feet. Enemy activity over the last month had decreased significantly. Even VC Charlie appeared to have gone on a vacation. Mortaring incidents had become a rarity. Travis thought this was due to the success of their advisory programs. Sergeant Minh believed that enemy activity was down because they were up to something. *The old "Minh theory,"* Travis thought. On occasion, Sergeant Minh was a crank.

The nights were now kinder to Travis. He actually slept. Deep inside him, however, the fear remained. The question was always there, haunting him. If the chips were down, really down, a hard combat situation, could he measure up? This secret never left him. The team's major problem was the shortage of two people. A deputy had never been assigned and Hartwell's death reduced them to four men. It was difficult to function, and he had to persuade Commander Re to lend him a soldier to secure their hut when the team was gone on their many trips. He continued to bombard Province with requests for replacements, but nobody appeared to pay attention.

At the end of this very good day at Vinh Cheo, the group returned by sampan to Hoa Luu. Major Tho was happy. "This medical military—how you say it? MEDMIL go very well. RF is good. I think PF get better." He paused looking at the canal bank. "Everything better in district."

"Yes, Sir," Travis replied, feeling upbeat.

"Dai Uy Luom tell me you plan Firefly for Hoa Luu. He tell me you have good plan."

"We have a good plan, Sir, but I'm not sure we can get the aircraft. Major Cochran thinks we can."

"Very important. We never have Firefly in district. We must control the canals at night." He lapsed into thought, worried about security.

"If we get the aircraft, the operation will go later this week. I have worked closely with the staff to identify the targets."

"It will be a good thing." Tho flashed Travis his gold capped grin. "You must get the aircraft!" He added a puff of smoke for emphasis.

Gunships had apparently been added to Tho's cigar list, Travis thought. *But it was good to see Major Tho in such high spirits.*

****

Midnight in Hoa Luu. Three aircraft flew southwest over the Hoa Luu Canal in trail at 500 feet. All running lights were turned off. The lead aircraft was Flip Cochran's Bird Dog, flying throttled back at 60 knots. He was the battle captain, point man, and navigator for the Firefly mission. The lightship followed, a UH 1 helicopter equipped with powerful search lights. A single gunship flew tail, slightly offset from the lightship, ready to attack any illuminated target. They had requested two, but only one was available. This aircraft was the famed UH 1 Hog, the early gunship, armed with 2.75 HE rockets and 7.62 machineguns.

The Firefly team had just refueled at a small strip in Vinh Thanh after thoroughly checking out the Vinh Thanh Canal and its major tributaries. So far, negative contact.

Jack Travis and Bob Harris flew with the gunship. Travis was looking carefully at the map with a thin pencil light. He was disappointed. The Firefly team had flown over almost all the significant canals in the district and found nothing. They would have a hell of a time generating another mission like this.

There was a half moon. The stars glimmered and appeared to be flying with them in formation. You could almost reach out and grab one. Damp tropical night air rushed through the helicopter's troop compartment. Visibility was good; the canal streaked out before them like a silvery ruler, straight and true. Harris looked at the canal below through binoculars, trying to pierce the darkness under the palm trees on the banks. On signal from Cochran, the lightship switched on. The canal was instantly transformed from tropical night to a blazing, surrealistic brightness. Everything stood out, the ripples on the canal surface could be seen. The gunship pilot pulled the nose up a little bit for a possible gun run, but, again, nothing. The canal below looked like some hyper-illuminated movie set not yet populated by actors. Switch off, the whole scene disappeared, plunging the world into Stygian blackness. The crews tried to keep one eye closed so that switching from brightness to darkness would not destroy their night adaptation. They were like God playing with the sun's on and off switch.

Cochran was having fun, even though they hadn't fired a shot. Where else could you lead an aerial armada like this, except in this crazy Delta war where time was anchored in history. He checked his instruments. Everything was okay. He thought of the "Deep Option." He spoke over the intercom to Sergeant Minh, who was traveling in the rear seat as an observer.

"What do you think, Minh, buddy? Should we go deep?"

"Just a minute, Sir." Minh was studying his map. In minutes they would fly over the Vinh Cheo outpost complex. No enemy seen so far, and this didn't surprise him. It had been quiet in Hoa Luu for weeks. The "Deep Option" was to penetrate the Vinh Cheo Triangle and fly southwest along the Tao River. They all thought this would be good hunting. It was also disobeying orders. They had received no clearance from Province to fly outside the district boundaries.

"Sir, I think we should go deep," Minh replied.

"Roger, we will swing south using the Lighthouse as a checkpoint." The Lighthouse was the Catholic Church on the Tao River.

"Better check with Major Travis," Sergeant Minh advised.

"Roger; meanwhile, I'm going to temporarily change course." He banked right, turned to the northwest, and gained altitude.

"FIREBIRD, GUNBIRD, WATCH MY TURN." He turned on his running lights. "WE'LL CIRCLE THIS AREA AND HAVE A COUNCIL OF WAR."

The Birds "ROGERED" him.

"HEY, GOOD BUDDIES ON GUNBIRD. I NEED TO GIVE YOU GUYS A TASTE OF DELTA AERIAL COMBAT. RECOMMEND WE EXECUTE 'DEEP OPTION,'"

Bob Harris looked at Jack Travis in the wind-rushed darkness of the rear troop compartment. "Your call, Jack, this is your district," he said over the intercom.

Travis worried over the decision. Potts had been very reluctant to approve this mission in the first place. He could not understand why anyone would bother with this kind of operation. It wasn't their job. The helicopters were Division assets. Suppose they lost an aircraft? He had agreed, mainly because the province had been quiet, and Cochran had assured him he had the aircraft in hand. It had not occurred to Potts that Travis would consider entering the Vinh Cheo Triangle. But the Unholy Alliance had addressed this option in detail and had half decided to execute if they came up empty handed in the district. The air crews from the two helicopters agreed. They were eager for action. They had done nothing but search and avoid for the past few months.

"FLIPSTICK, THIS IS DELTA ALPHA SIX. I SEEM TO BE TEMPORARILY DISORIENTED ON MY MAP. RECOMMEND WE FLY OVER LIGHTHOUSE FOR ORIENTATION AND SWING SOUTH A FEW KILOMETERS ALONG THE RIVER TO MAKE SURE WE HAVE OUR BEARINGS, OVER."

"ROGER," Flipstick replied. Having established their cover story, the Firefly team resumed their original formation heading for the Vinh Cheo outpost complex.

They flew over the outpost complex and the confluence of the canal and the Tao River. The canal was straight and turned at geometric angles. The river was wide and undisciplined. From the air it looked like a straight arrow had transfixed a wriggling silver snake. The tree cover was heavier here. A small army could hide under the trees on the banks.

They flew south. Below, Cochran could pick up the Lighthouse; the church was plainly visible, even the large cross. Flip felt a momentary twinge. He remembered his Catholic youth.

Mother Maria awakened to the unfamiliar sound of aircraft. She could hear excited voices calling on the radio from the Hoa Luu Battalion forward command post behind the church.

The Firefly team continued southwest down the meandering Tao River. Just beyond the church Cochran ordered, "LIGHTS!" Brightness exploded over the river. Everything was visible in stark relief. Nothing. "LIGHTS OFF."

They continued. The rice paddies beside the river were disappearing, replaced by dark mangrove forest. No chatter over the intercom now. They knew they were penetrating deep into the enemy base area. Cochran peered out the Plexiglas cockpit. The river was visible, surrounded by dark forest, dotted with a few open fields. No villages could be seen. The Tao curved to the south, continued for one kilometer, and then swung west, a good killing ground. He oriented the lightbird and gunbird, and then offset his aircraft so he could give precise commands to the lightbird when it flew over the target area.

"LIGHTS!" he shouted in the small Bird Dog cockpit. Sergeant Minh jumped hard against the safety straps in the rear seat. Blinding light, a tangible smothering brightness engulfed the Tao River below. And they were there! "BANDITS BELOW, BANDITS BELOW!" Cochran screamed into the radio. A double line of sampans loaded with armed men were motoring to the north. The sampans and soldiers stood out on the river's surface like frozen mannequins. The gunbird opened up immediately with its machineguns, followed by 2.75 HE rockets. Tracers streamed into the river in a solid yellow wall; lines of water geysers slanted and crisscrossed the columns of enemy boats; sampans capsized; men jumped into the water. The door gunner had a field day as the gunship flew over the target area, pumping hundreds of tracers into the morass of men and sampans. The gunship shook with firepower. Cochran yanked his Bird Dog around and fired two 2.75 HE rockets at the target. One missed and the other exploded in the midst of three sampans that had jammed against each other in the middle of the river and were hopelessly adrift. There was an explosion of white water, splintered wood and flying bodies. "KILL THEM MOTHERFUCKERS!" somebody screamed over the radio. They passed over the target area. Lights out. Immediate blackness.

"TURN AROUND, FIREFLIES. HIT 'EM AGAIN," Cochran ordered. The two helicopters turned over the western bend of the river and flew north up towards the killing zone.

"LIGHTS!" Again the brightness. Like magic, the river had changed. Nothing could be seen except a few overturned sampans. Suddenly green tracers shot out from the western river bank. They experienced the strange sensation men feel when they are being shot at from below. Pencil thin green lights arced up, stopped and opened up again directly at the lightbird. The ship shuddered. The crew could feel the rounds thudding through the aluminum. One slammed through the small space between the pilot and troop compartment. Hydraulic fluid was spraying inside the ship; there was the acrid smell of burning wires. The searchlight flickered and went off.

A cool detached voice on the radio said, "MAYDAY, MAYDAY. WE'RE HIT, LOSING HYDRAULICS, FOLLOW ME DOWN."

The gunship took up a position on the tail of the lightbird. The pilot looked for a field in the heavily forested area. He was losing altitude fast. The controls were stiffening. He spotted a small clearing to his right front, about two hundred yards from the river. Bouncing the skids on the cleared field, he landed hard. The following gunship circled once and then landed fifteen yards from the downed helicopter.

Travis's heart was pounding. They had to get these men out before the VC attacked. He jumped out of his aircraft and ran over to the wounded bird. Harris was with him. The lightship crew evacuated the downed aircraft immediately. One man had been slightly wounded by aluminum splinters. Nobody was seriously hit. The two Majors directed them to their aircraft, which was picking up power about to take off. There were deep explosions beyond the tree line; Cochran was firing rockets at the enemy positions along the river bank. The gunship lifted off the ground. The lightship pilot shouted, "No! We've got to go back!" They had to get the weapons, maps and signal operations instructions out of the downed helicopter.

"Bullshit," said the gunship pilot, and he pulled up on the collective and leaned down on the cyclic to develop maximum air speed. Just as they cleared the tree line, the downed helicopter exploded in a ball of flame.

"ANY CASUALTIES?" It was Cochran on the radio.

"NEGATIVE, BUT SCRATCH ONE HELICOPTER."

"SHIT! IT WAS WORTH IT," Cochran replied and selected a heading for the airstrip at Vinh Thanh.

"GET ON MY TAIL," he ordered. The helicopter fell in behind him, and both gained altitude and turned on their running lights. They flew on into the night.

"HEY, ALPHA SIX, YOU'D BETTER BE ABLE TO EXPLAIN THIS TO POTTSIE. I AIN'T GOING TO DO IT."

Jack Travis and Bob Harris looked at each other in the dark crew compartment and then burst into laughter. The rescued air crew joined in. They roared and slapped each other on the back. "Man, we gave it to those sons of bitches. We kicked ass."

They stood at rigid attention in Lieutenant Colonel Potts' office. At least

95

Travis and Harris stood at rigid attention. Cochran slumped and looked at Potts with his usual quizzical expression.

Potts was pacing before the three men in a rage. 'What in the hell were you doing in the Vinh Cheo Triangle? You were lost? Goddamn it, Travis, you should know that area like your backside. To have a helicopter shot down! I've been on the radio explaining this disaster to Division all day!"

"Sir, I became temporarily disoriented while we were flying down the Hoa Luu Canal."

"Don't give me that shit! You want me to believe you remained 'temporarily disoriented' for ten kilometers as you traveled south down the Tao River into Indian country? Unbelievable!" He looked at Cochran. "You were the air battle captain; what in the hell were you doing?"

Cochran just continued to look at Potts.

Harris cleared his throat. Potts looked at the tall, dark, bespectacled major. "Well?"

"Sir, we finally realized we had made a mistake, but by that time we believed we had a rare opportunity to check the area out. We had never been that deep into the Vinh Cheo before. The point is, Sir, we engaged a large enemy force moving north up the Tao River." All this was delivered in a flinty, almost sepulchral New England accent.

"The point is, gentlemen, you disobeyed orders. I've told all of you time and time again, especially you, Travis, to stay out of the Triangle. My God, things have never been better in the province. What were you trying to do? Start World War III?" The tirade ended. The air seemed to go out of Lieutenant Colonel Potts. He slowly sank into his chair.

"Sir, if I may." Travis approached the edge of the desk. "Something bad is going on in the Vinh Cheo. We fought a large enemy force moving north. What are they up to? You remember my briefing to you a few months ago. Are they trying to secure the canal routes in Hoa Luu District? Are they preparing for an offensive? We've got to get in there and break it up."

At this point Cochran finally said something. "We killed at least a fucking VC platoon, Colonel Potts. Doesn't that mean a goddamn thing? We haven't had a body count like that in this province since I've been here."

Potts looked at Cochran exasperated then shrugged. He looked directly at Travis. "You don't understand the issue here. You men disobeyed orders and lost a helicopter. And you know what, fellas?" He looked at them, smiling tiredly. "Tomorrow you can explain this to the new Division Senior Advisor, Colonel Mason. He is coming to Huong Tho and personally wants to investigate this fiasco." Potts dismissed the Unholy Alliance with a wave of his hand.

That night, the Unholy Alliance was drinking beer at the Province Club. They sat at a table in the far corner away from the bar noise. It was relatively quiet, except for a few muted conversations. Earlier, Cochran had unplugged the jukebox and then glared around the club. Nobody said anything. The three had gained some notoriety, particularly since the helicopter incident.

Cochran was speaking. "This Mason is a bad ass. He was an assault aviation battalion up in III Corps and has a helluva reputation, a real fighter."

"This is the guy they call the Grey Ghost?" Travis asked.

"The same. He's done it all, including combat in Korea."

"He should understand our story then. Maybe we can get off the hook and persuade him to put 64th Division into the Vinh Cheo Triangle. He might actually be interested in winning," Harris said solemnly.

"Maybe," Cochran said, "but I understand he can be a real shit. Mason is a West Pointer, a stickler for order, a harsh disciplinarian and," he slapped them both on the back, "we're a little weak in that department right now."

A worried silence hung over the table.

Later that night, Travis shared a room with Harris. Because it was safer, with real bunks with clean sheets and air conditioning, a night at Province was luxury. Harris unpacked his gear and set up a picture of his family on the bedside table; the picture showed a dark haired, serious looking young woman and two little girls who had a marked resemblance to Harris.

"You have a beautiful family, Bob. I wish I had a family," he continued wistfully. "You know, something to come home to. It would give me some purpose, a real incentive to get back to the world."

"They're everything to me. How come you never married, Jack, a big stud like you from Tidewater, Virginia?"

"I had so many women after me, I couldn't choose." Jack smiled and said more seriously, "There were two. You know, I was engaged my last two years at VMI. The girl was my ring figure date. That's a big thing where I come from."

"Us Yankee farmers can't relate to those esoteric antebellum traditions, Jack."

Travis laughed. "Well, anyway, this one was a serious relationship. Her father was president of a big dredging company in Norfolk. My parents thought it was ideal, but it didn't work out. I wasn't cut out to be a Tidewater businessman, and she wasn't about to leave her mommy and daddy, the Norfolk Yacht Club and the Azalea Festival. I guess the Army destroyed that romance."

"You said there were two?"

"I met the other girl in Germany. She was an American school teacher. We lived together for a while." He paused, frowning slightly. "But then I came home early from an exercise one day and found her in bed with my roommate in the BOQ."

"Jack, you have been unlucky in love. They write songs about guys like you."

"Yes, but hell, Bob, I'm still young."

The conversation wandered on to their meeting with the Grey Ghost the next day. They worried about the encounter.

After the lights were turned off, Jack thought about his life. He wasn't that young, over thirty. The time had come when he couldn't consider himself a young man anymore. Life was slipping by him. Here's Bob Harris with a family. What did he have? The Army, this crazy Delta war, Co Linh? Yes, Co Linh. He thought of her, her smell, her figure dressed in an ao dai, her upbeat vitality. A great yearning came over him.

Travis awoke later that night. The room was black. He felt again that terrible sense of disorientation, almost terror. The nagging doubts continued. Hartwell crossed his mind. Had he killed Hartwell? Could he have prevented his death? No, the Hoa Hao killed him. In spite of Hartwell's evil, could he fight without him? Something was happening here, a growing sense of tension. All was quiet now, but pressure was building up. He closed his eyes, fighting for sleep.

The Grey Ghost stood before the three men in Lieutenant Colonel Potts' office. He had an athletic build, medium height, iron grey hair, a well trimmed mustache and piercing grey eyes. His jungle fatigues were emblazoned with Ranger tab, Master Jumper wings, Master Aviator wings and the Combat Infantry Badge with star, which indicated he had fought in Korea. He was forty-one years old and had just been promoted to full colonel. *A soldier's soldier, the way a commander should look*, the Unholy Alliance thought. Mason was the Senior American Advisor to the 64th ARVN Division and was responsible for the entire advisory presence in the Division area to include both ARVN and province advisory teams.

Potts had left the room to answer an urgent radio call. They were located on the map side of the Province briefing room. The Colonel stood before the map and the three sat on the first tier of chairs.

Colonel William E. Mason had heard and re-heard their explanations. He had asked many questions about the lines of communications in Hoa Luu District, the avenues of approach to the populated northern areas, the relationship between the Hoa Luu District Battalion and the U Minh Regiment, and the Hoa Hao influence. He appeared to agree, or was at least concerned, about future enemy offensive intentions.

After Potts left the room, he looked hard at the three men. "It was a good operation." There was steel in his voice. "In fact, I would have decorated you except for one trifling thing. You know what it is?"

Silence.

"Major Travis, never mind this disoriented bullshit. Did you fully intend to execute this Deep Option the entire time?"

Travis looked at the Grey Ghost levelly. "Yes, Sir, it was always our plan. It was always on our minds." He looked at the others who nodded.

"Get this straight: in my outfit you never lie, regardless of the provocation! I'll be straight with you. You goddamn well better be straight with me! Understand?" There was a sharp rising inflection. The Unholy Alliance jumped. Then there was a moment of pregnant silence.

"Now I know you guys have had some trouble," he glanced at the door where Potts had left, "but we're in a transition stage right now. Better officers are arriving every day. You men are the first of the new breed. Right now you're just going to have to put up with the situation.

"I'm new here, as you know. I served in III Corps and there the situation is different. I don't really have the picture here and I have some problems of my own. You hear rumors all over the Delta that the 64th Division is a search and avoid outfit. To be absolutely candid with you, there is some truth to this. The Division Commander is in severe need of a backbone operation. My job is to perform the surgery. Meanwhile, you guys on the province and district teams have to do your damnedest to win the war.

"Jack," he looked at Travis, "I'm not sure of the Vinh Cheo operation right now. What you say makes sense, but you guys must understand, I've got a lot of Vinh Cheos in the Southern Delta. Things are quiet now, and I can't afford to persuade the Division Commander to operate in the wrong place at the wrong time."

Travis raised his hand.

"I've heard your arguments, Jack, and they're good ones, but I've got to wait."

Travis warmed to this man who used his first name.

"Any questions, gentlemen?"

"No sir," they said in unison.

"And if you've got any more ideas about Deep Options, you'd better goddamn well tell the Grey Ghost about them."

The Unholy Alliance left elated. Their winning spirit had been restored. They found out later that the Grey Ghost had set up the radio call to get Potts out of the briefing room.

✳✳✳✳✳✳✳✳✳✳✳✳

Travis and Sergeant Minh were finishing the team briefing for two new team members. Capt. Donald Burns and Master Sergeant Calvin Washington had arrived the day before. These two had brought the team up to full, six man strength. Both men, at Travis's direction, were taking copious notes.

"And understand this," Travis was briefing, "the war is here, because this is where the people are. What we do down here might not appear to be dramatic compared to U.S. operations up north, but it counts. What you do in Hoa Luu is important. Any questions?"

There was a pause. Capt. Burns fidgeted. "It's very quiet according to Sergeant Minh's briefing on the enemy. There's little activity," he offered nervously. Burns was a small, slight, balding young man who worried Travis. He exuded insecurity.

"Maybe that's because our programs are working, or maybe the VC are gearing something up. We told you about the contact we had two weeks ago on the Tao River."

"Oh, and sir…" Burns went on. The words were drawn out, concerned. There was a long pause. Travis waited impatiently. Burns was preoccupied. He did not understand what he was doing here. When he left the States, he had orders to a supply depot in Da Nang. During in-processing in Saigon, MACV had prepared orders sending him to a district team in the Southern Delta, certainly not a proper assignment for a Quartermaster officer just graduated from the Career Course at Fort Lee. He felt isolated. There were only six Americans in a sea of Vietnamese. And, according to Sergeant Minh, there were many VC in the area. He felt a pang of homesickness. He thought nostalgically of his parents, his home in Louisville, Kentucky. Hoa Luu was primitive beyond belief: a plywood hut, the team slept in a single room, no electricity, and the ridiculous latrine facilities. He could not relate to the old team members who thought Hoa Luu was a Delta paradise. Weren't they the only district team in the entire Cau Mau Peninsula that had an honest to God flying shithouse?

By Delta standards, the District compound was now a palace. The screened porch covered with louvered wood walls had been completed. This was the new recreation room. The bunker had been reconstructed, and they had installed a protected, underground communications wire between the U.S. bunker and the Vietnamese operations center. The wonder of worlds, however, had been the construction of the only flying shithouse in the Delta. Travis had struck a deal with some engineers in Can Tho. For a pile of souvenir junk to include three ancient German Mausers, two pith helmets, five VC battle flags, a pair of black pajamas with VC bloodstains, and five WWII Japanese bayonets, they had received two objects of beauty, sacred icons which were, in U.S. advisory channels, to gain the historical stature of the pyramids of Egypt: two gleaming white porcelain commodes. These were appropriately installed in an airplane-shaped outhouse, complete with corrugated metal wings for a roof and a large white propeller fixed to the door, literally a flying shithouse. Flip Cochran had declared the outhouse aerodynamically sound. Billy Turner described the wonder of the Delta best. "If you could shit like an American, you felt like an American."

Capt. Burns fidgeted again, started to speak, paused, and then asked, "Sir, will you please review again what we do in an attack?"

"I'll review that later," Travis answered. He looked hard at Burns, worried. He had done everything to get a combat arms officer assigned to the team. On a district advisory team they all depended on each other. Every man had to carry his weight. He knew how hard up district teams were for company grade officers. Burns had literally been shanghaied in Saigon and sent here. He was going to have to work out. They'd get him out in the boonies. A few small operations with the Tigers would toughen him up. Anyway, Sergeant Washington looked like he would meet the challenge.

Master Sergeant Calvin Washington was a strapping non-commissioned officer of Infantry. With strong, broad features and a fierce look, he was uncompromisingly black. Previously, Washington had served up north with a U.S. unit and extended for this assignment. He actually wanted to serve on a district team. Washington was from southeast Washington, a depressed area of the nation's capital. The grimy streets, the segregated isolation, the feeling of helplessness he had left behind when he was 14 years old. After roustabouting around the country for four years, he had drifted into the Army looking for purpose and direction. A natural soldier and leader, he rose rapidly in the NCO ranks. He had been a platoon sergeant for over a year in combat.

Washington liked what he saw. He approved of the advisory programs because he had some experience in operating with the Territorial Forces, and he was impressed with Major Travis. This guy was dynamite. Washington was a professional soldier who was interested in winning.

"Any more questions?" Travis asked.

"Not for me," Washington responded in a deep booming voice.

"Sir, you said you were going to review, what did you call it? The mortar attack battle drills."

Travis reviewed the drills and looked hard at Burns.

"The big thing to remember is, don't stand up. The explosions go up, you go down. Every night, store your combat gear under your bunk. If we're hit, roll under the bunk, secure your equipment and crawl to the bunker. Look at the walls," Travis gestured, "you can see what I mean." Burns looked at the lace work of small holes in the wall. None were below the sandbag line.

"Anything else? Okay, that's it, guys. Glad to have you on board. Once again, remember this is an important place. We're out to win the war in our little piece of Vietnam. Also, stay alert, remember security and the team battle drills. In Hoa Luu you can have your shit blown away like that!" He snapped his fingers.

* * * * * * * * * * * *

Watching her serve coffee was a delight. Every movement, pouring, handing him the cup and saucer, offering sugar in a small china bowl was graceful. Yet there was a sense of purpose, too. This evening she was wearing a white ao dai bodice which set off her golden skin and black hair. She sat down in a bamboo chair before him, revealing her shapely legs snugly covered with black silk pants. There was a spontaneous goodness about her that filled this room, filled his soul, made this tiny piece of the world work. She looked at him with large dark eyes.

"Jack," she said. He had persuaded her to call him Jack when they were alone with great difficulty. Frequently they met after dinner at her small cottage behind the hospital. It was her way to repay him for the dinners that had become a weekly affair at the team hut. The cottage was small and sparsely furnished. She had given the cottage a sparkle, a style uniquely her own by placing blooming tropical plants in the largest room, her sitting room she called it. *The room looked like a tastefully decorated greenhouse*, Travis thought. The only jarring aspect of the decorations was a large framed color photograph of her late husband that always appeared to be looking down on him with disapproval.

They had been talking about the Hoa Luu medical situation, much improved but still bad. She had started a midwife training program with students from all the villages in the district. She was excited about this. The training would help curb the high incidence of infant mortality and infection from childbirth. Next month she and Sergeant Gonzales would start a district-wide vaccination program for all the children. Diphtheria, tetanus and pertussis took a heavy toll. The MEDMIL exercises would be spiced up with lines of screaming children waiting for shots. She laughed. Hector Gonzales was praised as a godly man of medicine. Travis felt a twinge of jealousy.

"Jack," she said again, louder, attempting to break him from his spell. He looked at her, really looked at her, in the sense that he was listening not just watching her.

"I have wondered why there isn't a Mrs. Travis."

"Why is it all my friends are asking me this?" He then told her of his two lost loves.

"Foolish women, I think they did not really love you. Also, I think you did not really love them."

"I did love them," he protested.

"No," she persisted. "You are a strong man, Jack. If you had loved them, they would have stayed with you."

Jack almost said, "I won't let you get away. You will stay with me." But he kept his silence.

She sipped her coffee, then set the cup down with a definite bang.

"Why are you so quiet tonight? You always talk more; are you worried? I think we are doing well in the district." She leaned toward him, her breasts pressing against the tight bodice of the ao dai .

He forced himself to concentrate. "Co Linh, I'm worried. You know the contact we had on the Tao River. The VC might be moving north." Travis liked to call her Co Linh, a combination of Miss and her last name. Everybody called her "Co Linh." The name had a romantic lilt.

"Soldier, soldier, soldier!" she exclaimed strongly. "There is more to this war than only the military. The people here, especially the families of the soldiers, are beginning to believe in us."

"In us?" Jack interrupted. "You mean the Government?" he asked doubtfully.

"These Delta people will never relate to the Government. That is a concept far beyond these rice paddies. They believe in the people they see, people of responsibility, people they trust here in the district to take care of them. Leaders such as you, Jack, Maj. Tho, Commander Re, maybe even me." She half laughed. "When you win this trust, you win the war. What goes on in Saigon does not matter to the people here." The last was said with emotion; her eyes gleamed.

"You really care, Co Linh, about these people?"

"Of course." She sounded slightly hurt. "*I* love these people. They are Vietnamese, I am Vietnamese. I want them to lead happy lives, but I also want them to have pride, self-respect. My people have seldom had self-respect and that is the trouble now on the Government's side. Perhaps, Jack, you help us too much." She looked at Travis to insure he was listening. She thought how handsome he was: dark hair, blue eyes, strong features, a strong feeling of masculine strength, but there was a sensitivity, a softness in his personality. He was much better looking than Ky, her late husband, and yet they were much the same—soldiers doing their duty, but somehow unable to define that duty. Something about this man stirred her deeply. She felt strong emotions and wanted to run her hands through his thick black hair. Barely perceptible, she shook her head. She could not fall in love again.

"And now, Jack," she looked at her watch, "you must go. People will talk." She sat up very straight. *Already she was all business*, Jack thought, *the little steel lady.* Her sudden mood changes always surprised him. He was being dismissed.

"Maybe I will spend the night."

"Don't joke, Jack. You know that can never be." She looked down as she said this, lacking her usual strength.

Travis reluctantly stood up. She came close to him to shake hands. Quickly he embraced her. She gasped and backed away, offering her hand again. "Good night, Jack." This time, she said it very firmly.

He stopped on top of the bridge on the way back to the compound. A light rain was falling, more of a mist. The western horizon flickered with lightning. Far off he could hear artillery. Travis thought of the Delta: the brilliant sunsets, the damp heat of the day, the black nights, the chocolate canals, the endless rice planting. Inexorably, nature went on as the planet spun in this part of the world. But what about the people? What was their fate in the timeless cycle of the Delta? What hope, what terror lay beyond the thunder? Travis shivered in the moist wind.

LE YIANG SINH

CHRISTMAS 1966

"I'm Dreaming of a White Christmas, Just Like the Ones I Used To Know." Bing Crosby's voice filled the team hut. The song was a lament for Christmas past, for holiday memories far away from the Delta. It was the GI Christmas carol. Jack sat on the single easy chair in the team's louvered-in porch that now served as the recreation room. He thought of home. He had experienced very few white Christmases in Norfolk, but somehow "White Christmas" described his memories. When he was in high school, his father had given him a sailboat for Christmas, a 25 foot sloop. It had been a cold, sunny day with a gusting wind. He had persuaded his father, against his mother's strong objection, to take the new sloop out for a sea trial. They bundled up in their foul weather gear and went down to the boat landing. Water was slapping over the edges of the floating dock and a three foot sea was running with foamy whitecaps outside the breakwater. The boat was gleaming white, gently rocking in the protected water. The wind whistled through the shrouds, asking them to take her to sea. *The Spirit, Norfolk, Virginia* was painted in bright red, white and yellow on her stern.

They rigged the boat. Jack convinced his father to use the large head sail, not the small working jib. This would give them more sailing power. His father, at first, balked because of the wind, but he was a Tidewater man, and Jack could see he was eager to sail the new boat in the running sea.

The outboard started on the second pull. He pushed in the choke until the engine was running smoothly. They backed out of the dock and motored around the breakwater. Once in the bay, the wind hit them full force. His father took the tiller and pointed *The Spirit* into the wind. Jack went forward on the plunging foredeck, loosened the main halyard and hoisted the main. The new sail sparkled white in the weak winter sun. Next, he hoisted the large head sail. As if it had a life of its own, the sail shook itself alive with the sound of gunshots. Jack wended his way back through the shrouds and exploding white canvas to the cockpit. His father handed him the tiller. Jack eased the boat over and filled the sails on a starboard tack. He reached down and cut off the outboard. There was a sudden sailing silence, strong wind, and water spraying over the foredeck. The sloop heeled over and leaped forward. Jack eased out the main sheet to reduce the heel. The sloop righted, the bow slicing cleanly through the waves. Jack looked at his father who was grinning widely. Now that had been a "White Christmas!"

The hut was decorated with things from home. A small, artificial tree stood in the place of honor, the bar. Green and red crepe paper festooned the common room. Various Christmas knickknacks from tiny reindeer to large Santas occupied every nook and cranny. They had even decorated that wonder of the Delta, the Flying Shithouse. The propeller was garlanded with palm fronds.

The music came from Billy's latest music box, a multi-speaker affair with large decibel output, a gift from his mother. Jack thought that after the holidays, this gift would be a mixed blessing. Cal Washington's wife had supplied them with a ton of cookies and other goodies. Doc was going to prepare one of his Mexican specials for Christmas dinner. His wife had sent him a small piñata, which hung in the corner ready for the traditional breaking ceremony in the morning. Don Burns had been sent some classical tapes that he promised to play sparingly after the team heard the first concert. Sergeant Minh informed the team that since he didn't have a family, his contribution for Christmas was his company and his sense of humor. *Considering Minh's personality,* Jack thought, *this gift demonstrated a real joke-making ability.*

In addition to the tree, Jack's parents had sent him a Daisy air rifle. The gift was an immediate success. The hut was infested with lizards and the Muckers needed a population control program. They started a "Lizard Ace of the Week" competition. Sergeant Minh agreed to design a special bulletin board where lizard tails would be tallied.

Tension on the team had eased since Hartwell's death and the arrival of Cal Washington and Don Burns. They had taken to calling themselves the Hoa Luu Muckers because they were always mucking about in rice paddy mud and mangrove swamps. They were a relaxed bunch on the surface and called themselves by their first names, except for Travis, who was referred to as Boss. Don Burns didn't quite fit into the camaraderie, but Cal Washington had made it his personal responsibility to make sure Burns got along.

The bar was loaded with gifts to be opened Christmas day. All the team members were going to exchange gag gifts and looked forward to their opening with almost childish excitement. Jack was giving Cal Washington a jar of Brylcream for his short cropped hair, Doc a large pill bottle that never emptied, Sergeant Minh a map of the Vinh Cheo Triangle autographed by the U Minh Regimental Commander, Billy a Stan Musial baseball card, and Don Burns a carefully wrapped quarter to remind him of the Quartermaster Corps and his logistical responsibilities.

Major Tho had invited them to Christmas Eve dinner that night. Commander Re and Co Linh would also attend. "Very American, I Hoa Hao but I love Jesus," Tho had said with his gold capped smile.

The Muckers, dressed in their best jungle fatigues and shined jungle boots, trooped over to Major Tho's hooch. The District Chief opened the door and ushered the team into a large banquet room. Major Tho walked a trifle unsteadily, and Jack suspected the tough Hoa Hao had a head start on Christmas celebrating.

The room was filled with the District staff and the leadership of the Delta Tigers. Co Linh nodded to him. The Americans were immediately given tall glasses filled to the brim with genuine Japanese bourbon. Chug-a-lug challenges were issued all around and the team was forced to gulp down the bourbon non-stop. The honor of the United States Army was at stake. Billy Turner looked green after the first swallow. When the first round was finished, Jack knew it was going to be a short night if the team didn't find a way to shorten the drinks. There was a bowl of ice on the table. Jack quickly beckoned the Muckers to fill their glasses with ice before the next toast. The Vietnamese never caught on. The Muckers maintained a fighting edge over their Vietnamese allies, except for Billy Turner and Don Burns, who had to retire from the lists. Commander Re didn't participate in these events. He enjoyed himself hugely, however, watching the action of his brothers without condescension.

Wonderful smells were wafting in from the open kitchen. Ba Tho, Mrs. Tho, came into the room and beckoned to her husband. She was an attractive lady, a full two inches taller than her husband. Then the food came in on overflowing platters. Glasses and whiskey bottles were cleared off the table noisily. Jack grabbed Co Linh's arm and motioned her to sit next to him. She was looking at him strangely. "Jack, you have had too much to drink," she whispered in his ear. He put his arm around her, and she quickly knocked it away.

They sat down, Re and Tho holding forth at opposite ends of the table. The centerpiece of the banquet was two large turtles. To Jack's bourbon-blurred eyes they appeared alive, about to crawl off the table. The Tokyo booze was doing something to him. Major Tho took a knife and deftly removed the bottom shells and entrails from the turtles. He then cut off the head. The turtles were placed upside down on a large dish and served to Commander Re and Jack. Jack looked down at the eviscerated turtle. He tasted the bourbon again. His stomach churned. Ba Tho gave him a generous helping. Tonight, on this Christmas Eve 1966, he would do anything for his country. He put a large chunk of turtle meat to his mouth with his chopsticks. It was delicious, a cross between rabbit and chicken.

Later in the dinner, Major Tho rose unsteadily to his feet for a final toast. He swayed back and forth, having trouble keeping the drink in his glass. "Major Travis," he called across the table, "to victory!" Jack stood with the help of Co Linh. He was handed a glass filled to the rim with a special victory drink, genuine Japanese brandy. Wildly he searched the table for ice, all gone. *Once more into the breach*, he thought as he lifted his glass.

Sometime later he walked with Co Linh to the compound bridge. A soldier from the Delta Tigers also accompanied them. Jack was determined to go with her to the cottage.

"No, Jack, this has been a wonderful evening. Do not spoil it."

"I'm not going to spoil it. Don't you understand? I love you." He laughed and swayed alarmingly on top of the bridge.

"You must return to the team hut and get some sleep. Remember, tomorrow is Christmas."

"Christmas?" he responded.

"Yes, Christmas. I know that means something to you. Jack, you will not remember this in the morning, but I am going to tell you something. Beyond all the whiskey tonight, beyond all the warrior talk that you must do in this place, you are a sweet, sensitive man." She stood tip toe and kissed him on the lips. Jack blinked at her and she was gone in the darkness with her soldier escort.

For a time on top of the bridge he stared after her. Then, unaccountably, he had an urge to sing, to sing a Christmas song from his Cadet days. He remembered a Christmas concert long ago when the Glee Club had sung to the Corps before Christmas leave. He stood on the bridge and in a clear baritone sang into the tropical night, "Mary had a baby, my Lord." At two o'clock on Christmas morning 1966, only the flowing dark canal heard him.

After Christmas all was quiet in Hoa Luu District. For the Americans, life had become almost routine. The training program continued with good results; Co Linh and Doc Gonzales were making progress in medical services and with the District-wide vaccination program; Don Burns had started to correct many logistical problems; the District Staff was becoming a more cohesive organization. The Muckers had developed into an outstanding advisory team.

Jack was almost content. Sergeant Minh warned him, "Complacency is a killer in the Delta war. For weeks, perhaps months, all is quiet and then one day this is shattered by a terrible, killing event. Remember, Major Travis, the enemy continues to grow in the Vinh Cheo Triangle. We have yet to attack the area."

"Maybe you're right, Sergeant Minh, but you're such a pessimist, gloom and doom all the time." He smiled when he said this, not wanting to hurt his friend. "I believe our programs are working. That's the reason things are quiet." But deep down Jack worried. He remembered the armada of sampans they had battled on the Tau River during the Firefly operation last fall. Jack and Sergeant Minh had many similar conversations. In the end, Sergeant Minh proved to be prophetic.

PART TWO

CHIEN DICH LUA BOC SAT

SILK OVER STEEL

JANUARY THROUGH MARCH 1967

****** 1 ******

Sleep was difficult for Captain Don Burns. Events of the past weeks whirled in his head. What in the world was he doing in this crazy place? Yet, he had found something in Hoa Luu, a purpose and a kind of pride. He thought of the letter he had written requesting a transfer. Rumpled and stained with canal water, it remained in his briefcase. He was not going to quit. Tonight he had made that decision. Burns had to admit that what Major Travis and the Vietnamese were doing down here was unique. The challenge and the advisory programs had captured him. Logistics were a nightmare in Hoa Luu. As the pace of operations and training had increased, logistics had become more of a problem, particularly ammunition resupply and weapons maintenance. He had started to work with the District S-4 and together they were designing a support system to fix the logistics labyrinth. Burns was, in Major Travis' language, "activating the logistics staff channel." Hoa Luu was a terrible, fearful place, but much of the work here was quartermaster business, and he enjoyed it.

He had never in his life been "one of the guys," but he had become a Mucker. Major Travis didn't quite approve of him and, perhaps, thought of him as a quartermaster puke, but this had softened over time because, Don liked to think, of his hard work. Don sensed a bit of arrogance towards tech service officers. The Boss was funny that way. If you weren't a fighter, you didn't quite measure up.

Cal Washington was Don's one man life support system. He had taught him Delta survival skills: personal hygiene, field stripping weapons in the mud, wearing LBE low on the hips for comfort, packing rucksacks, combat shooting at moving and area targets, and throwing hand grenades. "Down here you don't get any fire support. Grenades are your personal artillery. Never mind this John Wayne bullshit about shootouts. If you've got a VC holed up in a hooch, blow the fucking hooch away." Cal had explained all this to Burns in his deep voice. So far the training had not been put to combat use. There was very little contact on field operations, and they hadn't been mortared for weeks. In spite of having no combat experience, Don believed he had become a real Delta Tiger.

It was raining, drumming loudly on the aluminum roof. The syncopated rhythm was comforting. Don felt almost relaxed. He cuddled up beneath his poncho blanket.

The rain tapered off later. There were a few, far off booms of thunder then absolute silence. Hoa Luu was covered in a thick tropical blackness. The time was 2300 hours. At first Don thought the rain had started again; there was a drumming sound. Suddenly he realized it was small arms fire; the fire welled up like crashing surf and was underscored by the staccato roar of automatic weapons. Frantically he tore open the mosquito net, stumbled on the floor and stood up. A terrible fear engulfed him, shook him, destroyed all thought. He felt his urine go. The arms rack was six feet from his bunk. Must get his weapon. Then he remembered the battle drill: get under the bunk. Don turned and started to drop to the floor. There was a screeching yellow explosion behind him. A hard wind hit his back and knocked him to the floor. Must reach the bunk, get his weapon. He rose halfway on his arms and fell. A strange weakness assailed him. He reached under the bunk and grabbed his carbine. It was slippery; he couldn't hold it. Something was gushing on his arms, on the floor. He tried to breathe. His nose clogged; his mouth filled with metallic fluid. Again he stretched and gripped his weapon like Cal Washington had taught him. But everything was slick and wet. He was spiraling down an endless black hole.

"PAPA BRAVO: THIS IS DELTA ALPHA SIX. WE'RE UNDER HEAVY ATTACK. I SAY AGAIN, HEAVY ATTACK. REQUEST SPOOKY OVER." Jack was on the radio.

"THIS IS PAPA BRAVO. WE'RE RECEIVING MORTAR FIRE. WAIT. OUT."

Jack tried again, no answer, just the unbroken rushing noise of the radio. He tried again.

"Those goddamn bastards. What kind of support are they giving us?" Jack shouted.

The mortar bombardment was continuous. There were ear splitting, sharp explosions. Shrapnel thumped into the sandbags, dirt and gravel fell on the top of the bunker; the bunker floor heaved like an earthquake. "Don't hit us!" they all prayed in their own way. The bunker couldn't stand a direct hit.

Jack was fighting fear, that desolate feeling of disorientation, as if he wasn't really here. He was looking at himself through a mirror. He shook himself and fought for control. Huddled together, the team looked at him in the eerie red light of the bunker.

"Burns is missing, Boss," Cal reported crisply, like they were on a Fort

Benning exercise. This pierced Jack's consciousness. Command action! He had to do something physical to destroy this awful sense of isolation.

"Cal," he said, "see if you can raise the District TOC on the land line. I'll get Burns." Cal started to protest, but Jack hunched down and took off through the bunker door like the VMI plunging back he had been. Once inside the hut, he immediately dropped to his knees in a fast low crawl. The rear of the hut and the porch were a mass of flames. A body lay like a huddled doll halfway under a bunk. Jack's hands and knees kept slipping on the blood covered floor. He reached the body and turned it over. Don's face was deathly pale in the firelight. His eyes looked at him accusingly. Jack swung the body over his back in a fireman's carry. He could feel Don's blood ooze out on his back. Halfway out of the hut Cal met him and helped drag the inert body into the bunker.

"Doc, Doc, check him out! He's alive!" Jack screamed at Gonzales. Doc put his flashlight on the body and checked for vital signs. Nothing. Don's face peered up at him with a pale red pallor in the bunker light. Blood covered his jaw. The eyes had already begun to glaze over.

"Boss, he's dead."

"He can't be dead." Silence. Jack was numb. Slowly, like stoking a blast furnace, a rage built up in him. A knot of hate and revenge, mixed with deadly control, defeated his fear. These motherfuckers would pay for this, the killing of an American, a teammate, his friend.

"Drag the body into the corner," he ordered calmly, coldly.

"Cal, any contact with the District TOC?"

"Negative, Boss, the line must be broken. Do you want me to check?"

"No, stay here. Keep trying to raise Province on the radio. Tell 'em our situation and get Spooky."

Mortar rounds now exploded at uneven intervals. The crescendo of small arms fire had increased, but it was outside the compound. The PF outposts were being hit hard.

"Sergeant Minh, come with me. Doc, get your gear ready to go to the Vietnamese aid station. Billy, keep this goddamn radio humming. Make sure we've got spare batteries."

Jack and Minh left the bunker at a dead run. Tracers arced across the sky, but there were no mortars. The District TOC was bathed in pale red light. Shrill Vietnamese voices screamed on the radio. Dai Uy Luom was trying to raise the PF outposts. Major Tho and Commander Re were locked in deep conversation beside a map of the District compound.

117

Travis reported, "Captain Burns has been killed. We have no contact with Province; they are under mortar fire." Both men nodded.

Commander Re briefed, "I think the PF outposts are lost. Radio contact was broken ten minutes ago. We have identified elements of the Hoa Luu District Battalion and the 309th VC Battalion of the U Minh Regiment. You know, Major Travis, when they operate together it is a serious attack."

"What will they do now?" Jack asked. Tho and Re exchanged glances.

Tho spoke in his guttural English, "They want destroy the District, kill us. We must have air support; Spooky must come, or we lose."

"We're working on it. Sergeant Washington is trying to get Province on the radio."

"We must have Spooky," Tho shouted, slamming his fist on the map. "This time they must forget we are Hoa Hao; they must help us."

Jack looked at Re. "Can't we move the 123rd RF Company up from the Vinh Cheo outpost and hit them from the rear?"

"They cannot break out. They cannot fight their way up the canal. The company is surrounded. This is an all-out attack on the District Headquarters. Outside support has been eliminated."

Jack's inside rage increased. "They won't win! We're strong here. I'll get air support!" He looked fiercely at the two men. "Sergeant Minh will remain in the TOC. I am going back to raise Province on the radio. Also, we must get the wire fixed between here and our bunker. And," he paused forcing a fleeting grin, "Major Tho, we'll never win without your cigars. Do you have them with you?" Tho smiled weakly.

Jack turned to leave the bunker. Re grabbed his arm. "Co Linh and the hospital patients are safe. I sent a platoon over the canal to rescue them."

Jack looked at his friend. "Thank you."

The mortaring had stopped. There was still sporadic small arms fire coming from the eastern side of the canal. Stars were visible; the sky had cleared. *Good flying weather*, Jack thought. A figure was crouching on the ground just in front of him. He leveled his weapon. "Hold it, Boss, it's me, Billy." Billy Turner on his own had been trying to repair the land line between the two bunkers.

"The line's in," he reported. Travis tapped him on the shoulder and they both returned to the bunker.

Cal was on the radio. "Still no luck, Boss. Can't get through to Province."

"Keep trying. Where's Doc?"

"He went to the Vietnamese aid station."

"Okay, the Vietnamese are going to send a communications team over here, that way we'll have both land line and radio working here on the ground. Not that it means a goddamn thing if we can't reach Province for support."

Suddenly the radio belched forth. "HEY DELTA ALPHA SIX, GOOD BUDDY, THIS IS FLIPSTICK. DON'T APPRECIATE A GODDAMN BIT BEING PULLED OUT OF MY SACK IN THE MIDDLE OF THE NIGHT. WHAT'S THE SITUATION?"

Jack grinned widely, gave the situation and finished, "WE MUST HAVE SPOOKY!"

"ON THE WAY DELTA ALPHA SIX, KEEP YOUR PANTS ON. I BYPASSED PROVINCE AND WENT DIRECT FOR SUPPORT. WILL GIVE YOU AN ETA, SOONEST." Jack wondered briefly how Cochran got to his Bird Dog through a mortar bombardment.

Tension hung over the District; there was a sense of impending violence. Soldiers whispered to each other in their positions, some cleaned their weapons, others peered into the impenetrable gloom. They were waiting, waiting…

Commander Re and Jack were inspecting the compound. They reassured many soldiers, got down behind machineguns to insure fields of fire were correct, and assessed damage. In addition to the Delta Tigers, the District compound was reinforced with three PF platoons who were rotated after a month's tour of compound security duty. Re and Jack had dispersed these units at squad level and placed them under the strong leadership of the Tigers. Re cautioned his platoon leaders to keep an eye on the PF squads.

Considering the size of the bombardment, the mortar damage was amazingly light. Most of the rounds had landed in the center of the compound. Some family quarters and District offices had been destroyed, the team hut was half blown away, but the important wall fortifications remained.

"They often make this mistake and direct fire into the center of the compound without hitting the defensive positions. A waste of ammunition and very lucky for us," Re observed.

Mortar rounds had pockmarked the parade ground and blown up the foundation of the flagpole. The pole lay forlornly across the parade ground, the Government colors missing. *A depressing symbol*, Jack thought. At his urging, Re ordered some soldiers to remount the flagpole and fly the battle standard of the 122nd RF Company, a yellow tiger's head on a field of green. No one thought to fly the Government flag. "The Tigers will not lose their honor, Commander Re," Jack said and saluted the colors.

"Sometimes, Major Travis, I think you are living in the wrong century."

"Are you sure they will come again?" Jack asked.

"Yes, they have over run the PF outposts and are regrouping for an attack on the compound. Probably there is some confusion. They are short mortar ammunition. I have never experienced such a bombardment. I have placed a platoon in reserve near the District TOC as a reaction force if they penetrate."

Cal approached them out of the darkness.

"Boss, Flipstick wants you on the radio. He has contact with Spooky."

"Good!" Re exclaimed. "If we can fire up the area around at least one PF outpost before the attack, perhaps the Tiger battle standard will see daylight."

"FLIPSTICK, THIS IS DELTA ALPHA SIX, PLACE SPOOKY FIRES JUST OUTSIDE THE PERIPHERY OF THE SOUTHERN AND EASTERN OUTPOSTS. DO NOT, I REPEAT, DO NOT FIRE ON HOA LUU TOWN BETWEEN THE EASTERN OUTPOST AND THE HOA LUU WALL FORTIFICATIONS. TOO MANY CIVILIANS. BE PREPARED TO FIRE ON THE HOA LUU CANAL SOUTHWEST OF THE CAPITAL ON MY COMMAND. WE CAN KNOCK OUT SOME OF THEIR SAMPAN LOGISTICS SYSTEM. OVER."

"ROGER, OLD BUDDY."

With the spare PRC-25 radio on his back, Jack left the bunker to watch the Spooky fires. He joined Commander Re just outside the District TOC. Re had just finished giving his orders to the reserve platoon leader who had the mission of repelling any penetration into the compound.

"Remember to continue to attack, never stop; if you stop forward movement, the counterattack is lost."

Spooky began its work. With a loud hum, thousands of rounds poured down in a continuous sheet of flame, isolating the eastern outpost. The Vietnamese called it the death ray.

"ON TARGET, FLIPSTICK, DO THAT A FEW TIMES AND THEN SHOOT UP THE AREA JUST SOUTH OF THE SOUTHERN OUTPOST."

The soldiers in the reserve platoon started talking excitedly, relieved that Spooky was on station, feeling reassured by the awesome firepower. A few looked at Jack like he was some kind of god to call upon such destructive power.

Explosions, mortars, hand grenades and a growing cracking of small arms fire all concentrated on the south wall.

"They are coming over the south wall!" Re shouted. "Get Spooky fires just south of the wall."

Jack gave the fire mission to Flipstick. "THIS IS AN EMERGENCY, FLIP, THE BASTARDS ARE COMING OVER THE SOUTH WALL."

The mortars stopped; small arms fire with grenade explosions increased and then suddenly subsided.

"TAN CONG! Attack!" Re shouted. A whistle pierced the night. The platoon fanned out in the dark. Jack shed the radio and went with them. He checked his sawed off shotgun; it was a better weapon for close work than the carbine. A machinegun positioned on top of the District TOG opened up; yellow tracers sprayed overhead into the south wall. Dark shadowy figures ran on top of the parapet. Jack moved forward at a half crouch. Confusion. Soldiers who had defended the wall fell back into the attacking platoon. Commander Re and the platoon leader shouted to continue the attack. Many whistles. They must retake the wall! The Viet Cong could not decide whether to enter the compound or to defend the southern wall from counterattack. Another Tiger machinegun opened up and raked the southern parapet. People were running around and through the attacking platoon. Jack fired at everything not wearing a bush hat. Suddenly there was a shadowy figure to his direct front; with a yellow flash, something scathingly hot cracked by his cheek. He pumped the shotgun three times. He heard buckshot splat against human flesh. The VC crumpled before him.

The lead Tigers hit the southern wall. Firing increased. There were struggling figures on top of the parapet. The Tigers were clubbing the enemy with their M-1 rifles, going from position to position rooting out the Viet Cong. Jack reloaded. He saw men running in the open field just beyond the wall. "BAN! Fire!" he screamed. The platoon opened up on the retreating VC. Jack pumped the area with buckshot. The field beyond the wall became a killing ground.

Abruptly, Spooky opened up; there was a sheet of yellow flame a hundred meters beyond the wall. Geysers of dust and dirt exploded over the field. Jack realized he was screaming, a modern version of the Rebel yell. The attack on the southern wall was broken.

Major Tong was grim faced. The attack was not going well. He had reported this by radio to Colonel Truc, who had ordered him to make one more assault on the eastern side of the compound. Tong explained that Spooky had disrupted their attack, and he did not have enough troops and mortar ammunition to continue. "You have your orders," was the response.

Tong looked at the 309th Commander who was with him in his command post, a farmhouse just off the main canal, one kilometer south of Hoa Luu Town.

"You must overrun the compound. Infiltrate the built up area of Hoa Luu Town and surprise them. Even if you are discovered, I do not believe the Americans will place death ray fires on the town. Too many people will die." The 309th commander nodded grimly.

"Comrade," Tong continued, "if they had only given you an additional mortar section. It would have made a difference."

"Yes," said the 309th commander. "And if the enemy had not received the death ray, it would have made a difference."

"It is the American advisor again. He and the Hoa Hao have become a very dangerous combination."

The two commanders coordinated the timing and fire support for the next assault. The 309th Commander stood up. "We will do our best. I will need all the mortar fire you can give me."

"It isn't much; use your M-l rifle grenades for support when you get close to the wall."

"I know how to fight," the 309th commander responded contemptuously, thinking that if he had not had to operate with a district battalion, if he commanded the operation with another battalion from the U Minh Regiment, they would have victory. He nodded to Tong and left the farmhouse.

Major Tong reflected on his losses, the better part of a company on the southern attack. The battle plan could have worked, but the death ray stopped the eastern attack, and the defenders were allowed the luxury of massing their combat power on the southern wall. Battle losses were just coming in, terrible losses and good men, too. Training replacements would take a long time. These men were not just fighters; they knew the people, the ground, the political apparatus. They provided the conduit between the U Minh Regiment's main combat forces and objectives in the pacified areas. If the Hoa Luu Battalion was eventually destroyed, the U Minh Regiment would be blinded for future offensive operations. This was a level of sophistication the 309th Battalion Commander, in Tong's opinion, would never understand.

Other thoughts entered his mind, non-professional, dangerous thoughts: his dead wife and son, was he too old to marry again, he would die in this war, Mother Maria's humility and goodness amid all this crazy death. He shrugged. These thoughts he locked away, perhaps forever. For now he must be a warrior.

Jack had climbed to the top of the half destroyed team hut. It was the only good vantage point in the compound. The PRC-25 was set up precariously on the crumpled aluminum roof. With a deadly hum across the canal, Spooky was shooting up the area around the eastern outpost. Before him, just beyond the team bunker, lay the huddled structures of Hoa Luu Town. In the gloom, only the first row of buildings could be seen, jammed up against the eastern wall.

He thought about the battle. Gambling that he would not place Spooky fires on the population, the VC would probably infiltrate the town and attack the east wall. Jack looked at the town through binoculars, trying to pierce the gloom. What were they doing? He could imagine the Viet Cong crawling up the small alleyways toward the east wall, the people cowering in their hooches.

One hour before, Commander Re had sent out some reconnaissance patrols. They had returned. "No contact," they reported, but Jack could see they were afraid of the Viet Cong and the town spies who must be all over on a night like this. Every alley was a possible death trap.

During this break in the battle, Jack felt all-powerful on top of the destroyed hut armed with his PRC-25 radio. He could direct Spooky at will. A finger of death and destruction could be directed anywhere by pushing the radio transmit button.

The radio spoke, "DELTA ALPHA SIX, WE'RE GOING TO LOSE SPOOKY IN THREE ZERO. THEY NEED TO REFUEL, REARM, AND HAVE BEEN DIVERTED TO ANOTHER TARGET AREA."

"BULLSHIT, FLIPSTICK. YOU GET THEM BACK HERE. THIS THING AIN'T OVER."

"NEGATIVE. THEY SAY SOME PLACES HAVE A HIGHER PRIORITY. AFTER REFUELING I'LL RETURN TO STATION. I'VE STILL GOT SOME ROCKETS. OVER."

"ROGER, GET BACK ON THE FIRE REQUEST NET AND TRY AGAIN. OUT."

Problems gnawed at him: Spooky gone in thirty minutes, they were dangerously low on high explosive and illumination mortar ammunition, they would not fire the mortars until the VC assault started, and they lacked fields of fire in front of the east wall where the attack was expected because of the buildings. He and Commander Re had devised a plan to pull back from the east wall to shallow positions the reserve platoon was preparing. They had planned to blast the east wall with Spooky fires after withdrawing, but no more Spooky.

Jack knew something had happened to him after the death of Don Burns. He wasn't looking inward, concerned with his own performance and fears. The battle and this tragedy had forced him out of himself. There was a direction, a cold-blooded focus on this battle that had never experienced in other fire fights. Fueling this change was a deep, controlled rage, which allowed him to make and execute combat decisions pitilessly. A cleansing had taken place, a warrior conversion. Different gods ruled in the Delta and you had to play by their rules. You had to fight their way to survive.

To Jack, these rules were intermingled with his own heritage and values that gave direction to the Hoa Luu war. You fought the Hoa Hao way to give a few thousand Vietnamese new hope, a better chance. Battle courage based on self would always fail. He could just make out the colors gently waving in the darkness over the parade ground. He was a Delta Tiger. The Delta Tigers would win the victory. They waited. The attack would have to come soon or the Viet Cong would run out of night.

A lone shot interrupted the dark silence on his right, then came the crashing of small arms fire. Bullets ripped through the air. Jack vaulted off the building and entered the team bunker.

Cal reported, "It's starting up again, Boss." Wham! Grenade explosions rocked the bunker; a fusillade of bullets thunked into the sandbags. They all hit the floor. A furious fire fight was taking place on the east wall, ten yards in front of their position.

Cal was on his feet, looking out the bunker slit.

"Goddamn it, it's hand to hand; those fuckers are coming over the wall. They're going to break through, Boss."

"Cal, you and I stay. Billy, you and the Vietnamese radio team get the hell out of here and back to the District TOC. Tell Commander Re or Major Tho to get ready to execute the plan. And run, goddamn it, don't let anything stop you."

The "plan" was to ready the reserve for counterattack and prepare to withdraw the east wall defenders to the fall back positions.

Jack grabbed the radio handset. "FLIPSTICK, FLIPSTICK, THEY'RE HITTING THE EASTERN WALL. WE NEED SPOOKY, WE NEED EVERYTHING!"

No answer. He remembered with a sinking feeling they had just broken station.

He peered through the bunker slit. Not ten yards in front of the bunker figures, enemy figures clad in nothing but shorts were milling around. They looked confused.

The Tiger defensive positions were quiet. They must be wiped out. A Viet Cong leader was screaming orders.

Jack grabbed Cal's arm and they left the bunker. They squatted in the small space between the bunker and the team hut. Jack unsnapped a grenade from his LBE and pulled the pin. *Shit*, he thought, *he was getting to be a real John Wayne.* He stood up and threw the grenade up through the small space between the bunker and the team hut. The grenade arced through the opening, hit on the edge of the bunker and fell at Jack's feet. He threw it again with more effort. The grenade disappeared over the top of the bunker. With a clink, clink, clink, there was the sound of something rolling; the grenade again fell at his feet, looking at him evilly. Time stopped. He couldn't move fast. Everything was in forced slow motion. He snatched the small, baseball shaped sphere which could blow them to pieces and threw again, this time keeping his throwing arm stiff like a basketball hook shot. The grenade disappeared over the bunker. Both men hit the dirt. There was a high pitched, crashing explosion. They were smothered in dust and sand. The bunker roof collapsed in a ruin of ruptured sandbags and shattered timber.

Jack looked at Cal. "That was an enemy mortar."

"Shit, sir, I'll never tell, but are you sure you played ball at VMI?"

Both men tore off for the District TOC.

Withdrawal orders were given to the east wall defenders. A few survivors fell back in confusion. Commander Re opened fire with his 60MM mortars, firing illumination first. White blinding light poured over the east wall. Near naked, gleaming figures, chests strapped with bandoliers of ammunition were clearly visible. The Tigers opened up with every weapon they had. Cal fired the team's M-79 grenade launcher. Everything was concentrated on the eastern wall.

The reserve platoon moved to the southernmost part of the east wall where it intersected the south wall. Jack and Cal went with them, Jack again carrying his sawed off shotgun. He felt no fear, only a sense of murderous exaltation. They had done this before and won. Taking the Viet Cong in the flank, they attacked up the eastern wall. There was a deafening roar of small arms firing at point blank range, grenade explosions, hand to hand combat, rifle clubbing, knifings and screaming. There was a chilling cry from the Tigers up and down like a symphony of death. Jack and Cal were yelling with the rest. The enemy fell back into the town. The east wall was restored.

A dark quiet descended on the battlefield, as if both sides were in mourning. The attackers and the defenders were low on ammunition. The Delta Tigers had no more mortar rounds. Tho, Re and Jack were holding a council of war. They were a disreputable bunch, covered with mud and filth. Re's and Jack's uniforms were ripped in a dozen places. Both of them had numerous cuts and bruises. Jack's right cheek was black and swollen, and he could barely see out of his right eye. *But, they had not been hit*, Jack thought. He was still in one piece. He had never felt so alive, so fully charged with vitality and purpose.

Tho was tired, depressed. Fatigue oozed out of his squat body. "If they attack again, we lose. We have nothing left. Even bandage in aid station gone. Many soldiers dead and women and children. The south and east walls damaged. Major Travis get support back. Spooky, fast movers, anything."

"Sir, we have no communications with Province. They were mortared earlier and the TOC took a direct hit. My only contact for outside support is through the Army observation plane, and Major Cochran has not returned to station." He paused. "Sir, I think we can hold. Their losses have been heavy, too."

Re nodded in agreement. "I have sent out patrols. On the east, the Viet Cong have pulled all the way back to the canal bank. They cannot have much left."

Tho interrupted, his deep guttural voice louder with concern. "Unless they have reserve. They put much into fight. They lose face if they not kill us."

The discussion continued. Re and Jack tried to reassure Tho that the situation was not hopeless.

An excited officer approached them.

"The VC are talking to us, come outside."

They left the bunker. A hollow, disembodied electronic voice came to them over the east wall from Hoa Luu Town. Sergeant Minh translated.

"Traitors, lackeys to the Americans. Hoa Hao fanatics. You are dead men. He know you are out of ammunition. The next attack will destroy you to the last man. Then we will kill your women and children. We are merciful. We are men of honor who represent the true honor, the true Vietnam under Ho Chi Minh. Give us your American advisors, and we will not attack. Let us have the imperialist dogs. You have fifteen minutes to decide. Fire three shots into the air and we will negotiate a place for you to hand over the Americans."

The American team suddenly felt very conspicuous and alone. They returned to the TOC. An embarrassed tension filled the operations room. The Vietnamese would not look at the Americans. There were muttered,

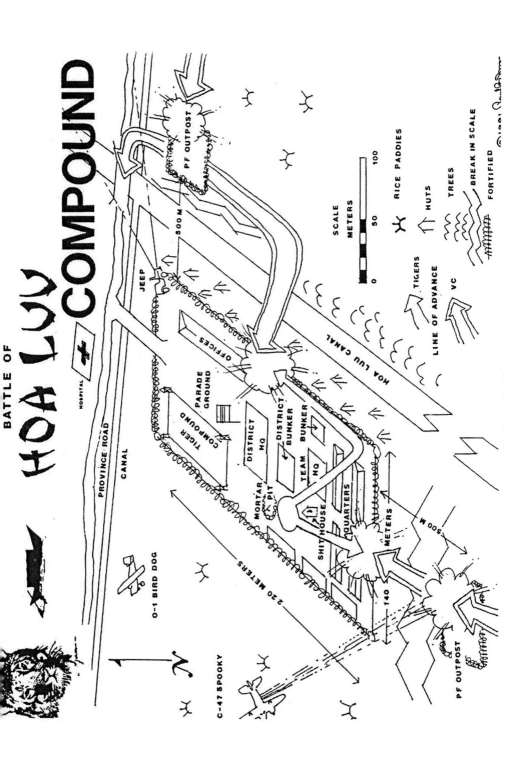

whispered conversations.

"This is going to be a long fifteen minutes," Jack whispered to Cal.

There were loud voices at the entrance of the TOC, a commotion. Captain Giao, the S-2, entered, followed by three armed soldiers who Jack had never seen before. They were not Tigers. Captain Giao was highly agitated. He screamed at Major Tho, "Give them the Americans. They do not matter. If they attack again, we will lose the District. He," he pointed at Jack, "is no good. Since he came here, we have started to lose the war. Everything has gone wrong. Many soldiers agree with me." The soldiers with him fingered their weapons. Looking somewhere over the S-2's head, Tho stood stock still.

"Our soldiers want to get rid of this American. He is a DU MA." DU MA is a gross Vietnamese insult pertaining to parentage. Catching his breath, Captain Giao paused, gasping.

Tho looked at him without expression. "Do you have anything else to say, Captain Giao?"

The Captain looked wildly around the room, trying to gather support. "He is not a Vietnamese. He has started up this war, which will kill many of our people, and then as we live in a hell he created, he will return to America and live in comfort." Captain Giao's face was suffused in blood. His hand hovered over his pistol. Jack thought the S-2's body was about to explode in bloody globs all over the TOC.

Major Tho spoke with dignity. "We are Hoa Hao," he said simply. "You come from another place. Viet Minh many years ago killed our leader who was a saint. We will always hate the Viet Minh. God hates the Viet Minh. We honor hospitality, we honor friends, and above all, we honor brave warriors who fight with us. I am the District Chief. Tonight I lose face because you dishonor a man who has fought and bled with the Hoa Hao." Tho walked slowly toward the S-2. He seemed to fiddle with his belt. There was a small muffled explosion. Captain Giao fell to the floor. His lifeless body was dragged unceremoniously from the TOC.

"Arrest those three soldiers," Tho ordered. He turned to look at Jack. "You my friend," he said with a gold toothed smile. He fished a Dutchmaster Panatella out of his breast pocket, which he lit, Jack thought, with a bit of a flourish.

"That is that," Tho said.

Re and Jack were again checking compound security. The fifteen minute hand-over time had come and gone and still silence. Silence from both sides. The Tigers had nothing much to shoot. Flipstick was back on station, without

Spooky.

They arrived at the northeast corner of the compound. A lieutenant ran up and reported. It was a short, intense conversation. Re turned to Jack. "He says they hear noises on the province road bridge. We remove the center spans of the bridge every night. They must be crossing through the girders. If they cross the bridge and occupy the high ground at this end, they can deliver deadly fire on the compound and threaten the north wall." Even Commander Re was finally worried.

Jack spoke over the ever present radio and explained the situation to Flipstick.

"STAND BY WITH 2.75 HE ROCKETS. WE ARE GOING TO GET SOME LIGHT ON THAT BRIDGE, THEN I WANT YOU TO HIT IT."

"HOA LUU'S OWN FIGHTER BOMBER GIVES YOU A ROGER, OUT."

Jack examined the fortifications at the northeast corner of the compound. At the juncture of the north and east wall was a raised machinegun position with an open observation position on top. *If some sort of light could be installed on the observation position*, Jack thought, *they could light up the bridge like a flare.*

Jack explained his plan to Re. Soon soldiers were widening the entrance of the observation position. Others ripped planking from destroyed buildings and metal matting from the walkway across the parade ground. A small incline was being constructed, which climbed six feet to the top of the observation position. Soldiers stood on both sides holding it erect.

Re displaced every automatic weapon he had to firing positions which could hit the bridge. The signal to fire would be the light. Re conducted a small conference at the foot of the incline. The plan was ready.

The engine ticked over, backfired, and caught. Jack worked the gear shift, eased the clutch out and accelerated across the parade ground. There was a slight bump as the wheels hit the lip of the incline; the wheels spun. Jack pushed down on the accelerator and the jeep slightly fishtailed up the incline. The incline swayed; the men grunted, holding the structure upright. The jeep skidded as it hit the top of the observation platform. Jack braked. Christ! The jeep was going over the wall into the canal. There was a sickening downward lurch; the entire position was collapsing beneath the weight. The jeep halted and settled on top of the ruined machinegun position. Jack saw the outline of the bridge before him. He fumbled with the light switch. White light smashed into the bridge. Figures climbing through the girders froze looking at the blazing headlights like frightened deer. Stunned, neither side fired.

The jeep was canted slightly to the right. Jack struggled to get out. The light switch should have been turned on after he left the jeep, a mistake. Absolute eternity. The whole world was ready to blow him apart. Anticipating bone shattering bullets, his body trembled. With a final wrench, he extricated his right leg and rolled down the rear of the position.

There was tiger fire and a throaty roar of ten machineguns. Yellow tracers converged on the bridge; figures dropped like tumbling sacks into the water below; bullets whanged and banged through the girders.

With the growing volume of fire from the other side, green tracers streaked over the wall, lowered and slammed into the jeep. Still the jeep lights burned like some eternal fire, oblivious to destruction.

Flip pulled the nose up slightly, eased the throttle, and rolled in. He armed his rockets. The bridge rushed up at him. He pulled the trigger on the stick. Whoosh! Two rockets boomed on the bridge, a direct hit. Flip pulled the stick back, applied full power and looked over his left shoulder. Nothing. Desultory tracer fire. Blackness.

The battle for the Hoa Luu District compound was over.

****

Sampans in a staggered column hugged the riverbank, motoring slowly back to the Vinh Cheo Triangle. A light moist wind was blowing. There was a feeling of dawn in the air, a peaceful contrast to the noisy death of the Hoa Luu battle that ended a short time before.

Major Tong had cautioned his commanders to maintain a vigilant air watch. They were very vulnerable withdrawing from an attack in the early dawn.

"All we need," he reflected, "is to have the death ray or a firing helicopter shoot up what is left of my command."

Many sampans were empty; the lost men and equipment would be hard to replace.

But, not everything is bad, he thought. They had destroyed two PF platoons. They had overrun part of the District compound even if they had not held it, and they had killed many Regional Force soldiers in the compound. The 122RF Company will not take to the field in strength for some time. Hopefully they had started—how did Colonel Truc say it?—popping the cork out of the bottle. Much of the Hoa Luu Canal would be open to the north for attacking forces. Nothing can be allowed to stop the future offensive.

Major Tong settled back in the lead sampan. He refused to look at the beautiful dawn or to think of the future beyond his immediate mission. He would never think of the deaths of women and children in the Hoa Luu battle.

****

They zipped Don Burns into a body bag and carried his stiff body to the MEDEVAC helicopter ticking over on the province road. That ended the battle euphoria. Exhaustion hit the team like a body blow. Without battle adrenalin it was hard to move; there was an enervation coupled with an awful, hopeless depression.

Jack thought Hoa Luu looked like a Beau Geste movie where the Foreign Legion lost, or how Dien Bien Phu probably appeared after being overrun by General Giapp. The two outlying outposts were totally destroyed, burned to the ground. A stomach turning smell of burning wood, wet ashes, and putrefication filled the air. At first light, Jack and Major Tho had walked through the ruins of these two positions. Twisted, scorched aluminum sidings and posts sticking grotesquely out of the ground were all that remained of the family dwellings. Bodies lay scattered about like discarded pieces of laundry. Blood was everywhere. Many PF soldiers had been beheaded and their private parts mutilated.

The District compound, however, was not seriously damaged. There were some destroyed family huts and fortification damage to the south and east walls. Men with picks and shovels were already repairing the damage. The parade ground was pockmarked by numerous mortar explosions. The jeep remained sitting on top of the destroyed machinegun position, like a large wheeled bird sitting on a crushed nest. The team hut looked like a half deflated dirigible, the common room and the porch totally destroyed, the sleeping area still intact. Some giant had reached down from above and thrust his finger through the top of the team bunker, collapsing the roof to the center of the floor.

Two important symbols survived: the Tiger battle standard stood out bravely in the light breeze, and the only flying shithouse in the Delta was unscathed. *Their indomitable fighting symbols remained intact*, Jack thought. *They had not been defeated.*

Casualty figures were high: 42 soldiers KIA, and 70 seriously wounded out of a rifle strength of 300. Most of the casualties came from the two destroyed PF outposts. According to the book, they should have been defeated. Civilian casualties were still being counted and promised to be higher than the military. Almost everyone was slightly wounded.

Jack had visited Co Linh and Doc at the aid station. There was the smell of rotting blood mixed with medicine; patients lay on ponchos in rows; flies were everywhere; babies cried; women wept; the soldiers lay fighting for life in stoic silence. Co Linh nodded to him and continued to work. She was not fazed by this terrible medical situation.

Doc reported, "Sir, we have to move some of these people over to the district hospital. There's no room here. Medical supplies are almost out. We've used everything, even the special emergency drugs in my medical bag." He gave Jack a long list. Jack had relayed this to Province, which since dawn had been up on the radio. The MEDEVAC bird which flew Burns' body out had brought some supplies, promising to return with more.

Only eight VC bodies were found, though there were many blood trails. The VC had taken their casualties with them or had dumped them into the canal tied to a heavy rock. Clearing the battlefield of their dead and wounded was a great pride to the Viet Minh.

The MEDEVAC bird took off. The team slowly trudged back to the half destroyed hut. Billy was waiting for them with a radio message. An entourage was about to descend on Hoa Luu: Brigadier General Wells, the V Corps Senior Advisor, Colonel Andrews, his chief of staff, Colonel "Grey Ghost" Mason, the 64th ARVN Division Senior Advisor, and even Lieutenant Colonel Potts was going to temporarily leave his air conditioned office. Apparently, the battle for Hoa Luu had created quite a stir at senior headquarters. The ferocity of the attack stood out in stark contrast to the relative quiet in the rest of the Delta. "The VC had really wanted this one— the question is why?" the Grey Ghost had asked.

They all sat down on their bunks. Jack's hands, his entire body began to tremble. He looked at the team. They were looking at Burns' bloodstains on the floor. Even Cal Washington seemed down. Jack did not know how he, or anyone, was going to brief the VIPs who were due in an hour.

"Okay, Hoa Luu Muckers, stand by for orders," Jack barked in his best VMI parade ground voice. "We're going to set an example around here. I want everybody in their jungle best, including your spit shined boots. Then I want you to line up for a little cocktail party." Jack reached under his bunk and pulled out an intact bottle of Jim Beam bourbon. Everybody's eyes widened at this. They dug out their fresh uniforms with gusto.

The Muckers stood before him. Four canteen cups were on the table, each loaded with four ounces of Kentucky's finest.

"Now, gentlemen, drink this slowly. A toast to our victory." They toasted.

"To Hoa Luu District."

"To the Tigers."

"To the Hoa Hao."

"To us, the Muckers, the best goddamned advisory team in the Delta."

"Now finish it off."

The bourbon exploded in his empty stomach, spread through his entire body, flushed his face and steadied his hands. A feeling of camaraderie and well-being settled over the team. "Now, lighten up. Things are pretty low around here and we're going to fix that. The Muckers are going to fire up our visitors. We haven't lost the war here. In fact, we're going to use this battle to get Province and Division off their asses and persuade them to operate in the Vinh Cheo Triangle. We're going to sell our advisory programs; we're going to convince these guys that the VC have a dangerous offensive capability. Now, Sergeant Minh, get the briefing charts ready. We'll brief over at the District TOC. I'll talk to Tho and Re and get their act together."

Jack felt confident, all-powerful. The team grinned back.

"Boss, I'm a bit woozy." Billy suddenly excused himself. He headed for the flying shithouse at a dead run.

"Make sure you guys squirt some toothpaste into your mouths," Jack said.

The Muckers waited for the VIPs.

Four helicopters were parked head to tail on the province road. The air crews fiddled around, kicking skids and checking rotors. The biggest challenge was to keep the kids off the aircraft. They faced a long wait in the intermittent rain, waiting for their passengers.

The briefing took place in the District TOC. After introducing Tho and Re, Jack gave the visitors the usual overview of the District and then concentrated on the battle. He had divided the battle into four phases: the destruction of the two PF outposts, the battle for the south wall, the east wall, and the final fight for the province road bridge. He did not mention the VC demand for the American team or the killing of Captain Giao. He concluded with what he thought was the enemy's intent behind the battle, to open up the Hoa Luu Canal for future VC offensive operations.

General Wells, sitting in an uncomfortable folding chair, squirmed at Jack's conclusion. As the V Corps Senior Advisor he commanded all Americans in the Southern Delta. He didn't like upstart young majors telling him how to do his job.

"Look, Major, I don't believe the enemy has the capability to launch a major offensive in the Southern Delta." He went on at some length in this vein, citing lack of training, lack of weapons, and lack of soldiers. Wells was a tall, stooped, almost cadaverous officer with a bad ulcer. His great professional ambition was to return to the pristine, confrontational beauty of the cold war in Europe. He had fought there as a young officer and had served many tours in Europe since. He understood armor warfare in the comfortable, linear configuration of NATO versus the Warsaw Pact. The VC, Hoa Hao, sampans, enemy base areas, refugees, and the terrible confusion of the Southern Delta were beyond him. Wells wanted an armor division guarding the Fulda Gap. A promotion to Major General and the assignment were already half promised to him. He had six months to go and now this, an unexplained violent attack on a district headquarters and the crazy theories of this young Major. His chief of staff, Colonel Andrews, backed him up.

"I agree, sir, I think the enemy was hassling us. Occasionally they'll launch a major attack so we don't misread the tea leaves and attack them thinking they've given up. It doesn't portend anything like a large offensive."

Colonel Harvey Andrews was fond of words like "portend." Years ago he had graduated from the Harvard Business School and had a reputation for being an "intellectual." He was a short stocky man with a constant five o'clock shadow. Andrews and Wells had served together before on the playing fields of central Europe. The Colonel had commanded a brigade in Europe on his previous assignment. It was well known in V Corps that he was bucking for a star. Part of the bucking program was to keep things quiet, since that is what General Wells told him every day. Keeping things quiet was a strategic objective in V Corps.

Jack felt bold. He knew he had briefed well and could barely suppress an irrational desire to laugh. Nothing like a few shots to get ready for a briefing. He dove in.

"Colonel Andrews, nothing has happened like this in this region for over a year. When you look at this operation in the context of the intelligence we are receiving, intelligence that indicates that the U Minh Regiment is retraining and refitting, I believe this attack is alarming. It could 'portend' future offensive operations." Jack was heavy on the word "portend."

Colonel Andrews appeared to ignore his inflection. He smiled smoothly at Jack, but his eyes were cold. "What would you recommend, Travis?"

"Sir, I'm not sure the enemy plans offensive operations. But, we must get into the Vinh Cheo Triangle to disrupt his activities and find out what the hell is going on." Jack paused; he was on a roll. He turned to General Wells. "I would also suggest, General, that V Corps conduct large scale operations into the entire U Minh Forest area for the same reason."

SILK OVER STEEL

BOUNDARY

PHU LONG

PROVINCE ROAD

TRAM CUA

PROVINCE ROAD

HOA LUU

122

125

VINH THANH

INTERDICTED

PROVINCE ROAD

123

VINH CHEO TRIANGLE

HOA LUU CANAL

VINH THANH CANAL

NUONG THO.
PROVINCE CAPITAL

BOUNDARY

TAO RIVER

BOUNDARY

RICE PADDIES

LINE OF ATTACK

TREES / FOREST

© 1990 Donald Rowe

SCALE

0   5 KLM

General Wells started at this. He looked at Colonel Mason. "What do you think, Bill?" He asked this question with a clipped tone, like he didn't want an answer.

The Grey Ghost was not going to be stampeded either way. He looked at Jack and the General. "Sir, I think going into the U Minh Forest on a large scale at this time would be a mistake. We need more intelligence, more precise targeting. On the other hand, Jack has a point." The Grey Ghost always called junior officers by their first names in front of his superiors. "District forces here have been weakened as a result of the attack. Hoa Luu's ability to react to future offensive operations is diminished because of losses to the 122nd RF Company, the Delta Tigers. To improve the district security situation and," he grinned at Jack, "to find out what in the hell is going on, I strongly recommend we hit Vinh Cheo and do it soon."

General Wells stroked his chin. *Perhaps this is the way to go*, he thought, *a compromise.* He looked at his chief.

Colonel Andrews was shaking his head. "Sir, certainly we should not conduct operations into the U Minh. God, what a waste of resources! Also, I don't think we want to stir up the Vinh Cheo hornet's nest. The Vinh Cheo and U Minh Forest are operationally linked. The entire Southern Delta could go up in flames."

Jack interrupted, "Isn't that the point, sir? We need to attack. If they're up to anything, we need to destroy them. If you know where they are, if you think they are planning to attack, you attack them first. That's the way you win." Even Jack thought he had gone a bit too far this time.

A silence as if some obscure taboo subject had been addressed descended on the briefing. Barely perceptibly, the Grey Ghost shook his head at Jack.

General Wells cleared his throat and stood up. "We'll have to think about this one. I'll get back to you, Bill."

The Grey Ghost wanted to force some kind of commitment. "Sir, if we decide that the 64th ARVN Division should enter Vinh Cheo, your counterpart, the Vietnamese Corps Commander, must tell my counterpart in the strongest possible terms. If not, my general will never get off his butt."

"Bill, you sound like your young Major. Let the Vietnamese fight their own battles. It's their war. We're just here to provide some of the assets."

Jack noticed that Lieutenant Colonel Potts had not said a word during the entire exchange.

They trooped out of the District TOC after the VIPs had ceremoniously shaken hands with the Vietnamese.

"General Wells, I would like you to meet my team. If you have the time."

"Of course, Travis, I want to see the gallant defenders of Hoa Luu." This was said with a trace of sarcasm.

They walked over to the half destroyed team hut. Cal had the Muckers lined up in a sharp military formation wearing pressed jungle fatigues and spit shined boots.. They exuded high morale and good fellowship.

General Wells looked at the destroyed bunker. "God damn, you guys took a direct hit." He marveled at the destruction. "What a close call. I must say, I am deeply impressed by the professionalism and buoyant morale of this team. This battle, even the total destruction of your fighting position, did not sap your fighting spirit. You are a tribute to the American advisors serving in the Delta." General Wells' voice filled with emotion. He clapped Jack on the shoulder. Cal winked at Jack.

That night Jack was summoned to Commander Re's quarters. Major Tho, Commander Re, Dai Uy Luom, and the junior officers of the Delta Tigers were there. They stood around the table with the tiger head in the middle. The tiger's eyes gleamed alive in the kerosene lamplight. Re gave him a glass of Ba Si De whiskey, no western brandy tonight. Glasses were raised. Re toasted, "DOI VOI THIEU TA Travis, NGUOI CHIEN HUU DA CHIEN DAU SAT CANH VOI CHUNG TA, ONG TA THAT SU LA MOT CHIEN SI CUA HOA HAO. To Major Travis, a warrior who fought and bled with us. Major Travis is a true Hoa Hao warrior."

Re was followed by the remaining officers who all gave similar toasts. At the end, Jack was feeling woozy, because every toast required him to drain his glass. Major Tho was last. The District Chief stood before him, strangely shy. From around his neck he removed a thin gold chain and hung it around Jack's neck. Attached by a gold device to the chain was a tiger claw, the talisman of the Hoa Hao warrior. All present exposed their tiger claws to demonstrate they were warrior brothers. Major Tho embraced him. Jack knew this was a great honor, an induction into the Hoa Hao warrior society. Tho toasted, "Welcome to the Hoa Hao warrior society. You have demonstrated during this battle that you are a true brother. MONG RANG CHIEC MONG COP NAY SE MANG DEN CHO ANH LONG CAN DAM, SUC MANH VA SU DANH DU. May this tiger claw always bring you honor, strength and courage."

Jack replied in halting Vietnamese, "CAM ON CAC CHIEN HUU, TOI LAY LAM HANH DIEN LA NGUOI CUA HOA HAO. Thank you, my brothers. I am proud to be a Hoa Hao."

137

Jack looked at his brothers, these short dusky men in jungle fatigues standing around the table with the tiger's head, which now looked ready to pounce. Through the fiery Ba Si De, he thought, this is why he fought, to serve his brothers, their families, these people. The motivation was here, not in some obscure and distant litany of duty, honor, and country. True honor was to fight with these men and never let them down.

*******2*******

Three weeks after the Hoa Luu battle, the Silk over Steel campaign progressed to the next phase. The 123rd RF company, which secured the northern apex of the Vinh Cheo Triangle area, was ambushed in broad daylight on an open rice paddy. At the same time, a battalion of the U Minh Regiment overran their lightly secured outpost complex. The company was forced to withdraw northeast up the Hoa Luu Canal to new positions five kilometers south of Hoa Luu village. Major Tong let the company's families go up the canal to join their men. A foolish gesture, Major Tong thought, but he wasn't reduced to killing women and children in cold blood—at least not yet.

This battle cleared all government forces from the northern part of the Vinh Cheo Triangle. Terrorism, assassinations, ambushes, and snipings increased. The VC agents became more active, even in Hoa Luu Town. These agents provided the information to make the offensive work. It was not safe to travel the roads or canals in the district without mounting a military operation. The new medical program came to a standstill. Inspections and training visits to units became almost impossible. Jack requested the Province helicopter often for support but it was never available. District services, such as delivering food and building materials, stood still. A desperate problem arose as refugees began to pour into Hoa Luu Town. Among the refugees were many Viet Cong spies.

The three RF companies were constantly on operations, reaction forces, ambushes, resupply operations, and security stakeouts. Losses mounted up. The PF began to develop a "fort up" attitude. Stay behind the walls and give the countryside to the enemy at night. This had a devastating effect on civilian morale. The Government could not provide for their needs; even basic security was lacking. VC recruiting, even in pacified areas, increased along with subversion.

Jack had many talks with Colonel Mason, the Grey Ghost, and Lieutenant Colonel Potts. He hammered the point over and over again that the offensive in Hoa Luu District was not an isolated situation but was part of a larger plan. The VC needed the Hoa Luu lines of communication for future operations. Potts would not listen. He viewed Hoa Luu as a single situation, an abscess which should be isolated and left alone so it would not infect the rest of the province. Potts these days was polite to Jack because he realized he was one of the "Grey Ghost's boys," but there was no support. He also believed that General Wells, his boss's boss, did not want to heat up this Hoa Luu mess. Potts understood the "keep it quiet" guidance.

Colonel Mason halfway agreed with Jack. He believed the offensive activity fit into some grand design but was not convinced it telegraphed a major VC offensive. After the battle of Hoa Luu, Mason had done everything to pressure his counterpart, the 64th ARVN Division Commander, to enter the Vinh Cheo. The Division Commander would not budge. General Wells refused to discuss the situation with his counterpart, the Vietnamese Corps Commander. No command pressure was placed on the Division Commander to conduct an attack into the base area.

Six weeks after the battle of Hoa Luu, a major night attack occurred against Vinh Thanh Town by the 310th Battalion of the U Minh Regiment, reinforced with additional attachments. The 125th RF Company had been warned and put up a stiff fight. The Tigers and one platoon of 123rd RF Company maneuvered to the northwest and hit the attackers from the rear, a running melee of a fight on the open rice paddies. Flip Cochran had a field day with his little fighter bomber. In this battle, because they had positive identification of a U Minh unit, the Territorial Forces were given air support. They did not rate jets. A-1 Sky Raiders dove out of the sky. These aircraft pounded the VC with high explosives and napalm.

Jack did everything to call up reinforcements, but the 64th ARVN Division was not moving. Colonel Mason flew to Jack's CP. This was done at risk, and the helicopter took two hits.

"Jack, I can get you some more air, but no troops. ARVN will not budge with ground troops to reinforce you. My counterpart says we have other obligations, whatever the hell that means. Also, forget about Spooky. They're all tied up supporting U.S. operations in the north." The Grey Ghost could see Jack was exhausted. They had been through weeks of uninterrupted, end to end operations. And there was the stress, the surprise. The Government forces did not have the initiative. He offered to send some more advisors to assist the Muckers, but Jack refused. He was very jealous about who dealt with his Hoa Hao.

Colonel Mason spent some time trying to reassure Jack. In the end he put an arm around him. "You're doing a hell of a job, son." He was surprised at his emotion.

That night, the VC slipped to the west, rendezvoused with their sampan flotilla and began motoring back to the Vinh Cheo. Some small units were left behind with missions of interdicting the province road and the Vinh Thanh Canal.

The same night, the Tigers rushed back to Hoa Luu, a fifteen kilometer forced road march after contact had been broken. Major Tho had called Re on the radio. He was concerned about a major attack on the District which was vulnerable without the Delta Tigers. The force was totally exhausted when they arrived at Hoa Luu. The Tigers crashed for sleep. If the VC had attacked that night, they would have encountered a sleeping compound.

Lying on his bunk waiting for sleep, Jack reviewed the situation through a gray haze of fatigue: we can't keep this up; the team is exhausted; the regional forces are getting weaker; the PF won't leave their outposts; the province road and the Vinh Thanh Canal are cut; the VC have free run of the Hoa Luu Canal almost all the way to Hoa Luu Town; nobody is securing the northern apex of the Vinh Cheo Triangle, and the refugees, God the refugees! We have to somehow get them out of the Hoa Luu area. His mind refused to work. He fell asleep.

****** 3 ******

The Tigers were on the rice paddies. It was pitch black. A soft rain was falling. Thunder rumbled in the distance. They were walking along a narrow rice paddy dike made slick by the falling rain. The day before, intelligence had been received that the VC were setting up an ambush on the province road midway between Vinh Thanh Town and Hoa Luu Town to destroy a supply column coming to the district capital the following morning. The Tigers had deployed with two platoons, leaving the remainder of the company to defend the District. Cal was behind him in the column. A Vietnamese soldier carried the radio.

Jack thought, *another walk in the dark*. They had been doing this for weeks, or was it months? One good thing, he had honed his Tiger skills to a razor's edge. Here he was walking with tightrope finesse on top of an ice slick paddy dike toward possible death. And he was asleep, resting. That was Tiger style. The radio spoke behind him, good contact with Billy back at District.

Re was waiting for him at a bend in the dike. "The objective is five hundred meters ahead. My forward squad reports nothing."

Jack nodded, barely comprehending the situation. Re looked hard at Jack in the gloom. He could sense his friend's fatigue.

"Is the Tiger with you?" he asked Jack, a joke between them. Jack fingered his Tiger claw which always hung around his neck. He nodded.

"The Tiger is with me. At least this time we're ambushing an ambush, not the other way around." He knew this sounded weak to Re, but there was a body numbing tiredness upon him. Re went ahead to his forward elements.

There were shots, a burst of automatic fire from the head of the column. Cal, the Vietnamese radio operator, and Jack broke into a dead run, heading for the contact. In an instant Jack was awake, every sense alert. He grabbed the radio handset from the radio operator and reported the contact to Billy. "RELAY TO PROVINCE, TELL THEM WE MIGHT NEED SOME SUPPORT."

The firing slackened and then surged again. They had entered a wooded area. Bullets tore through the air, dropping pieces of palm fronds to the ground.

Jack reflected quickly; these Delta fire fights usually started the same:

142

shots from the front, the company deployed, automatic weapons employed, 60MM mortars registered and the Tigers maneuvered against the enemy. He considered this a good contact. Frontal fire normally meant no ambush, no surprise. When you were taken in the flank by short range killing fire, that tightened up your rear end. His young radio operator was out of breath. He was a headquarters type, a TOC radio shift operator. He looked soft to Jack, but the young soldier had been eager to go on this operation. Jack's usual Vietnamese operator was sick. Carrying the radio for the famous Co Van My, the American advisor, a member of the Hoa Hao warrior society, was a great honor for the young man. Face would be gained.

The bullets were lower now, slapping over their heads. They half crouched while running. CRACK! Jack whirled around; his radio operator lay on his face. Cal was kneeling beside him, checking for wounds. He removed the radio from the soldier's back with difficulty and gently rolled him over. The young soldier had a tiny hole almost exactly between his eyes.

"He's dead."

"Grab the radio and follow me."

Suddenly the firing stopped. They caught up with Re standing beside a small farm hut.

"A platoon size force, most of them escaped. We have two bodies." He guided them forward. Jack looked down at the two figures crumpled in odd directions. He kicked the nearest body.

"What do we do with them?" he asked Commander Re. Re looked at him, thoughtfully.

"We will take them back to District and decide."

All the way back to District, Jack thought of the young radio operator, his early death. He thought of the battles of the last weeks which had threatened the life of the District. And he thought of the VC spies living right in their midst who made enemy operations successful. The tiger claw warmed his chest. He knew what to do with the VC bodies. They would be a demonstration. Commander Re would not object. It was the Hoa Hao thing to do.

The small market square in Hoa Luu town had been cleansed by the early morning rains. It glistened in the sun beside the brown, flowing canal. The VC bodies were placed at the end of a covered concrete platform normally used for displaying bananas, melons, and large coconuts. They sat upright, arms suspended by ropes attached to the ceiling. The heads leaned against their shoulders. With terribly blank faces, the eyes were glazed over with the final sheen of death. Flies buzzed. Over all hung the smell of putrefaction. Jack had arranged the bodies, a gruesome example for all VC spies.

A small crowd gathered, mostly women and children. Their voices were hushed in contrast to the usual shrill market noise. They had an almost religious solemnity, like they were attending a sacred rite. Co Linh thought the platform with the half raised bodies looked like an obscene shrine, a symbol of futility, the hollow tragedy of young death. She was ashamed.

Jack slept most of that day, a dark dreamless sleep. He woke up and used the services of the newly constructed 55 gallon shower stall. He visited the District TOC, and for once everything was quiet. The radio in the team hut did not make a sound. Jack settled down in the team's only easy chair with a book. He couldn't concentrate. The words jumbled together. He could not relax. Perhaps he was too tired. A lethargy came over him, but also a sense of growing unease, a feeling he was too tired to define.

The afternoon wore on. The sun went down in another glorious colorful display enhanced by towering clouds. Jack declined dinner. The Muckers respected his silence. Cal and Doc worried about him. Jack sat in the easy chair, a book resting on his lap. His mind flitted over many images which floated through his head like the tide. He couldn't stop them, grip them. He thought of home in Norfolk, the pungent smell of the salt marshes, the white beaches, the slate grey bay, a white capped spring day with his sailboat heeled over in the freshening wind, tree lined Granby Street where the action was, his father and mother in the big white square house with the lawn going down to the water, and his younger sister and her baby boy. God! He was an uncle! The vault-like serenity of his church—did the Episcopalian God live in Hoa Luu? The battlements of VMI, the harsh discipline of the rat line, his brother's rats, his classmates, his friends, sports, girls, his lost loves, the Army, the responsibility, the thrill of company command in Korea, and now this. He fingered the tiger claw, then abruptly brought his hand down. Co Linh came in with the tide, her beauty, her smell, her love for the land and the people, bodies, dead, malodorous, grotesque bodies tied up—He had done this.

Somebody gently tapped his shoulder. He started slightly and looked up. It was Sergeant Minh.

"Sir, there are some visitors here to see you."

Jack, wide awake now, nodded.

"There are two Vietnamese women outside who want to talk to you."

"About what? Who are they?"

"They are the wives of the VC in the marketplace. They want to take their men down the canal for burial."

Jack felt a growing unease.

"How did they get here? Who let them into the compound?"

"Families travel easily up and down the canal. I let them into the compound."

"You!?" Jack's voice rose.

"Yes, sir, they are Buddhist. I am Buddhist. These men must receive a proper burial, or they will not achieve a rebirth. They will become spirits forever inhabiting a shadowy world between their past lives and rebirth. This will bring great shame and misfortune to the family."

"These women came up the canal, through all that danger to Hoa Luu, for their men? I can't believe it!"

"They're outside, sir; they want you to give permission to cut down the bodies. They want to take them back down the canal for burial."

Jack was suddenly furious. He jumped up. "Goddamn it, Minh, you hate the VC,;they killed your family. You thought this was a good idea. It is a warning to the VC. Paying these bastards back for all the horrible things they've done to us." Jack had more to say, but Minh interrupted.

"My tragedy has made me bitter. You cannot hate the dead. In death we are all brothers and sisters. In life we hate, but in death we are the same." He paused and looked at Jack. "Sir, we must allow these women to take their men home."

"Minh, you sound like a goddamned monk." This was said without emotion. Jack sat down slowly. A fog blotted his brain. He did not want to think, to confront this memory. It would go away with the tide like his dreams.

After a long pause, a low voice said, "Bring them in."

They were before him, dressed in simple black pajamas. The women were very clean and bowed in unison, as if they had rehearsed for this occasion. *No older than sixteen*, Jack thought. One woman started to speak in high pitched, singsong Vietnamese. It sounded like a young girl reciting her catechism. She looked at Jack and then quickly pulled her eyes down. Tears rolled down her cheeks; she started to tremble.

Jack turned to Sergeant Minh. "Tell them we will cut down the bodies and bring them to the compound. They will have their men back."

Minh explained; the women bowed in unison again and left, backing away as if they had entered some terrible den of evil.

The Muckers watched Jack, but not with accusation. They understood the reason for tying the VC up in the market.

Doc spoke, "Maybe what we did was wrong. I know all us guys feel different now after seeing those women, but at first it seemed right. Boss, if you saw the death in the aid station, treated the wounded, sewed up little kids, like I did after the battle…" He stopped, holding back emotion. "Well, maybe we made a mistake, but they sure deserved it." He had run out of words.

Again, the low voice spoke, drained of vitality. "Thanks, Doc. Listen, guys, I got some things to take care of with Commander Re. Cal, make sure things are squared away for the night." He left the hut.

There was a short, intense conversation with Commander Re, words of condolence from his friend. "Do not blame yourself. We did this, not just you."

He walked across the parade ground. There were fresh circles of earth where the mortar craters had been filled. At the top of the bridge he stopped and looked down at the flowing canal. There was a shout welling up in him, a yell over the dark canal, a need to howl to the world. "Yes, I did this thing! And fuck you!" Nothing came. He continued across the bridge to Co Linh's cottage.

She looked up from her chair at the far end of the room. He stopped in the doorway. They gazed at each other. Tears worked down his face. Suddenly he was on his knees before her. She placed his head in her lap and stroked his black hair. He wept, huge, convulsing sobs as if the world had died. After a time he stopped. Blindly, he reached out, slipping his arms around her waist.

"Co Linh, I'm sorry, sorry."

"We are all sorry, Jack. We are all at fault." She lifted his head up and pressed his face to her breast. Tears dropped from her eyes. This man was special, so unlike an American, so caring, so sensitive, yet so strong. Rocking gently, they remained like this for some time.

Desire began to move them. They stood; she placed her arms around his neck, breathing rapidly. She felt his hands run down her hips. Feeling his growing hardness, she moved against him. He kissed her softly, then with growing need. Her mouth opened. Their tongues met. The room was rolling; she could barely stand.

He picked her up and carried her into the bedroom. They stood awkwardly, looking at each other. Then she unsnapped the side of her ao dai and stepped out of her black silk pants. Jack struggled out of his jungle fatigues. She stood before him in white pants and bra. He unsnapped the bra and looked at her full figure in the half light. His breath caught. He touched her smooth breasts, then took the pink aureole in his mouth and ran his tongue over the rounded nipple, feeling it swell. She gasped and placed her hand on his penis which throbbed and hardened as she ran her fingers over the swollen head and across the small opening. There was growing moisture between her legs. He sat down on the bed before her and eased down her pants. She felt her stomach caressed by his tongue and then an electric shock as he went lower to the silky hair between her legs. He rose and placed her gently on the bed. She lay on her back and opened her legs. He gently entered her; there were warm, soft, caressing sensations. He came halfway out and then slid in farther, with more strength. She raised her legs and pushed against him. They were losing themselves in each other.

Faster and faster, she wanted all of him. She spread her legs wider. With a buildup of impossible desire, an explosion of love, they drove into each other with all their strength and all their joy, to become forever one.

Co Linh woke Jack up. She had dressed in her white nurse uniform. "You must go now. It is late." He reached out to put his arm around her, trying to bring her back to bed. She withdrew to the far side of the room. *Here comes another abrupt decision*, Jack thought.

"Co Linh, after this you can't just throw me out into the street. I love you. I will never leave you."

"Jack, this will never work. Everything we do here will be for nothing if people know we are—you know."

He became angry. "Is that all you think about, Hoa Luu District, this Godforsaken place? I love you. I want to marry you and bring you home to America."

"America! That is the trouble with you Americans, you think America is everything. It is not my home. I would never like your country. The crime, the boasting, think of Sergeant Hartwell. I could never leave my land and my people. We Vietnamese must settle our differences and restore the peace. I live for that day."

"Sergeant Hartwell? For God's sake, we don't have many Hartwells in my country. We have many good people. Look at this place, you and your people. It is hopelessly screwed up with war, corruption, terror, you name it. You need peace, children, love," and more gently, "my love."

She interrupted. "I had a family once. That will never happen again." She looked at Jack. "We must never make love again."

He rose reluctantly and began to dress. Jack knew this was a woman he could not lose. He looked at her beautiful, distant eyes, bright with determination. Linh, the woman he had made love to, was no longer in the room. The iron warrior, the heroine of her people had suddenly returned. He felt a sinking feeling, a vast hollowness.

They shared a handshake at the doorway.

"I will see you tomorrow, Jack. We must talk about the inoculation program."

Jack said goodbye. He had not told her about tomorrow.

The two new coffins were painted light brown, the Buddhist burial color. They were loaded carefully on a large utility sampan powered by a Johnson outboard that was running at low throttle. A large white flag flew from the bow of the sampan. Sergeant Minh stood on the dock holding the mooring lines, ready to cast off. Jack could not persuade him not to come.

"This is my problem, too, and you might need an interpreter."

Commander Re talked to Jack. "I think this will be all right." He paused, worried. "They will not fire on a sampan under a flag of truce bearing two of their comrades prepared for a Buddhist burial. The wives went down the canal last night with a letter from Major Tho explaining your trip. He explained you paid for all the funeral expenses, that it was not your fault that these young men were violated."

"That is not true. It was my idea."

"Jack." Re's exasperation showed through the use of his first name. He normally referred to him by rank, even though they both wore the tiger claw and were bonded together through many bloody skirmishes on the rice paddies.

"I do not want you killed. If you must do this, you must appear as a man of compassion, a man of mercy. It is your only chance." He paused. "You know I do not want you to go." Jack started to speak. Re waved him down. "I know you have to do this to fill some deep need in yourself. I admire living to a special code, even if I do not understand it." He squeezed Jack on both shoulders, backed away and saluted.

The Muckers were on the dock to say farewell, all very solemn as if they were there to pay their last respects.

"Look, guys, I'll be back." Jack tried to sound cheerful.

"Boss, you know I think what you're doing is bullshit, but I respect you. When these motherfuckers are trying to kill you, anything goes to survive and win." Cal shook his hand.

Doc was next. "Be careful. You are doing the right thing. Last night I prayed to the Virgin Mary for your safety. This is a Christian act. Keep this for the trip." He pressed a silver Saint Christopher medal into his hand. "It has kept me safe."

"Boss, are you sure you don't want a radio?" To Billy Turner the biggest sacrilege was to go anywhere in this country without a radio. "No, Billy." Billy nodded, and bit his lip.

Jack stepped cautiously into the sampan and cast off. The sampan moved slowly into the middle of the canal, then picked up speed and headed south for Vinh Cheo.

They passed through the 123rd RF Company's new positions. This unit had been the previous occupants of the Vinh Cheo outpost complex. People waved; children shouted. Here the canal turned to the southwest, and they were abruptly in Indian country. *The lines had dangerously shortened*, Jack thought. Indian country, five short klicks south of Hoa Luu Town.

The sampan motored on. The banks of the canal were now deserted. There was nobody to wave or shout a greeting to them. Sergeant Minh, in the bow, turned around to reassure himself that Jack was still there.

The contrast between the pacified areas and Indian country was startling. There was mile after mile of deserted huts and empty hamlet market places, as if the entire population had been vaporized by the war. But Jack knew they had not been vaporized. Most of them were refugees, huddled around Hoa Luu Town, close to starving. It was a bed of poverty and VC subversion. He thought again, *we must move these people.*

The outboard engine noise bounced off the banks, the only sound they heard. The wind freshened, throwing brown ripples across the face of the canal. The sky darkened, Jack put on his poncho. The rains slanted down on them like water from an overturned bucket. *The Delta climate*, Jack thought, *one moment you were drowning, the next you were sweating in the hot sun, the water steaming off your body and equipment.* The rain stopped, bright sunlight twinkled off the surface of the canal.

Jack studied the map. They had motored twenty-eight kilometers down the Hoa Luu Canal. The sampan was passing through the now deserted Vinh Cheo outpost complex. Not totally deserted, there was a VC flag with a single white star on a red and blue background flying from the outpost flagpole. Much of the outpost was destroyed; each corner fortification had been blown up. The canal widened here; they were approaching the Tau River. Jack slowly steered the sampan around in a circle. This was the rendezvous point. They circled for thirty minutes. Jack checked again to make sure the large fuel tank was on board. They had that tingly feeling of being watched.

There was a shot across the bow. Sergeant Minh jumped, rocking the sampan. Jack reached below the splash board for a weapon that wasn't there. A sampan with five men on board motored into view flying a VC flag. A man in the stern motioned them to follow, then executed a quick U-turn and moved back down the river. They followed. Jack looked hard at the VC sampan but could see no weapons. After four kilometers, the Catholic church, the Vinh Cheo lighthouse, came into view. Its blue and white walls and single large cross stood out starkly in the sun, like a relic from another world, Jack thought. The VC sampan headed toward the church. A large VC flag flew at the landing. A group of men stood on the wooden planking, watching them. Two were looking through binoculars. The VC driving the lead sampan gestured them to land. Jack throttled back and readied the mooring lines. They crept up to the landing. Two soldiers moved forward and took the lines. Jack started to rise; there was a violent gesture from one of the men on the landing. He sat down. After a low order, two more soldiers came forward. One at a time the coffins were carefully removed from the sampan. The widows of the two dead VC were not in sight.

Face to face with the enemy, Jack stared hard at the group of Viet Gong. They were dressed in the black pajamas of the Delta. Bush hats hung by cords down their backs. Extremely thin and hard, Jack sensed a quiet elan in these men which he'd never seen in the Government soldiers, with the exception of the Delta Tigers. Two of the VC wore pistol belts, but no pistols.

The coffins were carried off the dock. The taller of the two with pistol belts approached the end of the dock. He looked intently down at Jack then released the stern and bow lines. He gestured the sampan away and gave a sharp command to his soldiers. They came to attention. The man turned to Jack and saluted. Jack awkwardly rose in the sampan and returned the salute. Jack turned the sampan north to Hoa Luu.

The sun was down when they pulled into the Hoa Luu landing. Commander Re met them.

"Hello, my friend." He greeted Jack in the familiar form reserved for close friends. "What did you learn?"

Jack hesitated, then said, "I learned we are losing the war, and I thought of a way to win it."

PART THREE

PHU LONG

APRIL THROUGH JUNE 1967

****** 1 ******

Lee lived in a small hamlet next to the Vinh Cheo outpost with his father, a TRUNG SI, a sergeant in the Regional Forces, his mother, his nine-year-old sister and a small black and white dog named Chi. His grandparents had been killed two years before during a Viet Minh mortar attack. His mother and father had tried to have more children, but she had become sick after his sister's birth. The midwife was untrained and a bad infection set in that almost killed her. There were no more children.

The family inhabited a small thatched house perched over the canal on thin wooden stilts. There were two rooms. Lee and his sister slept in the large family room, which also served as the kitchen, dining room and place of worship to the family ancestors. Often the large room smelled of incense. His mother and father had the remaining room to themselves. Behind the house was a dock where Lee spent many hours casting a circular net for fish to vary the endless meals of rice spiced with nuoc mam, fish sauce, and chicken. Usually when Lee's father returned from an operation, he would bring a chicken, a Viet Minh chicken, he always said. The house was fronted with a small porch which faced the narrow hamlet road. Lee's father had been issued aluminum roofing from his unit which made the house stand out, the only home on the row with a shiny roof. This was a status symbol among the neighbors. He was, after all, a TRUNG SI in the 123th RF Company.

Being a member of the local RF Company, Lee's father was a full-time soldier. His only civic duty was helping, during harvest time, to transport the rice in large sampans to Hoa Luu Town, where the rice was processed in a Chinese owned rice mill. The other men in the hamlet were rice farmers and part-time soldiers. They were assigned to a PF platoon that secured an assigned area in the community and occupied a satellite outpost to the main Vinh Cheo fortification. The families would go to the outpost in times of danger. As soldiers, they performed local security missions on a scheduled basis. These farmers were good at it. They were dedicated to protecting their families and rice lands, and the PF training program had given them the skills and confidence to do the job well.

Life in the Southern Delta was oriented to the rice cycles, family, reverence to ancestors, and the Buddhist faith. It was measured out in toil on the rice paddies, occasional religious festivals, and important family ceremonies such as weddings, births, birthdays, and funerals. The people lived daily with the threat of death, the loss of a loved one. All had suffered from the war over the years. This didn't dim their spirits. They accepted life without lasting depression. But, in the constant face of tragedy, they wanted something better, to own their own rice lands, to build a better home, to get a better price at the Chinese owned rice mill, and to educate their children. These people were warm, fun loving, and emotional. They cried for their dead. They mourned their children. They weren't inscrutable, fatalistic, and uncaring people.

Above all, they wanted to end the war which always hovered around them and threatened to destroy the fabric of family, religion, and land that made life possible.

Lee had heard firing and distant mortar explosions the day his father was killed. Frightened men came running into the hamlet. There was a storm of rumors: all families must go to the outpost, then that the outpost had been destroyed, and, finally, that the 123rd RF Company had been routed on the open rice paddies and was fleeing toward Hoa Luu. The last rumor was correct. Then Lee knew his father was dead. He would never desert his family.

There was chaos in the hamlet; families threw their belongings into sampans or on their backs. Wails of mourning filled the air. A long column formed of people walking or boating northeast up the canal towards Hoa Luu Town, a sanctuary from the Viet Minh.

His mother was disciplined. She would cry for his father later. The family altar, furniture, matting, cooking fire stones, everything of consequence was thrown into their old battered sampan until the freeboard almost disappeared. His sister was crying. His mother told her to be silent. After an argument, she said Chi must stay behind. Lee told his mother that Chi was their talisman, a good luck token that would help them in the new place.

Lee rowed the overly loaded sampan to the middle of the canal. As the family traveled up the canal past the deserted hamlet, Lee could see armed men on the banks searching the abandoned dwellings. The Viet Minh! They made no attempt to stop the fleeing refugees.

The refugee column swelled as it moved up the canal, like a small glob of honey gathering bees. Family after family joined the exodus, abandoning their homes and rice lands. They knew that the Government couldn't provide security. Government control along the southern Hoa Luu Canal had been obliterated with the defeat of the 123rd RF Company.

The growing column of refugees was quiet, except for occasional cries from babies. There was the brooding silence of hundreds of dispossessed people whose future had been devastated by the war. Lee forced himself to concentrate on propelling the dangerously overloaded sampan. He told his sister to sit still as water lapped over the gunwales. His mother sat stoically in the bow looking straight ahead. Memories of his father kept entering Lee's mind: teaching him to fish, to operate the sampan, to shoot, counseling him on the troubling thoughts all thirteen-year-old boys have. He forced these thoughts away. What was ahead mattered. What lay beyond the bend in the canal was the future for his family. He was, after all, now the man of the family. Lee's father had reminded him of this each time he departed on an operation. His father was gone; he must take care of his mother and sister. Lee held back a sob. Chi, sensing his sorrow, snuggled against his master's leg. He reached down and patted the smooth black and white head. Chi thumped his stubby tail on the deck of the sampan.

There was no reception that first night in Hoa Luu Town, no food, no water. Sampans were secured to the canal banks for miles around the town. Hundreds of small cooking fires started. The refugees used small pieces of canvas for shelter. Cramped and cold, Lee's family spent the first night on the sampan. Chi whined for more food, but they had nothing but cold rice and a few scraps of chicken. The number of refugees grew to over a thousand, a mass of despairing humanity with no place to go.

The next morning soldiers gathered the refugees in the marketplace. The District Chief talked to them. Lee could barely make out the short, barrel chested figure from the back of the crowd. The voice was deep and carried loudly over the marketplace.

"This is a tragedy, but do not despair. Hoa Luu District will take care of you. We will give you shelter and food. Someday in the future we will attack back down the canal and liberate your homes and rice lands.

"The Viet Minh have done this to you. You must hate the Viet Minh! They treat you like trash, scattering you before the wind, killing your sons, your fathers and brothers. They steal your land and your honor. They insult the memory of your ancestors. The Viet Minh hate the people. Never forgive them for what they have done to you!" The District Chief's voice rose to a shout when he said this. Lee felt a surge of hate for those who killed his father.

The District Chief continued, "You must stay here for a short time. How long, I do not know. Soon we will build shelters for you. Today we can only give you food." Lee noticed there were stacks of food behind the District Chief:

bags of rice, bulgur wheat, and tins of cooking oil. The District Chief gestured to this mountain of food with some pride. "This will feed you for a few days. Later there will be more.

"Finally, today, let me tell you something which is very important. You must live as a family; you must all be brothers and sisters. Do not fight with each other. That is what the Viet Minh want. These will be hard times, and you will need a special belief in yourself as a people and your country. The Hoa Hao and the Government will help you. You know I am a Hoa Hao and the District Chief. Other Hoa Hao will be among you, talking to you, helping you. Cooperate with these people. They will show you the way to overcome the terrible crime the Viet Minh have committed against you."

After waving to the crowd and turning the meeting over to a deputy in charge of food distribution, the District Chief left the marketplace. Lee could feel the crowd press toward the food. Hunger and riot was in the air. The deputy started to speak. His voice was drowned by a large mob noise. The people moved forward and attacked the stacks of food. Lee fought against the pressed bodies but couldn't get through the crowd. Screams, fighting broke out. The stacks of food evaporated. Only the physically strong ate that day. Lee's family and many others continued to be hungry.

A few days later, the district registered all the refugees, and food was distributed based on family needs. There was never enough, however, and the food was of poor quality. More refugees arrived every day. Children developed distended bellies; pet dogs were eaten. Lee carefully guarded Chi. Starvation stalked the refugee camp.

Three large warehouse buildings were constructed for the refugees at the southern end of Hoa Luu Town. These were divided into family areas. There were no running water or latrine facilities. The Hoa Luu Canal had to serve both purposes. A terrible stench covered the refugee area. An epidemic of dysentery broke out; small children began to die.

The Hoa Hao went among them, preaching to the people in small groups. "Respect the District, respect the District Chief, support the Government, revere the example of Huynh Phu So, the Hoa Hao founding father, a warrior priest who loved his people and his nation." Pamphlets were distributed to the people, though few of them could read, outlining the precepts of the Hoa Hao faith. The refugees were indoctrinated with the Hoa Hao creed.

"We are united in thought to be Buddhists, to be Vietnamese individuals who believe in the worth of life on this earth, to assist in the construction of an upright nation, to fight communism and to destroy the Viet Minh."

Many grumbled about this. You could not become a Hoa Hao and support the Government when you were sick and hungry.

Others came in the night. One evening Lee went into Hoa Luu Town. He had heard there were visitors who wanted to talk to young men. He was large for his age; he was a young man. The meeting would take place in a restaurant on an alley off the main town road.

Lee entered the dimly lit restaurant. The small dining room was choked with cigarette smoke; a heavy smell of fried fish mixed with the staleness of dead cigarette butts. To the rear of the single room, a small group of young men had gathered around a scarred round table. A tall, very thin young man stood before them. He glanced briefly at Lee and then continued to look at the group. The tall man began to speak.

"Do not believe these Hoa Hao. They are worse than the Government. They speak nonsense. The Hoa Hao creed is a pack of lies. Look how you live. The children are starving. Many of you are sick. The Hoa Hao and the Government leaders live like kings while you perish under their feet. Consider the Chinese merchants in this town. They own the rice mill. They own your lives. You work for them. The Chinese pay the Hoa Hao and Government so that they can exploit you. We must own the rice mill. That way everything we accomplish is for ourselves, the people. We must destroy the Hoa Hao, the Government leaders, and the Chinese or this land will never belong to the people."

The tall man was a compelling speaker. A cause burned within him. He riveted the group with his hard black eyes. Lee felt a chill go down his spine.

"There is a way," the tall stranger continued. "A way to return the land to the people. You!" He punctuated you, looking at each man in turn. "You young, brave men, you warriors must fight for the Viet Minh! Only the young men of our people can save the country." After a pause, the young men looked at the speaker with nervous expectation. "Do you want to join us? Do you want to join the saviors of your country, the Viet Minh?" All the young men said, "yes," including Lee. He didn't want to stand out. Suddenly, he felt his thirteen years. He was younger than the others. Joining the Viet Minh was too big a thing to contemplate. The tall man brought out a notebook. "Let me have your names," he said with a sense of discipline, as if they had already been recruited. Slowly Lee backed out of the group. Nobody noticed. They concentrated on the speaker. He left the restaurant and ran down the alley toward the main street.

Later Lee told his mother. "I thought of joining the Viet Minh. We cannot

157

continue to live like this."

She grabbed his shoulders. "Remember, my son, your father fought with the 123rd RP Company. He supported the Government. Your father hated the Viet Minh. You shame him. Remember who you are."

Lee bowed to his mother and went to his mat beside his sleeping sister. Sleep was long in coming. He thought of life back down on the canal, of riding water buffalo on the rice paddies when he was younger, of his loving mother, now so careworn, and his laughing sister, who now only cried, and finally his father, the strong soldier.   Life had changed forever. They had been visited by a terrible evil. Chi curled onto the mat with him. Lee wept into his soft fur.

Often, during the day, older men and women would visit the refugees. They blended in, and the Government did not notice. These visitors held small meetings, sometimes in the marketplace but more often in the warehouses. They did not talk about the Viet Minh recruiters; they talked about the new safety of the countryside.

"Move back down the canal. The Viet Minh will welcome you. Your young men must leave the Popular Forces. You can have your old homes back and farm your own rice paddies. The Viet Minh did not molest you when you came up here. They will welcome your return. Become a part of our movement. We will grow and prosper, a true country for the people."

"But how will we market our rice?" many people had asked. "The rice mill is here in Hoa Luu Town. The Viet Minh do not own the rice mill."

"The Viet Minh will take care of the rice mill. Soon everything will belong to the people."

"But when will the Viet Minh own the rice mill? We would starve down the canal. Life is terribly hard here, but at least the Government does give us food, though it is poor and not enough."

When the visitors heard this argument, they would become very quiet. Then they would say softly with a slight trace of menace, "We are family people like you, not warriors. We want what you want, a safe place for our loved ones. The Viet Minh believe as we do, but they are worried. Time is running out. The Americans are becoming stronger in our country. The people must all come together and fight them and the puppet Government. If some people do not support the Viet Minh, then the Viet Minh will regard these people as the enemy."

"What does that mean? We are not an enemy." The refugees wondered.

"It means that if you stay here in the refugee camp and do not return to your own rice lands, the Viet Minh might attack you."

"Attack us? But many of us are women and children and old people. The Viet Minh would not kill us if they loved the people." But as the refugees spoke, there was a chill in their hearts. They had seen it happen before.

The visitors left. The refugees talked. A few left at night to go back down the canal. Some young men joined the Viet Minh. Most of the families stayed. The Government was the lesser fear. At least, here they had a little to eat and some shelter.

Life in the refugee camp began to improve a week after Lee first saw the American Major. The Major had walked through the refugee warehouses speaking in a guttural language. A Vietnamese officer was writing down everything the Major said. Lee thought the Major looked like a god, impossibly tall and strong. He moved with the athletic grace of a warrior. That day the Major had seemed angry. He gestured violently to the dirty sleeping mats on the floor, kicked a pile of rubbish on the earth packed floor and wrinkled his nose at the stench of human waste and unwashed bodies. The Vietnamese officer took notes furiously. The American Major had looked at Lee and smiled. "CHOU, MANJOI KHONG, hello boy, are you in health?" The accents were wrong, but Lee understood. He was nervous. He could only nod. The Major reminded him in a strange way of his father. The strength was the same.

After the Major left, his mother said, "That is the Co Van My, the American advisor. It is said he is Hoa Hao, a great fighter and a friend of the people."

The next week all of the refugees received more food. Armed truck convoys had brought it in from Huong Tho, the province capital. The convoys had to be protected because the Viet Minh had interdicted the province road in many places.

Later, rumors began to circulate through the refugee camp, rumors about a new place up the canal, a place where a new village would be established. They would be given new homes and rice lands. The American Major said it was so. At first, nobody believed this. "It is more District propaganda. They are bribing us so that our young men do not join the Viet Minh, and we will not leave the refugee camp."

Lee believed the story. The man who reminded him of his father would not lie. His mother had no opinion. "I have seen too much suffering to believe anything anymore. We must live day to day."

But, the story was true. The heads of the families were called to a meeting. They were told of the new village. Each family would be given a home. The rice lands would be divided among them. A marketplace would be constructed and later a school. Medical services would be provided from the district hospital, including a midwife who would live in the village. Most reassuring, an ARVN battalion would be assigned to the village to protect them from the Viet Minh. The family leaders were shown a map of the village. Family registrations would be rechecked and building lots assigned.

Overnight the refugee camp changed. The people had a future. A better chance was up the canal. Lee was happy: a new home, a place to become a man. His sister laughed again. Even his mother began to hum while washing clothes in the canal. Chi sensed a better spirit. He and Lee played again like boys and dogs should do.

The Hoa Luu Canal was jammed with watercraft of every description: ARVN Navy landing craft, a variety of sampans, log rafts, and an incredible mixture of houseboats with thatched living quarters over hulls as long as forty feet. All the boats were decorated with red and yellow crepe paper and loaded to the gunwales with refugees, bedding, cooking utensils, furniture, chickens, dogs, and religious altars. The red and yellow Government flag bravely flew from the stern of every craft. The fleet was stationary in a loose nautical formation facing north, just south of the Hoa Luu Canal bridge. The District Chief was on the bridge talking to the assembled fleet. Lee's sampan was well to the rear. Only snatches of the speech reached his ears over the idle of hundreds of outboard motors.

"A glorious day."

"A new opportunity."

"Own your homes and rice lands."

"Educate your children."

No matter, he had never been so excited. Even Chi quivered with anticipation, surveying the scene with his paws up on the gunwale.

It was early morning, a clear blue day of sun, green palms, flowing brown water, and the shining refugee flotilla.

The District Chief raised a pistol over his head and fired a flare which arced brightly over the bridge, the signal to start. Outboard engines revved up. The Government flags stiffened in the breeze. Two thousand people were headed for a village named Phu Long.

******2******

Major Tong brooded about the Silk Over Steel campaign. Many of the objectives had been met, but now, a surprise. A village was being established 10 kilometers northeast of Hoa Luu Town. Hundreds of refugees uprooted by the campaign were being transported to the site. Most alarmingly, an ARVN battalion had been moved to the village to secure the refugees. This force had the capability of blocking northeast movement up the canal, which would disrupt the major offensive. The Hoa Luu District Battalion had been issued a warning order to attack the new village. A pitched battle with an ARVN battalion was hard to contemplate because of the reinforcements and enormous fire power the enemy could bring to bear. Tong had great respect for enemy air power, a non-problem when fighting the Territorial Forces. They were seldom supported. An ARVN battalion brought a whole new dimension to the Silk Over Steel campaign.

He leaned back in his chair on the church patio and looked over the wide, green lawn rolling down to the river, sparkling in the early morning light. *A quiet place*, he thought. Colonel Truc would soon destroy this tranquility. The Regimental Commander was coming by sampan up from the U Minh Forest. He expected him at any moment.

Tong rehearsed again the anticipated conversation with his commander. He would ask for at least two battalions from the Regiment to reinforce the Hoa Luu District Battalion. Perhaps Colonel Truc would command the operation himself. Massive fire support would also be required, more mortars and automatic weapons than they normally employed. His mind ran on about the military requirements then encountered a blockage, the refugees. What would they do about the people, who were, after all, the objective? He feared Truc would want to make some sort of an example, something related to the GIET SACH policy, no survivors. He turned in his chair and looked through the open door of the church. It was dark; he could not see inside. The cross felt cold against his chest. Mother Maria was inside. It was her morning prayer time. She would never forgive GIET SACH. God would never forgive such an atrocity against His creation. Many bad things had been done to the people during the war. And for what purpose? Were all crimes to be expiated on the altar of a free Vietnam, or were there acts so vile that it would be better to lose the war than to abuse the people further?

Tong's thought process was broken by the soft chopping sound of muffled outboard motors. Two sampans motored into view, hugging the river bank under the trees. Waiting soldiers secured these craft to the boat landing. Colonel Truc nimbly stepped out of the sampan and strode up the lawn. Tong rose to meet his commander.

The conversation was shorter than Tong expected. Colonel Truc brushed aside his request for reinforcements. "No more than your usual task force for this operation." Tong questioned this, amazed at the response. In his view, it was tantamount to suicide to operate against an ARVN battalion without reinforcements.

"Kinsman, trust me. I have some work to do, but be confident. Remember, the people are the objective. The ARVN battalion will not fight. We will defeat them politically. We have ways to render ARVN ineffective. Their tactical object is always to remain 'in being' for some obscure future battle, which they hope never occurs. This means they will always avoid decisive combat until another distant day. You also know that if ARVN commanders sustain too many casualties, they will be relieved. We will exploit these twin desires to avoid both fighting and casualties. There is a political aspect in our favor. The Hoa Hao situation, which will take some preparation, but we will do it."

Tong looked at his kinsman with some surprise. "How do you communicate all this to the other side, the Government?"

"Again, little brother, have faith. You have seen this before."

And, indeed, Tong reflected, he had participated in many battles in which ARVN refused to fight and even allowed the Viet Minh a way to escape back to their base areas. He continued to worry, however. Truc was not going to face the guns. The Hoa Luu District Battalion would take the brunt of the fighting.

"The serious problem is the people," Truc continued. "Here, we must make some sort of an example. I fear the Government has had some success in the new village. Some people believe the Government cares, that it will secure and feed the people. We must think of GIET SACH." He looked at Tong, knowing he was going to hear the usual arguments. He was not disappointed.

"You have heard me speak of this before. GIET SACH turns the people against us. It is a two-edged sword. We terrify the people to stay with us, or the alternative is death. If the motivation for their liberation is based only on terror, then the people will not sincerely believe in our cause. They will desert us at the first opportunity. For those outside our sphere of influence, those who are not subjected to our terror, they will hear about GIET SACH and fear us. This forces them closer to the Government. The policy cannot work."

Colonel Truc lit a cigarette and squinted at his kinsman through the smoke. "Tong, you do not understand terror and the state. They are inextricable. If people do not believe in the state, the state would rather kill them. Terror is a coercive factor aimed at the people. It is always present and must be successful. Terror is an extension of the state. Liberation, our cause, is focused on the state, not the individual. Understand, the state is everything."

"Colonel Truc, you are sounding more Marxist every day. I remember a time when it was the other way around—the people mattered."

The silence between the two men was filled with tension. Truc leaned forward, eyes blazing at Tong. "Be careful," he said, his voice thick with menace, "I allow much in Vinh Cheo, to include this church and people like Mother Maria because you are my kinsman. But, if you do not obey my orders..." He snapped his fingers. Tong felt a surge of fear. "I will decide about GIET SACH and you will obey."

"Yes, Sir," Tong responded.

"I will let you know my decision soon after I have made some arrangements. This will be the final large battle of the Silk Over Steel campaign." He stood to go. "Please, give Mother Maria greetings and good health. And, cousin, smile. This enterprise will go well. You Christians think about God too much. Think now about the state." Truc walked down to the boat landing.

＊＊＊＊＊＊＊＊＊＊＊＊

"Sir, welcome to Phu Long Village. As you can see this place looks a lot different from your first visit."

The Grey Ghost agreed. "I can remember my first visit here two months after the Hoa Luu battle, Jack. It was Indian country then. You've done a helluva job!"

Jack continued, "I believe we've followed the concept to the letter. Two thousand refugees have been moved to our present location." Jack tapped on the map at a point ten kilometers northeast of Hoa Luu Town at the bend of the canal . "As you recall, Sir, these refugees were displaced as a result of the ongoing VC offensive conducted by the Hoa Luu District Battalion and elements of the U Minh Regiment. Most of these people originally lived along this same canal thirty-five kilometers southwest of here, just north of the Vinh Cheo Triangle. They were forced from their homes because of the recent enemy attacks."

Colonel Mason nodded. They were seated in a newly constructed sandbagged hut in the middle of the ARVN battalion security perimeter which was under construction. The ARVN Battalion Advisor was with them.

"You know the district security situation," Jack went on. "We do not control the Hoa Luu Canal beyond our outpost five kilometers southwest of Hoa Luu Town. The Vinh Thanh Canal is interdicted in many places south of Vinh Thanh Town, as is the province road in the western part of the district. It takes a company size force to get through these areas.

"Our biggest problem has been the resettlement of refugees. Two weeks ago we moved them up the canal to this village. It was a massive undertaking; we had to commandeer everything that moves in the district to haul them up here. USAID has given us massive support in building materials and food. You saw some of the results on the way up here."

Colonel Mason responded, "You know, Jack, this is a monumental accomplishment. You've established a spanking new, functioning community in a month. The people are resettled, housing is going up, rice paddies are being worked, the marketplace is complete, and the aid station is seeing patients. I understand the school will be completed next month. The entire Pacification Task Force concept appears to be working," he paused, "and I'll tell you something, it's one of the few things working in the entire Goddamned Southern Delta."

"Sir, I think the task force is a success. It's the first time we've put all these agencies together. Even the Vietnamese information service is here, indoctrinating the people, though I don't think these Delta farmers understand a damn thing about the Saigon government. District and Province are working together as if they belong to the same organization, which is unbelievable, and, of course, ARVN is supporting us. You know, Colonel, in the past we have always been treated like a Hoa Hao foreign country. This is different."

Mason turned to the ARVN Battalion Advisor. "How are you fitting into this situation, Mike?"

Captain Michael Baker, the newly arrived advisor to the 2nd Battalion, 3rd Infantry Regiment, 64th ARVN Division, was amazed the Grey Ghost knew his first name. He had been commissioned two years before through ROTC at the University of Washington. He had attended the Basic Officers

Course at Fort Benning and, after a brief troop assignment, had returned to Benning for Ranger School. Baker was uncomfortable. This situation was a long way from the mountainous beauty of the Pacific Northwest and the rigorous but straightforward fighting skills he had learned at Ranger School. Here he was in Phu Long village as the U.S. representative of a vast undertaking. He had advisory responsibility for the security of 2000 refugees in an area carved out of Indian country just weeks before. His battalion was training five PF refugee platoons and, additionally, had to be constantly prepared to repel a VC attack on the new settlement. To compound the challenge, the battalion had been detached from the 64th ARVN Division and placed under the operational control of Hoa Luu District. He was under the direct command of Major Travis. This command arrangement was new to ARVN. A battalion had never been detached from its parent division before. It was the heart of the new Pacification Task Force concept. Hoa Luu had been given the necessary security to protect the refugees. Baker didn't think the chain of command was clearly defined. He would rather have worked through the 64th ARVN Division. He stood before the Grey Ghost, medium height, blond hair. He looked like he was eighteen years old, Colonel Mason thought.

"Sir, as you know, I'm new here, but I think things are working out. The PF platoon training is going well. The battalion is learning the area, and you can see we've made great progress on the fort."

"Let me tell you something about this goddamned fort," Mason interrupted, suddenly angry. "Your battalion is here to protect the people and that is a tough job. You are not here to hide behind forts. If Phu Long is attacked, I want you to get your ass out of this fort and counterattack. Also, make sure you have an active patrol plan. I don't want any surprises. And, remember, the battalion works for District, and you work for Major Travis. Do what he tells you. There's a lot riding on the task force concept, and it must not fail. You understand, young man?"

"Yes, sir," Captain Baker said standing at attention. Jack thought this was pretty hard on a new guy, but the Grey Ghost was under a lot of pressure.

"Now, Mike, if you will excuse us, I want to have a few words with Major Travis." Baker saluted and left. "Jack, you know this is a stopgap measure. The real answer was to attack the Vinh Cheo triangle after the Hoa Luu battle, but I received no support." Mason tensed when he said these words. "Goddamn it!" He rose and paced the small hut. "What a fucked up war! We know where the enemy is, we're attacked from a major base area, and we do

165

nothing. This is happening all over my area of operations. I'll tell you, Jack, the Vietnamese jumped on this Pacification Task Force idea of yours because it was not dangerous. They knew they had to do something after the Hoa Luu battle, and this concept saved face without fighting, a favorite tactic on the part of our allies. My American highers haven't given me any support either. General Wells absolutely refused to place any pressure on the Corps Commander to conduct operations into known enemy base areas such as Vinh Cheo. 'Keep it quiet,' he says, and his Chief, Colonel Andrews, is a real political prick. His sole objective is to get a star, and then get the hell out of this Godforsaken war. He has got his head stuck up Wells' ass so far that if Wells turned around fast, Andrews would break his neck. Christ, Jack, we Senior Advisors are as bad as the Vietnamese. The major American functions of this war are to survive and get your ticket punched. Little thought is given to winning at the rice paddy level. The people that suffer are the folks in Phu Long village."

Mason abruptly stopped, embarrassed. He actually blushed. Jack was surprised. This was not the Grey Ghost's style. Professional in everything, he never discussed personalities or his superiors. A long silence followed with Mason staring steadily at the wall map as if it would give him the answer.

"Just forget all this crybaby crap on my part, Jack. The point is the Pacification Task Force must work. It's the only operational initiative we've got going for us." Mason buckled on his pistol belt and prepared to leave. He stopped and looked at Jack. "Tell me more about the Hoa Hao. Some of the Vietnamese and American hierarchy are worried about these people."

"Sir, you know their basic political and religious philosophy. In my view, at this time they are an important third force in the Delta. There are certain unfortunate overtones: they're aggressively evangelical; they can be brutal; and they believe in political subversion to include assassination. Many of them, however, are honorable men dedicated to their nation. I am proud to fight with them. The point is, they hate the enemy, and we hate the enemy. At this stage in the war, this is the stuff alliances are made of. Hating is enough."

Mason stiffened. "Many Vietnamese leaders do not believe this. They think Phu Long, this little village, could be the start of a Hoa Hao revolution."

"Sir, that's bullshit. The Hoa Hao are sincere. They want to defend Hoa Luu from the enemy and take care of these people. I admit, they are converting many of these refugees to the Hoa Hao faith, but that makes them more cohesive as a group, a needed characteristic in an area like Phu Long."

"Just understand, Jack, important people are worried. This entire task force structure could collapse in a microsecond if the Vietnamese Corps Commander and the 64th ARVN Division Commander, my counterpart, see any subversion in this operation."

"I'll keep the lid on, sir."

Mason turned and then faced Jack again. "Another thing, there is rumor around that you're a Hoa Hao yourself." He looked half jokingly at Jack.

"I wear the tiger's claw. Not many Americans are given these," Jack said seriously. He showed Mason the talisman of the Hoa Hao.

"Certainly you don't believe in all that mumbo jumbo?"

"I believe in winning the war in Hoa Luu, and here things are different. There is a different spin on values, which must be learned if you believe in surviving and victory." He paused. "Sorry, sir, I didn't mean to get preachy. To answer your question, yes, I halfway believe in 'that mumbo jumbo.' It works in Hoa Luu." He stroked the tiger's claw according to custom before placing it under his shirt.

"Well, Jack, you've done a hell of a job down here. I guess we've both let our hair down a bit today. We've been under a strain. You know I'll support you to the hilt. Keep your powder dry." Their eyes locked. The two men vigorously shook hands.

****

The district hospital was getting a facelift. New aluminum roofing was replacing the old leaky plywood, and ground had been broken for a new maternity wing. Co Linh and Jack were standing on the province road, watching the construction.

"This will be a beautiful hospital." She walked back and forth, throwing her arms about as if embracing the half finished building. Her energy was contagious. It seemed to spur the workers to greater effort. Jack had never seen such industry in Hoa Luu.

"But there are problems." A frown interrupted the curved lines of her eyebrows. Jack believed he could read Co Linh like a headline. He didn't have to hear her, just watching the fleeting expressions cross her face was communication enough.

"The vaccination program is suffering because we can't move around the district. Many children will die because we can't reach them. There are few students at my midwife school. The people cannot travel the canals or the province road. You know, Major Travis"—she called him Major Travis when they were not alone, which was now most of the time, Jack reflected bitterly—"the VC attacks are hurting the people." She turned from the building and looked at Jack, expecting an answer. *Not paying any attention,* she thought. He was gazing at her with that dumb schoolboy expression.

"We have to concentrate on what we can do, take care of the people we can reach," Jack eventually replied.

"We must do better than that. If we cannot care for the people, if they come to believe we are helpless in this attack to even deliver babies and care for children, we will lose the war. Major Travis, you must secure the area so we can travel again. Perhaps I will go alone. The VC will not kill a person who heals the sick."

This alarmed Jack. "They would blow you away in a minute. You don't understand these people. The VC are barbarians!"

"Do not tell me I do not understand my own people! The VC are not the only barbarians. The war has made us all barbarians, even you Americans. I suppose you consider Sergeant Hartwell a saint."

He thought, *Sergeant Hartwell again.* "Can we talk in private, in your cottage?"

"Absolutely not." She faced him with rising anger. Her rapid mood changes always disturbed Jack. Some of the construction workers looked up.

"And I will go where I please. I know Sergeant Gonzales will go with me anywhere in the district. Like me, he is a healer. He is not afraid."

Jack stood erect, towering over her. "I absolutely forbid it!" he thundered. She turned to go. He grabbed her arm and whirled her around. With the strength that always amazed him, she broke his grip with a wrench of her arm.

"You become more like Sergeant Hartwell every day." She turned and stalked to her cottage. Half stooped, like he had received a body blow, Jack stood in the road. He followed her to the cottage.

She stood still, her back to him. Jack could tell she was crying. He waited. She turned. "I'm sorry," they both said almost at the same time. Co Linh rushed into his arms. "It is sad, these people deserve so much more," she said muffled into his chest. Jack felt her body against him, the softness of her breasts. His arms tightened around her, then he looked over her shoulder straight into the eyes of her dead husband. He gently pushed her away. Co Linh did not cry for their love.

"Co Linh, I know this is a bad situation, but there is much to do here. The refugees are coming in every day. The Pacification Task Force is working. Phu Long village gets larger and larger. For now, let's make this tiny part of Hoa Luu District work."

She looked at him, suddenly bright-eyed with an idea. "Jack, we need a hospital in Phu Long village—not just an aid station. You must get the building materials and the medical supplies. I have trained four assistants, so we have enough people to work in Hoa Luu hospital and in Phu Long. I know Doctor Gonzales and I can supervise both locations." She was jumping up and down with anticipation. Jack wondered at the level of medical support—four "trained" assistants, an Army medic, and a nurse to treat thousands of people. And now they were going to open another hospital. How would that go down in Norfolk, Virginia?

Co Linh had made up her mind. She would never be deterred from her course of action. That day the Phu Long hospital was born.

****

The bottle of Jim Beam was half empty. They sat around a battered table on the screened-in porch of the Tram Cua District hut. A thousand insects buzzed outside. The Unholy Alliance was in session. Flip considered the Tram Cua meeting place a hardship tour. There was no flying shithouse for comfort, a deficiency that severely hurt his thinking process at these strategy sessions. Bob Harris, the host, understood the problem. In his view, Flip was being hurt where he did his thinking. They poured drinks all around. Flip was talking about his favorite subject.

"You know, guys, we never went on R and R. We canceled twice. Jack, you're always talking about this strategy bullshit, but I miss sex. In fact, lack of nooky has taken on strategic importance. The Goddamn Hoa Luu District Battalion has cut off my dick. They have struck this Irish boy a terrible blow. Remember all the plans we made? Australia, Hong Kong, Bangkok, and for what? To sit around this miserable place and get boozed up with you fuckers."

Flip leaned back in his chair and took a deep swallow from his drink. It went down smoothly; earlier it had been like gulping fire. "You know, Jack, you've lost your soul, your love for women. You live and breathe Hoa Luu. You're like a goddamned Hoa Hao. Of course, on second thought, if I had Co Linh living around me—" Jack shot him a look which temporarily silenced Flip. Then he looked at Bob. "I think Bob, being married, has an excuse, but, Bob, variety nooky is the spice of life as long as you're careful. I wasn't careful with my first marriage." Bob waved Flip down.

"You know, what we were talking about before," Bob started in his sepulchral tone.

Flip jump started again. "Your problem, Bob, is you're a one woman man. That makes for a boring life." Bob and Jack looked hard at Flip. He started to speak, then sputtered into silence.

Bob continued, "I agree with you, Jack. Hoa Luu and Tram Cua Districts have got to run a joint operation into the area just north of the Vinh Cheo Triangle where the canals run into the Tao River. We've got to disrupt this new base area. The VC are staging operations against your district at will along those canals, and I know Tram Cua will be next if we don't do something."

Jack nodded. "We're gonna need air support, Flip, buddy. Can you deliver your usual magic? Tell Division we'll try to keep all their birds in one piece this time."

Flip was immediately alert. "It's gonna be tough, guys. You know there's a lot a weird shit going on in the Southern Delta. There's more than one Vinh Cheo in the V Corps area. Another problem, the U.S. forces up north are tying up a lot of air assets. There just ain't enough to go around."

"Well, you're going to have to make your usual hellfire and brimstone case. You know, Bob, if we can get the two districts to work together, it would strengthen our argument for more support. Hell, they might even Chinook some artillery in here."

Bob mused, "Well, it's going to be tough. You know, Jack, the Hoa Hao thing is a simmering affair. My Chief thinks you guys are starting a new country in Phu Long. There is a school of thought around here, and you have to know this, that the Government situation down here would be strengthened by a Hoa Hao defeat. You know, wipe out the Hoa Hao around here once and for all."

Jack gestured with his glass. "That kind of thinking will lose the war for us. You've got to tell them it ain't so."

"It's the Hoa Hao conversion with the refugees. Do you have to do that?"

"I don't do 'that,' but I agree with the conversion. It gives those folks the cohesion they need in Phu Long. You know, setting up a community in Indian country ain't for sissies. They have to hang together."

"It's like the goddamn Catholic Reformation," Flip interjected.

A pause. They refilled their glasses. The insect buzzing faded. Jack spoke slowly. "You know, thank God for the Grey Ghost. He got that Pacification Task Force established. If he hadn't kicked the Division Commander in the ass, there wouldn't be much left of Hoa Luu District right now."

"Yeah, too bad he couldn't have leaned on the Corps Commanding General as well. We gotta attack the Vinh Cheo Triangle. You guys know I fly all over Ngoc Hoa Province every day. Jack, I agree with your Sergeant

Minh's theory. There's something going on down there. You can smell it. We damned well better find out. I think they're planning an attack."

"The problem is the V Corps American leadership," Bob said. "Old 'Keep It Quiet' Wells and his erstwhile Chief, Andrews. I hope the Army promotes them both so we can get on with the war." He reflected. "And General Westmoreland. I wish he would stop saying we are going to win the war in the Central Highlands. There ain't any people in the Central Highlands. Nobody is watching the store in the populated areas. And, our own cross to bear, Pottsy. We all know he extended for another six months. Something about another shot at full colonel. When you think about it, like Pogo says, 'We have met the enemy and he is us.'" Bob said this with emotion that surprised Jack. Usually the New Englander was more reserved.

"At any rate," Jack said, "the Grey Ghost is a good shit, even if he is a West Pointer." They all laughed.

"I propose a toast," Flip said solemnly. Flipstick often became solemn at the end of an evening. "To the Grey Ghost, the best fighting son of a bitch in the Delta." He hesitated. "Next to the Unholy Alliance, of course." They drained their glasses.

"A refill," Jack ordered. "We must continue the Hoa Hao tradition even though some of you find it rank heresy." He glared at Bob Harris. "Don't worry, I won't try to convert you."

"To victory." The Unholy Alliance shattered their glasses on the concrete floor of the porch.

"For Christ sakes! That's the end of the Jim Beam," Flip observed.

"In my honored position as the host, I strongly suggest we all hit the sack," Bob Harris ordered. The Alliance called it a night.

171

******3******

Jack was sick. He knew what was wrong with him. The dreaded Delta drizzlies had struck again as a result of drinking crystal clear rainwater which had collected in an earthen jar. He knew it was a mistake at the time, but he couldn't resist the temptation of a taste of untreated water. Days later he started erupting at both ends. Doc reached into his medicine bag, but nothing worked. Jack tried to ignore his condition but grew weaker. On a short daytime security operation just south of Hoa Luu Town, Jack bit the dust. He was walking along the usual slippery dike. His bowels ached even though he had just returned from the bushes; his head felt like a balloon; the world was canting right and left; a loud buzzing sound drowned out reality; his sight fogged over with thousands of black dots. Suddenly there was blackness.

A large fan rotated overhead. The room was white. There was the sound of a generator in the distance. Cold, the room was deliciously cold. Jack awoke to an icebox-like paradise.

A figure in white hovered over him. "Major Travis, can you hear me?" Jack nodded, not opening his eyes. "You passed out on an operation and were MEDEVACed here to the field hospital at Binh Trang Army Airfield. You are suffering from severe diarrhea, dehydration, and exhaustion. A few days rest and you should be as good as new." The voice faded away. There was a muffled conversation in the background, then total, cold silence. Jack wouldn't open his eyes, afraid all of this would go away.

He rested and semi-slept all day, basking in his cold heaven. From time to time somebody gave him some pills. Once, he got up to store his gear Hoa Luu style under the bunk. That night he sank into a deep sleep.

Jack opened his eyes. It was morning. Sunlight streamed through the window. "Time to eat, Bucko." He looked into the tough face of Lieutenant Colonel Irene Bellingham. Rough hands forced him into a sitting position; a tray was thrust on his lap. He was given a bowl of tasteless soup. "Eat hearty!" the Colonel said. She was dressed in battle dress, right down to a pistol belt which accentuated her huge bosom. Her bare arms indicated she could beat most men in an Indian wrestling contest. Her voice was high and rough. She loomed over Jack, a huge camouflaged presence hell bent on administering medical aid. "After the soup, Bucko, I want you to pick up your combat gear

172

which you threw under the bed when you arrived and hang it neatly in the wall locker. And then it's shower and shave time. You're smelling up the whole hospital. I'll be back later." She left in a swirling smell of disinfectant.

All that day, as Jack was about to fade off into his arctic oblivion, Colonel Bellingham would charge in to check his vital signs, give him pills, or ply him with another bowl of soup. At midday he did laboriously get out of bed to stow his combat gear in the wall locker. Instinctively, he checked the action on the M2 carbine.

Late that afternoon Colonel Bellingham barged into the room again. She was flushed and agitated. "We just received an intelligence report. Tonight we might be mortared. When the siren goes off, you must follow the signs to the bunker. Bring your combat gear." She paused. "Open your eyes, Major!" Jack kept them squeezed shut. "You know, Bucko, I know your type. You're one of those officers who thinks he's winning the whole war single handed. Let me tell you, there are others..." Her voice droned on. Jack fell asleep.

A siren wailed through the hospital; there were running feet and blinding fluorescent light in his room. "Major, Major," Colonel Bellingham was shouting. "You must come to the bunker! We are being mortared." She was jumping up and down, her huge bosom undulating above the pistol belt.

"Fuck off!" Jack said.

"What did you say?" Her voice rose to a scream.

"I said, 'Fuck off,'" Jack repeated tiredly. He mentally shut his ears. Crump! Crump! Crump! Distant exploding mortar shells could be heard. The Colonel rushed from the room. Jack rose slowly from his bed, gathered his gear from the wall locker, and threw it under the bed. Then he returned to his blissful air-conditioned heaven. If a round landed on his private parts, he wouldn't care.

The room was exploding, moving, heaving him up in the air. Maybe a direct hit. Jack opened his eyes. Colonel Bellingham was back on station. She was at the end of the bed, shaking the footboard like it was a mortal enemy. "Major Travis," she said primly, "you are ordered to report to the hospital commander in twenty minutes. If you're not there on time, the MP's have been alerted to escort you." Jack kept his eyes screwed shut. She left the room.

Slowly he rose and dressed. He reached under the bed and retrieved his combat gear. He swung his LBE over his shoulder and left the hospital .

The heat hit him like a burning wall. Jack walked through the shimmering brightness across the airfield to Flight Operations. He spoke to the OPS sergeant. "I need a lift back to Hoa Luu District." He was cured of the Delta drizzlies.

*******4*******

The Delta Tigers were beautifully deployed, moving across the rice paddies two kilometers north of the old Vinh Cheo outpost. The lead platoons moved in extended columns along two parallel rice paddy dikes one hundred meters apart. Each had deployed its lead squad forward for ambush security. The remaining platoon was positioned to the rear, mid-way between the lead platoons, forming the apex of the company vee. The 60MM mortar section was with the rear platoon for fire support. *By the book*, Jack thought, but he was worried. They were two hours late. The sun glinted off the rice paddies. Flooded areas to the north had delayed their progress.

Jack walked with the rear platoon. It was hot, an enervating, sweating, tropical hotness which drained his energy. His jungle fatigues were stained dark with sweat. He started to unsnap his canteen, but thought better of it. Have to conserve water. God knows how long we're going to be out here, and God knows what was going to happen to them. Jack looked at the BINH SYs, the private soldiers, walking beside him. Not a drop of sweat. Hell, they were even smiling. Since the sun had come up, they had been horsing around with each other as young men do. The smallest BINH SY looked at Jack. "MET KHONG?" he asked. "Are you tired?"

"KHONG MET, no," he replied. As often happened, a bantering conversation in Pidgin English and Vietnamese started. It passed the time on a hot, dangerous rice paddy.

"You think VC today, THIEU TA, Major?"

"Maybe, maybe many VC."

"It is light; they can see us, but I am not afraid. The VC fear the MONG COP, the tiger's claw." The young man laughed. The men in the squad laughed with him.

Another BINH SY joined in. "You are too young and small to wear the tiger's claw. You are a kitten with a loud voice and a small penis." Loud laughter.

"How old are you?" Jack asked the small BINH SY.

"I am seventeen," the young man said with dignity.

"He is sixteen," a soldier said. "Look how small he is. The rifle is taller than he is." Jack noticed this was almost true.

175

"Where is your family? Do they live near Hoa Luu?"

"Yes, my father is a rice farmer. He and my uncle own many hectares."

Another squad member said, "His father owns a tiny patch. Maybe two rice plants."

"It is much land." The small BINH SY said, chastened, looking at the ground.

The soldier behind the small BINH SY moved forward and slapped him on the back. The small BINH SY immediately brightened.

"Does your father want you to fight?"

"All of our fathers want us to fight. We are Hoa Hao. We hate the Viet Minh!" the small BINH SY replied with passion.

"Is that the only reason you fight?" Jack pressed.

The small BINH SY pondered this question, his smile fading.

Another soldier said, "My father says we fight for land; the Viet Minh want our land. My father says we would die without the land." The squad members all nodded.

"But the Chinese own most of the land?"

"Not all. We are Hoa Hao. We own some land."

"What else do you fight for?" Jack pursued.

"Women," replied the young BINH SY.

"You do not know women! He sleeps alone and plays with himself." There was loud, raucous laughter.

Sensing a deeper meaning to Jack's question, a soldier added, "We fight for Hoa Hao, for land and rice, and for family. We would lose our life, our faith, if the Viet Minh win." The squad members strongly agreed with this.

The small BINH SY showed Jack a cellophane wrapped photograph of a girl. "This is my girlfriend. Do you think she is beautiful?"

A squad member said, "Do not believe him. That is a picture of a movie star. She lives in Saigon."

"She is still my girlfriend," he said defensively. "I look at her picture every night." He said the last softly, so the others could not hear him.

Jack took the picture and studied it. "She is very beautiful, BINH SY," he said formally, looking at the entire squad.

The small BINH SY put the picture away with a slight swagger. Face had been gained. The CO VAN MY, the American advisor, thought the girl in the picture was beautiful. That was enough.

"Are you very rich?" a BINH SY asked.

"No, I am not rich."

"We hear the Americans are very rich. That is why they fight for us. They fight to make us rich."

"We fight for you to make you free."

"But we are free," the small BINH SY said. "Look." He gestured to the surrounding rice paddies. "We walk free. We fight free."

"You are all free," Jack said. He waved to the squad and moved up the column. He could hear them laughing behind him.

The BINH SYS always made him feel good. They never lost their good humor, which was amazing considering the tactical situations they encountered. The BINH SYS joked and played like young boys. These young men didn't mourn openly for their fallen comrades. Jack had seen them many times joking with each other after a serious fire fight where many of their friends had been killed. And yet, there was a serious purpose here: a religious faith, family, land, and a strong warrior ethic. Behind the laughter, the silly behavior that some Americans considered childish, they were deadly fighters.

ARVN soldiers didn't fight as well. Jack had heard complaints of their performance from advisors in the 64th Division. The raw, manly material was the same, but fighting for ARVN lacked the intimate, tactical urgency of the Territorial Force War. Here, young soldiers fought directly to defend the institutions which propped up their lives. For ARVN the motivation was remote, hard to define. Their families and beliefs were not at stake on the immediate battlefield. Jack wondered if MACV understood the key role of Territorial Forces. Probably not, he reflected, if the support they received in the Southern Delta was any indication.

The Tigers had moved out the day before, heading northwest toward Vinh Thanh. When night fell they had established a perimeter and rested a few hours. At midnight they had moved southeast toward Vinh Cheo. The concept was to surprise the VC in the suspected new base area between the Hoa Luu and Vinh Thanh Canals where they joined the Tau River. The Tigers were alone. Tram Cua District forces were not allowed by Province to participate. *A good opportunity to have the Hoa Hao bushwhacked*, Jack thought. Major Tho would not release additional RF forces because he feared for installation and canal security. Jack had even requested a rifle company from the ARVN battalion in Phu Long. He had been strongly reminded that, under the charter of the Pacification Task Force, they could not leave Phu Long village. There was no air support except for Flip's ubiquitous fighter bomber which was on call.

The night before, Jack and Re had a conversation while in the perimeter position. They had occupied a farm hut which was deserted but swarmed with paddy rats. Before dinner they deleeched themselves with burning cigarette butts. Jack experienced some difficulty dislodging one large black and brown slug from a sensitive part of his anatomy, an operation that deserved a Purple Heart. After this Delta tradition, they hunkered down on ponchos for their usual dinner of what Jack called LDSC (liberated, destroyed, and stewed chicken). The men ate quickly in silence. After finishing, Re observed, "This is a dangerous operation."

"Yes, but we must operate against the new base area, or they will build up for an attack which we can never stop."

"We agree, but it is very difficult. Even our 'brothers'," he laughed silently, "refuse support."

"We'll be all right, Commander. The Tigers can beat anyone in the Delta."

"No, my friend, even the Tigers can be defeated. We place these fine young men at grave risk, but there is no alternative. When we reach Vinh Cheo, we can easily be surrounded, isolated." Re paused, thinking. "If only we Vietnamese could work together. If only we had a clear insight into the heart of the war. The Government cannot avoid the enemy. This is not a strategy. He only grows stronger every day and will destroy us. We must do more for ourselves. The Viet Minh, though he is supplied by others, fights on his own. He has no overwhelming fire support, and the battle plans are his alone. There are no advisors. You understand, Major Travis, that for them this is a source of great pride. Our dependence on the Americans is a great shame to the Vietnamese. Face is very important here, and as a people, we have lost face. I sometimes think we can never overcome this shame. The only thing left is the pursuit of greed. You see this all over Vietnam. Corruption has become a substitute for honor. No people can build up a fighting spirit in this situation."

"But the Hoa Hao have fighting spirit."

"Some Hoa Hao in this area and a few others in the Southern Delta. In other places, particularly up north, our leaders are as venal as the Government's."

"You talk of the people losing face, but you really mean the leaders."

"You must understand, Major Travis, for years we were under French rule. Our people, especially the Delta people, have never controlled their lives. They are used to a leadership dictating everything they do. Nationalism and a sense of individual worth are new emotions for many Vietnamese. The crime of the leadership, the Government, is that they are betraying the people's trust. The people want to improve their lot, but all they see is corruption. The people lose face because they are a part of the corruption as long as they support the Government. The Viet Minh leadership sets a far better example. They give the people pride."

"But you hate the Viet Minh."

"I hate the Viet Minh because I understand them. They employ a double cloak strategy. On the one side, the side the people see, you have honor, concern for the people, and gallantry on the battlefield. On the other, you see their true purpose, the establishment of a collective, centralized state which destroys the individual and God. If the Viet Minh win, the country will become a soulless, police state populated with dead people with no chance for good works on Earth or salvation. This is the terrible evil we are fighting against. Remember, my friend, here we see the fighting side of the cloak, not the true side if they win. And even on the fighting side, the cloak sometimes turns and we see, for a brief moment, the other side. The Viet Minh doctrine of GIET SACH, no survivors, where they indiscriminately slaughter women and children, is an example of their evil side."

"Does the Government have a chance?"

"That is not the correct question. There is no civilized, spiritual alternative to Government defeat. We must win or this country will descend to a living hell on Earth." Commander Re stood, nodded to Jack, and left the hut to ready the Tigers.

Crack! There was a single shot from the rear. The rear platoon went to ground. Adrenalin pumping, Jack grabbed the handset from Billy. He called Cochran's ground station. "FLIPSTICK, FLIPSTICK, GET YOUR ASS UP HERE. WE'VE GOT COMPANY." He then reported the contact to Province. A bullet zipped through the air. Cal Washington called to Jack, "I'm worried, Boss. Those motherfuckers are behind us."

Jack yelled to the platoon leader to get some fire on the tree line behind them. Two machineguns went into action. Re returned from his position between the lead platoons at a dead run. As he hit the wet rice paddies next to Jack, small arms fire exploded to the direct front. Between gasps, Re said, "We're surrounded, as I feared. We need fire support." Over the radio he ordered the lead platoons to move forward and sense the enemy position. The 60MM mortar section went into action. Small arms firing increased. The lead platoons made some headway and then were stopped by a wall of automatic fire. They reported losses. Suddenly, the rear platoon was smothered by a hail of fire. The mortar section was knocked out. Two crewmen were killed instantly. With a constant tearing sound, bullets smashed into the paddy dike just above Jack's head.

Suddenly there was a deeper sound, the crump explosion of mortar shells. The VC were zeroing in on the Tiger position. Jack could see the explosions, small geysers of mud thrown into the air. He looked at Re, two feet away. His sweaty face was furrowed in concentration. He had told Jack many times, "In a combat emergency, many people tell you doing something is better than doing nothing. This is nonsense. The worst thing you can do is make the wrong decision, because men will die. Take some time, even seconds, and come up with a sound plan of action before you issue orders. This is hard to do because of your own fear and the confusion of battle, but sound reflection when faced with danger is the mark of a good field commander. Often the best action is to do nothing, let the situation develop." And, in this case, Re followed his own counsel. His platoons were ordered to take up defensive positions and stand by for further orders. The enemy mortar fire increased. The VC was finding the range.

Jack shouted on the radio giving Province the situation and demanding air support. "I'M DECLARING A TACTICAL EMERGENCY. THE TIGERS ARE PINNED DOWN TWO KILOMETERS NORTH OF VINH CHEO. WE ARE FIGHTING AT LEAST A BATTALION. WE NEED FAST MOVERS AND WE NEED THEM DAMN QUICK!" He was given the usual laconic "ROGER OUT." Jack requested to speak to Lieutenant Colonel Potts, the Province Senior Advisor, who eventually came on the air.

"DELTA ALPHA SIX, THIS IS PAPA SIX. ARE YOU SURE YOU'RE NOT OVERESTIMATING THE SITUATION?"

Jack keyed the radio set to the battle noise. A cacophony of small arms fire and mortar explosions went over the radio. "DOES THAT SOUND LIKE I'M OVERESTIMATING THE FUCKING SITUATION? OVER."

"DON'T USE PROFANITY ON THE RADIO. I'LL SEE WHAT I CAN DO—OUT."

Jack knew their only hope was to go through Flipstick channels. Suddenly that cocky voice was on the air.

"KEEP YOUR SHIRT ON OLD BUDDY; FLIPSTICK IS HERE TO SAVE THE DAY. FAST MOVERS DENIED FOR NOW. I PUT OUT AN APB FOR THE GREY GHOST. HE IS THE ONLY GUY WHO CAN DELIVER. MEANWHILE, YOUR OWN LITTLE FIGHTER BOMBER'S GOT SOME HE ROCKETS. GIVE ME SOME TARGETS."

"ROGER, HOLD FOR NOW. I NEED TO CHECK WITH THE COMMANDER."

Re was giving orders over the radio. He ordered the two lead platoons to pull back to a designated perimeter position. The right platoon would start to withdraw covered by the left. The soldiers were told to withdraw in reverse rushes, covering each other. The rear platoon was ordered to spread out and form the base of the perimeter.

"The signal to start the withdrawal of the lead platoons would be Flipsticks's HE rocket fire to their front. The same for the rear platoon's redeployment on the opposite side of the perimeter." Re nodded and passed on the orders to his platoons.

Flip's basic load of rockets will be used up after this mission, Jack thought. Their only fire support would have to break station immediately after the withdrawal. Jack explained the maneuver plan to Flipstick .

"FLIPSTICK, STAND BY. EXECUTION IN ZERO FIVE." The minutes ticked by. Time! "FLIPSTICK, FLIPSTICK, FIRE NOW." Whoosh! A rocket boomed on the far tree line. The right platoon started to withdraw. Enemy fire didn't increase. *I hope they think they're under heavy aerial attack,* Jack prayed. The right platoon reached its new position. The left platoon started to withdraw. Small arms fire increased, snapping at eye level across the rice paddies. Men fell; the left platoon went to ground. "FLIPSTICK. FIRE EVERY GODDAMN THING YOU HAVE AT THE TREE LINE." The enemy side was quiet. Re and Jack worried. They were sure the VC were maneuvering more forces behind them to prevent their escape. Without Cochran they would be buffalo meat by now. His little aircraft constantly rotated between his private ammo dump in Huong Tho and the battlefield. The enemy appeared reluctant to risk his forces in an attack across the open rice paddies. The VC couldn't believe the Tigers would be this deep in Indian country in broad daylight without air support.

Jack called Flip. "CHECK THE HOA LUU CANAL EAST OF OUR POSITIONS. I'LL BET THE BASTARDS ARE TRYING TO END RUN US."

"ROGER, JACK." Flip was having a wonderful day. He loved his 0-1 Bird Dog, this relic of the Korean War. The old craft was reliable, maneuverable and rugged, ideal for Delta aerial warfare. The three hundred and sixty horsepower engine sang like a bird. He ran his eyes over the primitive avionics: altimeter, air speed indicator, needle and ball indicator, vertical speed indicator—all O. K. This was really flying. None of this Mach shit for him. Right on the seat of his goddamn pants, like the Red Baron.

Nothing was moving on the canal, an empty chocolate line running like a ruler to the northeast. He went lower, attempting to see under the tree lined bank. He saw them! Armed men moving at a half run up the western canal bank. Suddenly green tracers crossed the Bird Dog's nose. He flip kicked the stick right, jinked and gained altitude. He reported the target to Jack.

"COMPANY SIZE UNIT MOVING UP THE WESTERN BANK OF THE CANAL. I'M GONNA HIT 'EM FROM THE WEST." Flip leveled off at 1500 feet and rolled in at a forty-five degree dive. The air speed increased from 90 to 130 knots. He reached up with his left hand and armed the rockets. At just under 1000 feet, he pulled the trigger on the stick. The ship shook slightly. Smoke trails went into the canal tree line. Flip broke left full throttle; the engine roared, fighting for altitude. He flew over the canal at 2000 feet, then approached the target complex from the opposite heading. The enemy had gone to ground.

"JACK, BUDDY, I DIDN'T KILL ANYBODY ON THAT RUN, UNLESS THE NOISE SCARED THEM TO DEATH, BUT THEY STOPPED MOVING."

"ROGER, FLIPSTICK, KEEP IT UP. THAT'S WHERE WE NEED YOU." Jack thought—not for the first time—that he would owe Flip a beer if they ever got out of this mess.

The mortar fire was starting again. The ground heaved up around him in muddy clods. The noise was deafening. Casualties mounted. A small aid station had been set up in the middle of the perimeter. Jack missed Doc. He and Sergeant Minh were setting up the hospital in Phu Long.

During a conference of war, Cal Washington was speaking. "Boss, we've got to get out of here. They're going to shoot our asses off in this perimeter one by one. Tonight should be our best bet."

Commander Re shook his head. "A good idea, Sergeant, if we had more cover and the enemy had less ammunition. We must withdraw today, and we must do it soon. We cannot survive under this bombardment all day." He looked hard at Jack. "Major Travis, we must have air support. With air fire we can blow our way out of here to the rear."

"Commander, we're trying to contact Colonel Mason. He's the only officer who can get air down here."

"I have a plan. With or without air, we will break out this afternoon at 1400 hours. You have two hours, Major Travis, to get the air support. We will attack full strength to the east, heading for the canal. Major Tho, with elements

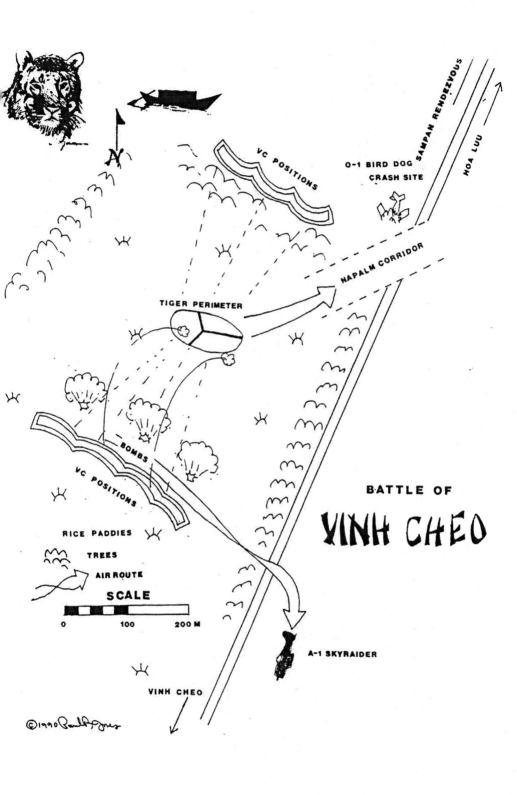

VC POSITIONS

SAMPAN RENDEZVOUS

HOA LUU

O-1 BIRD DOG
CRASH SITE

NAPALM CORRIDOR

TIGER PERIMETER

BOMBS

VC POSITIONS

RICE PADDIES

TREES

AIR ROUTE

SCALE

0   100   200 M

BATTLE OF

VINH CHEO

A-1 SKYRAIDER

VINH CHEO

©1990

of the 123rd RF company, will move down the canal and rendezvous with us at the bend in the canal with a flotilla of sampans. He doesn't dare come any farther south because Hoa Luu Town is undefended. Major Travis, you and I will discuss the details of this plan later." Re left to talk to his officers.

Billy Turner looked at Jack, eyes wide as saucers. "Sir, Boss, I'm scared shitless."

Wham! The team buried their faces in the paddy mud as a nearby explosion sent shards of shrapnel whistling over their heads.

"Don't worry, man, it don't get no worse than this," Cal reassured Billy.

The day blazed on. There were sporadic mortar fire and occasional green tracers. *Probably saving ammunition for tonight*, Jack thought. Humid heat wrapped around them like a wet blanket. The distant tree line shielding the enemy floated in the air. The sun glared off the rice paddies. The Americans felt a growing thirst.

The radio barked, "DELTA ALPHA SIX, THIS IS GREY GHOST. AM INBOUND TO YOUR POSITION, REQUEST LANDING INSTRUCTIONS." Amazed, Jack grabbed the headset.

"DO NOT LAND. I REPEAT, DO NOT LAND. WE ARE UNDER MORTAR AND SMALL ARMS FIRE."

"THIS IS THE GREY GHOST. YOU CAN GET AWAY WITH ANYTHING ONCE IN THIS WAR. I'M COMING IN. GIVE ME A GRID AND A LANDING HEADING."

Jack sent the location and a recommended landing heading.

The Huey hopped over the tree line two kilometers west of the perimeter, then, with skids just off the paddy dikes, bore across the open paddies at one hundred knots. Jack was convinced the chopper would catch a skid and crash. At the last instant the ship flared up and stopped four feet off the ground. The Grey Ghost jumped out of the rear cargo door. The helicopter executed a quick 90 degree turn and roared for the nearest tree line. The helicopter was half way across the paddies when the perimeter erupted with incoming fire. Too late, the VC had been caught napping.

Jack crawled over to report to Colonel Mason. The Grey Ghost was convulsed in laughter. "Shit, Jack, this is the most fun I've had all week. I envy you guys. You get bombarded like this every day?" Tension eased. Jack laughed with his Colonel.

"I couldn't get fast movers, Jack, but I got the next best thing, A-1 Sky Raiders. They fit in better around here. We wouldn't want anyone to think we're modernizing the war. They should be on station in an hour. I damn near had to see General Westmoreland to get them." He looked around the Tigers' tiny perimeter, frowning when he saw the wounded. "What's the plan, Jack? How are you guys gonna get out of this goddamn place?"

Jack explained the withdrawal plan. "Sir, I don't want our Sky Raiders carrying all iron bombs, just a few 250 and 500 pounders. I want napalm. We're gonna burn our way out of here."

"Okay. I'll get that word back. Anything else?"

"Not at this time, sir."

"Okay, it's been great to see you. Get my aircraft back."

"Already? Don't you want to wait a while? Let the VC calm down a bit?"

"Hell no, nothing will happen to ruin my day. Jack, you've got to believe in BARRACA, the Foreign Legion word for combat luck. I've got good BARRACA and so do you."

And, on that day, the Grey Ghost did have good BARRACA. As he flew away, Jack felt ten feet tall. They would get out of this mess. He, personally, could lick an entire VC battalion.

Flip had rearmed his aircraft with four white phosphorous rockets for marking air strikes and four HE rockets for the fighter bomber role. As he waited for the incoming Sky Raiders, he cruised over the battlefield at 1500 feet. The plan was to napalm a corridor northeast of the perimeter to the Hoa Luu Canal while simultaneously plastering the VC position south of the perimeter with iron bombs to suppress enemy fire. The Tigers would fight through this corridor, move up the canal and rendezvous with Major Tho and the sampans.

Flip called on the radio. "GUNFIGHTER AIRCRAFT, THIS IS FLIPSTICK, FORWARD AIR CONTROLLER FOR THIS FRACAS IN HOA LUU DISTRICT. RECOMMEND RENDEZVOUS AT BEND IN TAO RIVER AT GRID." He read the coordinates.

"ROGER, FLIPSTICK, THIS IS GUNFIGHTER. ETA AT RENDEZVOUS IN ZERO TWO."

"THIS IS FLIPSTICK, ROGER, REQUEST ARMAMENT. OVER."

"NAPALM AND IRON BOMBS, 250 AND 500 POUNDERS, WHAT YOU GUYS WANTED."

Flip picked up the aircraft, four black specks flying southward towards the rendezvous point. He informed Jack.

"FLIPSTICK, THIS IS GUNFIGHTER, I HAVE A VISUAL ON THE RENDEZVOUS POINT. WHAT IS YOUR SITUATION?" Using the air strike checklist strapped on his left leg as a guide, Flip explained the situation as the aircraft loitered at 4000 feet above the rendezvous point where the entire battlefield was visible. He covered every aspect of the battlefield: the Tiger perimeter, enemy locations, the escape corridor, and major landmarks.

"EXPECT HEAVY GROUND FIRE, RECOMMEND EAST WEST ATTACK HEADING WITH RIGHT BREAK FOR NAPALM TARGETS. WEST EAST ATTACK WITH RIGHT BREAK FOR IRON BOMB TARGETS. WILL POP YELLOW SMOKE AROUND THE PERIMETER. MAKE SURE YOU'VE GOT A GOOD VISUAL ON THE FRIENDLIES."

"ROGER, FLIPSTICK."

"I'M ROLLING IN HOT FOR MARK." Flip marked both targets and designated the corridor location to the canal with WP rockets.

"ROGER, FLIPSTICK, GOOD VISUAL, READY TO EXECUTE."

"WAIT. BREAK. JACK, BUDDY, IF YOU'RE SQUARED AWAY DOWN THERE, THE BOYS IN BLUE ARE ABOUT TO WIN THE WAR."

"ROGER," Jack replied. "WATCH FOR YELLOW SMOKE." Flipstick relayed this to Gunfighter. Jack could just make out the aircraft circling three kilometers south of the perimeter. He nodded to Re who gave the signal to fire. Every machinegun the Tigers had raked the VC position.

"FLIPSTICK, THIS IS GUNFIGHTER, I RECOGNIZE YELLOW SMOKE."

The Sky Raiders dive bombed out of the sky, an artifact of the Korean war. WHOOM! WHOOM! The ground shook; the bombs hit first, obliterating the enemy position in dust, then the napalm exploded behind the perimeter. The Tigers could feel the searing heat. Whistles blew, the Tigers were up and running for the tree line east of position, which was a mass of flames. At first no enemy fire, then bullets zipped over the rice paddy. Men fell. Cal effortlessly threw a wounded Tiger onto his back and continued to run.

"FLIPSTICK, WATCH OUT FOR THE FRIENDLIES, WE'RE MOVING FOR THE TREE LINE."

"ROGER, WE'RE GONNA MOVE BACK THE NAPALM."

They entered the tree line: abandoned firing position, burning corpses, the sweet smell of burning flesh. Suddenly there was a burst of bullets to their front. The Tigers went to ground on the old VC positions. Jack screamed into the radio. "FLIPSTICK, NEED MORE NAPALM, IRON BOMBS, ANY FUCKING THING ON THE POSITION IN FRONT OF US."

"ROGER." And the Sky Raiders came in again.

Jack spoke to Re. "We've got to move, Commander. These aircraft can't keep this up forever."

With shouts and whistles, the Tigers were up again, moving sluggishly this time, but moving forward. Napalm exploded to the front. With the white heat, many men stopped, dazed. Jack screamed, "DI! DI! Move! Move!" They continued to move through the burning wasteland.

"FLIPSTICK, THIS IS GUNFIGHTER, WE'RE BONE DRY. NOTHING LEFT TO SHOOT. HAVE TO BREAK STATION."

"CAN YOU COME BACK?"

"WE'LL TRY, BUT YOU KNOW HOW IT IS. ENJOYED WORKING WITH YOU, FLIPSTICK."

"HEY GUNFIGHTER, THANKS FOR THE SUPPORT AND DAMN GOOD BOMBING."

The Sky Raiders assembled above the rendezvous point and left the battle.

The Tigers made it through. Jack could see the glistening brown canal through the fire blackened palm trees. They rushed for the canal as if the water held some magical healing powers.

"FLIPSTICK, WE MADE IT. WE JUST GOT TO MOVE NORTH TO THE SAMPAN RENDEZVOUS."

"YOU HAVEN'T MADE IT YET, OLD BUDDY. WE'VE PISSED OFF SOME PEOPLE BACK HERE AND THEY'RE COMING AFTER YOU. GET THEM TIGERS MOVING UP THE CANAL. I'VE STILL GOT A FEW HE ROCKETS LEFT TO COVER YOU. "

Flip saw fleeting figures in the tree line just before the canal. No hope for kills, but he hoped the noise would scare them and make them think the Sky Raiders would return. He picked out a small clearing as a target reference point. This one had to count. The tiny airplane rolled in for another rocket run. The reference point disappeared; he went lower and lower. He knew he was hanging it out, six hundred feet; the clearing appeared at one o'clock; he adjusted the dive. A green Christmas tree of tracers exploded under him. He fired his rockets, jammed the stick back and applied full throttle; the nose came up, too slowly. THUD! A shudder went through the aircraft. RPM dropped and there was no power. The aircraft slid into a slow right bank. There was no response to controls, and there was a metallic sound behind him like tapping a church key against a beer can. The Plexiglas shattered above his head. Then came a shock to his right leg. He looked down: the leg below the knee dangled by a few cloth threads; arterial blood spurted out onto the control pedals. Flip keyed the radio set. "JACK, JACK HANG—" The bird exploded on impact.

187

A hush fell over the battlefield. Absolute silence. The VC could not believe they had shot down an airplane. The Tigers could not believe the Bird Dog, their reassuring companion on many operations, was down.

Jack, stunned, refused reality. If you back up a few picture frames, Flip would still be alive, still giving him all that cocky chatter in the face of death. He grabbed the radio handset. "FLIPSTICK, FLIPSTICK." No answer. "ANSWER GODDAMNIT!" he called hoarsely. Cal took the handset away from him.

"Flipstick is gone," he said softly.

"Bullshit! Men like Flip don't get killed. They can't die."

Commander Re came up. He placed his hand on Jack's shoulder. "Major Cochran was a brave man; he wore the Tiger's claw."

"But you never gave him the goddamned claw," Jack interrupted.

The Commander continued, "The Tiger claw is not a material thing; it is a spiritual symbol for brave warriors. Major Cochran fought like a Tiger. He is one of us. And, now, my friend, we must move up this canal so that his brave death will not have been in vain."

******5******

On the day of Co Linh's parade, the sun shone all day in revolt against the weather. Music played up and down the Vietnamese scale, a mystery to American ears. Lines of shining children dressed in their best and carrying miniature Government flags lined the newly constructed roadway. A special arch had been built over the hospital's entrance and decorated with crepe paper. At the top of the arch a freshly painted red and yellow sign read BENH VIEN PHU LONG, Phu Long Hospital. Between the posts of the arch stretched a light blue sash. Major Tho, with a flourish, cut halfway through the sash, then gallantly offered the shears to Co Linh to complete the task. She bowed to Major Tho, then firmly severed the sash. The people cheered. A scratchy record played the national anthem and all present, which included the entire village, the ARVN battalion, and an honor guard from the Delta Tigers, stood at attention.

Major Tho was the first speaker. He spoke of security and working together against the common enemy. On Jack's advice, he only mentioned the Hoa Hao once. The ARVN Battalion Commander was next. He wore a camouflaged scarf like an ascot, and a pair of Ray Bans covered the upper half of his face. Jack had heard from a 64th Division Advisor that this man was all politician, with heavy connections in Saigon. Gesturing with a polished wood swagger stick, he said the 2nd Battalion, 3rd Infantry Regiment, 64th ARVN Division was pleased to work with Hoa Luu District to secure the new village. The VC would never attack as long as the battalion was here because they were fierce fighters. The new village chief shakily approached the microphone. He said he was proud to represent the people and some other things nobody could hear. He visibly trembled before the crowd and appeared to be afraid of the microphone. From time to time the loudspeakers of the ancient sound system emitted a loud humming sound which could only be eliminated by a member of the District's Public Affairs Division who worked magic with the wires.

The applause was sporadic for the three men. Co Linh was introduced. There was loud applause. "BA CHUA BENH, the healing lady," many of the villagers shouted. Co Linh stood in the sunlight, radiant in her starched white nurse's uniform. Jack's eyes misted over. Her voice was clear and strong. Her message was simple, to the people.

"I am honored to speak to you today. Phu Long Hospital is a symbol of the entire village. Here, we work together as brother and sister. We must love each other. There will be no wicked words or deeds. Though we are Buddhists, Hoa Hao, and Catholics, we will work together in harmony. Phu Long, this tiny place, will set an example for the entire nation. We will demonstrate that a community of farm people such as we can flourish. We are all refugees here, uprooted by the terrible civil war which engulfs our country. But in Phu Long, all of us have been given a new chance. We own our land. Bountiful crops of rice will grow. The village will be made beautiful through our common labor. Soon the school will be completed to educate our children. Our young men will provide security in the PF platoons. We are certainly most grateful to ARVN for providing the 2nd Battalion." She smiled beautifully at the Battalion Commander. "And," she gestured with unconscious grace, "we will heal the sick at this wonderful new hospital." More applause.

"As you know, after this ceremony there will be a delicious feast prepared by the women of Phu Long. I can smell the roasting pork now." She visibly sniffed. The people laughed. "The feast will be followed by a gift presentation to all of the children. Later we will visit our beautiful hospital.

"At this time I would like to recognize a man who has made most of this happen, Doctor Hector Gonzales." The Doc stood and made a short bow, trying to be modest, but hugely enjoying the recognition.

Co Linh concluded, "We have lived long amid hardship and death. Phu Long was created by war. Let us dedicate ourselves to live here in love and peace."

There was loud applause. *These people believed in Phu Long and Co Linh,* Jack thought. She could be the next village chief or higher. She wasn't real. Loving her was like loving Joan of Arc. Sergeant Truong of the Viet Minh Hoa Luu District Battalion, on a reconnaissance mission, was moved. He applauded with the rest.

Bob Harris had come by jeep and sampan from Tram Cua District to attend the ceremony. He approached Jack as the people went to the marketplace for the feast.

"Not hungry, Jack?"

"Maybe later."

"We should have a wake for Flip."

"Careful, Bob, I'm having a helluva time handling this one. You know, he saved our butts out there on that Vinh Cheo rice paddy. You should have seen him, a one man air force. The Grey Ghost has put him in for the Distinguished Service Cross."

"He would never wear it."

"That's the damn truth."

"You know, I never realized how much he did around here. Every morning at Tram Cua I looked forward to his chatter on the radio. It made my day. He acted as a great cheerleader in sharing information and pulling all the district teams together."

"Yeah, I know. Like Commander Re said, he wore the Tiger's claw. Flip worked and fought hard, but he wasn't motivated by advancement. Flip simply believed in this war, because he was ordered here to do a job. It sounds corny, but he just wanted to do his duty and win."

"There was more, Jack."

"Yeah, he was a hell-for-leather soldier, the best goddamn aviator in the Army. He enjoyed his profession. Let's face it, he loved combat almost as much as he enjoyed giving the finger to the brass."

"Do you love combat, Jack?"

Jack hesitated. "I don't love combat, but there is something addictive about the excitement. I'll have to sort that out if I ever get back to the world."

"How was the memorial service? The Tram Cua guys were out on an operation. I couldn't come."

"The usual thing. Pottsy presided. Some chaplain came down from Can Tho and made a lot of platitudinous comments about doing your duty, young men dying for a cause, that sort of crap. They didn't know Flip. The words didn't fit. Only one thing got to me." He looked hard at Bob. "They were sorting out Flip's stuff to send it home. His boots had to be displayed for the ceremony. You know how they do it. Line up the deceased's boots. Well, Flip's boots looked like hell. Shoe polish had never touched them. I volunteered to shine them up for the ceremony. I sat there shining those fucked up, scruffy boots and I could see Flip looking at me laughing. That was Flip. I cried, Bob." He abruptly stopped talking. As both men controlled their emotions, a silence fell between them.

"Well, we're short, Jack. Just about thirty days for me, and you have less than that. Leavenworth orders should be out soon."

"Yeah, the Command and General Staff College, the 'must' ticket for us studs." Jack looked around him and waved his hand at the village. "You know, Bob, Phu Long is my big accomplishment in almost a year. This is it.

I hope the idea grows." He turned to his friend. "There will be adjustments when we return to the real Army. You and I will never have a job like this again. We have been running our own little war down here. Majors don't do that."

"I know."

Jack accompanied his friend to the dock.

"Keep your powder dry, Jack," Bob warned in his somber New England way. "We're not home yet. I think the VC might hit Phu Long."

"Perhaps, but I think we're in good shape with the ARVN battalion here." They shook hands on the dock.

A large crowd, mostly women and children, went on the hospital tour. Co Linh presided. Most of the tour was spent showing the women the new delivery room, explaining new equipment and her midwife education program. She showed them the maternity ward where each bed had an accompanying crib. These women had lived in Indian country. They had their babies at home, often in combat conditions where infections took a terrible toll of mother and child. They viewed these facilities as a rare luxury. In the pharmacy, the ever-present Doctor Gonzales distributed some low power medicine for minor complaints along with hard candy for the children. This was a wonderful treat. The children laughed with joy. Each of them had already received a present. The women completed the tour feeling reassured about health care for their families, as important as any victory on the rice paddies, Jack thought.

Co Linh was in her element. Jack had never seen her so motivated. This was her special day. Phu Long, and particularly the Phu Long Hospital, had become a reality. After the tour, Jack finally had a few moments alone with her in the hospital waiting room. The room smelled of drying plaster and wet paint. Everything was fresh, new and clean. Co Linh belonged to this place, a house of healing and hope.

"Will you return with me tonight?"

"No, I will stay here. There is much to do and tomorrow morning my assistant and I will conduct our first treatment."

"I will miss you. Don't spend too much time up here; it might be dangerous."

"It is more secure than Hoa Luu Town. Here I have an ARVN battalion to defend me."

"In Hoa Luu you have me. I'm worth at least two ARVN battalions." He moved close to her and put his arms around her waist. He could feel her skin under the white starched material. Her breast pressed against him. She hugged him, sighed, quickly kissed his cheek, then twirled out of his arms and went across the room.

"We've been through this, Jack. It is safe here, and I belong here."

"You belong with me. I have thirty days left. Soon I will leave Hoa Luu. For us time is running out."

Her eyes became very bright. She sobbed once and caught herself. "Please, do not make it difficult for us, Jack. You and I have accomplished so much together—Phu Long, the hospital, the entire district. For us it must be enough." Jack knew it would never be enough.

Before he left Phu Long, he had a short conversation with Captain Mike Blake, the ARVN Battalion Advisor.

"Remember, if you are attacked, you must react, and that means get the fuck out of that huge fort you've built and defend these villagers. Do you understand?"

"Yes, Sir, don't worry, Major, the Battalion believes in this mission. We look at Phu Long as our own little town."

"Get this straight, Blake, and this is very important. These people must believe they are protected by ARVN. If that trust is broken, the word will spread throughout the Southern Delta, and many people will go to the other side."

"Yes, Sir," the young captain said again, but Jack was uneasy.

Jack always enjoyed the short sampan journey between Phu Long and Hoa Luu Town. Sergeant Minh and Doc Gonzales were returning with him. He had made it countless times since the Pacification Task Force went into operation. The trip was usually made at the end of the day when the sun was setting, the most beautiful time in the Southern Delta. Jack loved sunsets. It was as if God had declared a hiatus on all terror. For a few moments each day, there was rare beauty when the sinking red sun highlighted the pink and gold of the sky and the brown and green of the Earth, making them, for a glorious instant, one. God forgave men in these few colorful seconds for their terrible deeds on His Earth. The black tropical night soon followed. Jack knew that often the sunset was an illusion, that often violence and sudden death occurred when the sun went down. But, yet, he believed in the sunset. He would always believe in the sunset.

Sergeant Minh wanted to talk. He kept trying to catch Jack's eye. Finally, he made contact. "Major Travis, you know my background, how my family was murdered by the Viet Minh years ago." Minh rapidly opened up the conversation in his stilted, academic English. "I became a bitter man who lived on hate. Revenge was my motivation. But, you know, Sir, two events have occurred in Hoa Luu District this year that have changed my life, given me new hope. Remember when we took the VC bodies back to Vinh Cheo?" Jack nodded. "I learned there was honor on the other side. Those women loved their husbands, as we love our families. They have faith. All of us are much the same: we hate, love, fight and grieve. This terrible war has divided us over issues which few of us understand, but we are the same people. That is the terrible tragedy of Vietnam, good people, many with the same fundamental beliefs, fighting each other." Minh paused. "Do not misunderstand me, Sir, I continue to hate the Viet Minh leadership. Their purpose is an abomination. If they win, Vietnam will become a wasteland. Human spirit will be destroyed, but many of the Viet Minh are honorable people. I respect them." He stopped.

"You said there were two events," Jack prompted.

"Phu Long, Sir, the whole idea of the Pacification Task Force. You deserve great credit for this effort, though I am not sure your superiors will ever understand. The idea to combine all these governmental agencies, District, Province, ARVN, USAID, the Vietnamese Information Service, into a single pacification effort is strong and has application throughout Vietnam. If the many sides of the Government pull together, we can defeat the Viet Minh. In war we must forget our differences and concentrate on defeating the enemy. Projects like Phu Long provide a beacon for victory."

"I totally agree, Sergeant Minh," Jack said.

Doc had been following this conversation closely. "You know, Boss, I've traveled all over the district on medical missions. Sometimes the people are happy, sometimes they are sad, often they live day to day just not giving a damn. I've been poor. I understand not giving a damn. The folks in Phu Long are really happy. You could tell that through the mothers. They have the happiness that comes from believing in the future of their kids. They know the danger of the other side. The mothers believe that the Government really cares for them. They can see the security because of the ARVN battalion and the caring because of the hospital. And, Boss, the person who has made most of this work is Co Linh. She is an angel for healing."

Jack smiled. "You and Co Linh should organize a mutual admiration society." He slapped Doc on the back. "You played a large part in making the hospital work. You're a living legend in the district." He paused. "In fact, both of you guys are super warriors. We've done many great things together. Both of you are Hoa Luu Muckers and wear the Tiger's claw. That is the best compliment I can pay you." Both men felt pleasure. Jack wasn't too open with

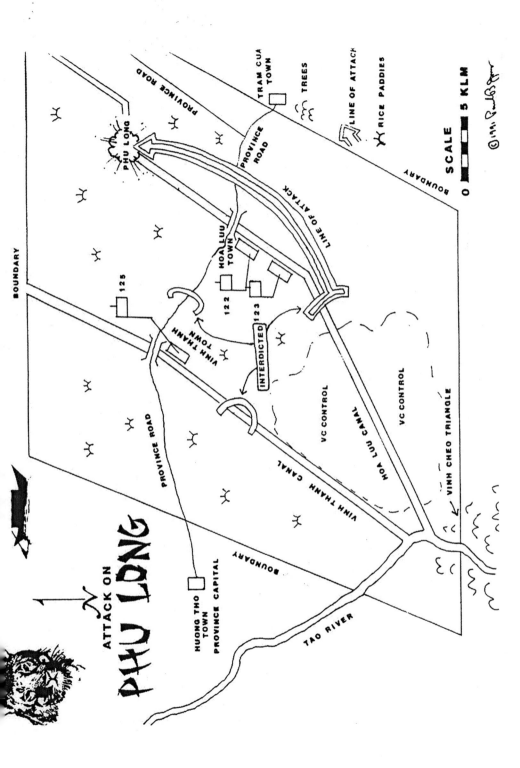

ATTACK ON PHU LONG

N

BOUNDARY

PROVINCE ROAD

PHU LONG

125

HOA LUU TOWN

122

VINH THANH TOWN

123

INTERCEPTED

PROVINCE ROAD

TRAM CUA TOWN

TREES

LINE OF ATTACK

RICE PADDIES

BOUNDARY

SCALE

0   5 KLM

© 1971 Doube Byron

LINE OF ATTACK

VC CONTROL

HOA LUU CANAL

VC CONTROL

VINH CHEO TRIANGLE

VINH THANH CANAL

PROVINCE ROAD

BOUNDARY

HUONG THO TOWN PROVINCE CAPITAL

TAO RIVER

compliments.

Billy Turner was waiting at the dock. He looked worried. He was always worried when Jack wasn't around. Billy thought Jack made it right, that he would somehow guide him through this mess back to St. Louis, his girlfriend, and the Cardinals.

"Boss, Cal's on the radio with Province. There is an important message for you."

Jack could tell the message was serious. Cal was standing outside the hut. The steel had gone out of his usual impeccable bearing; he slumped. "Boss," he said so low Jack could barely hear him, "the Grey Ghost is dead. He was shot down over a hot LZ this morning."

****

The two men were drinking cognac in the living room of the Commanding General's villa. They had just finished a served meal of coq au vin, prepared by the General's French trained Vietnamese chef. They were stretched out on padded easy chairs. The living room had an eighteenth century motif with flowered carpets and delicate cherry furniture. The easy chairs jarred with the décor but had been installed by General Wells for comfort. Both men were dressed in exquisitely tailored, starched jungle fatigues and spit shined boots. These clothes strangely suited the room.

"The meal was delicious, General, and the wine, Chardonnay 1962 I believe." Colonel Andrews gave an approving gesture, holding his hand up touching the thumb and forefinger.

"Glad you enjoyed it, Harvey. You know I'll miss you around here. You've done a great job for me."

"Thank you, Sir, and, as I told you before, I really appreciate being given the 64th Division job. It's a great opportunity."

"I think the 64th Division will really set you up for the next one star board which meets in sixty days. This will give you time for an efficiency report in your new assignment. With your colonel command time in Europe and the division advisory job in combat, you should be a shoo-in. You've got all the tickets for flag rank."

"Well, Sir, I owe it all to you. I hope we can serve together again, preferably in Europe."

"You've earned it, Harvey. As my Chief, you've kept it quiet in V Corps. Believe me, if I get another star and a division, you'll be the first brigadier I'll ask for as my Assistant Division Commander."

"I wish I was going down to the 64th under different circumstances, though. Tough about Bill Mason. He probably would have been on the top of the next one star list."

"The famous Grey Ghost?" There was anger in General Wells' voice. "I don't think so. Mason was too much the fire eater, and he fought the problem. He never should have been over that LZ. He personally got too involved in combat. Remember, Harvey, you're a manager down there. I don't want you leading any charges like the gallant Grey Ghost."

General Wells reflected, "You know, I could never talk to him. He was never in his headquarters, always flying off some place. Another thing about Mason, he was overly aggressive, pressing me to attack one VC camp after another based on very sketchy intelligence. My God, Harvey, here's Westy trying to win the war up north, especially in the Central Highlands, and Mason down here is trying to start his own major battle. All that bullshit about hitting suspected enemy base areas and defending the population and rice economy. The Westmoreland strategy is to target the NVA main forces up north, and it's right on target. Remember the crap Mason was trying to sell us about the tremendous offensive capability the VC have in the Southern Delta." At this point they broke eye contact; there was a pause in the conversation. Colonel Andrews cleared his throat.

"Damn," General Wells continued. "He always wanted to put pressure on the Vietnamese Corps Commander through me to run off somewhere looking for a battle. I never did it, though occasionally word would reach my counterpart that Mason didn't believe we were prosecuting the war, like we were a bunch of goddamn cowards or something. Christ, Harvey, this isn't my first war; I know how to fight a war; a lot of dead Germans could tell you that."

Noticing the general was becoming more agitated, Andrews said soothingly, "I understand your guidance, Sir; I'll keep it quiet."

"One last piece of guidance before you leave, Harvey. You know about the Pacification Task Force in Hoa Luu District. What's the name of the village?"

"Phu Long," Andrews provided.

"Yes, Phu Long. Harvey, that place is a ticking time bomb, an open challenge to the VC for combat. You recall, after the battle of Hoa Luu, we had to do something. Establishing Phu Long village for all those refugees and providing an ARVN battalion for security seemed like a good idea. Now, I'm not so sure. Phu Long is an invitation to the VC in that area for battle, and there we sit with an ARVN battalion. It's not the civilians I worry about, but ARVN counts—you know what I mean, Harvey. ARVN is fighting strength. Their numbers count on reports; civilian casualties don't count. Also, there is the problem of American casualties with the battalion advisory team. We can't stand that."

General Wells sat up in his chair and looked intently at Colonel Andrews. "Now listen up, Harvey. I don't want that ARVN battalion put at risk. If there is a major attack on Phu Long, defend the fort; don't counterattack into the village and don't set up defensive perimeter positions around the village. Hopefully, the presence of the battalion will deter attack, but if an attack comes, the battalion defends the fort only. The Corps Commander agrees with me. He doesn't want any casualties defending Phu Long. He is also concerned about the Hoa Hao thing. You know the rumors going around that the Hoa Hao are starting a minor revolution in Phu Long. He doesn't want to jeopardize ARVN lives to start a Hoa Hao rebellion. 'If the VC attack, let the Hoa Hao die.' Those are his words. We don't want to become involved in the middle of a revolution between the Hoa Hao and the Government."

Colonel Andrews was busy taking notes on a stack of 3x5 cards he always carried in his breast pocket. He looked up between notes. "Anything else, Sir?"

"Yes, Harvey, one more thing. Keep a lid on that young firebrand down there. What's his name?"

"I remember Major Travis, Sir." Colonel Andrews half smiled.

"Yes, Travis. I think he is a good man but was badly influenced by Mason. Keep him alive and out of trouble. He should be on the next Leavenworth list."

There was another note on the 3x5 cards. "Anything else, Sir?"

"No, Harvey, and I apologize for all these last minute orders. You know how us old farts are. It's just that the war and you and I have reached a critical juncture. How about another brandy?"

"No, Sir, and I thank you for a superb evening. Please, don't get up. Your man can show me out."

******6******

Major Tong gave the signal to fire. With a hollow, explosive noise, the mortar section fired in unison. The target was the fort occupied by the 2nd Battalion, 3rd Infantry Regiment, 64th ARVN Division. The bombardment of the fort would continue until the Hoa Luu District Battalion and the 309th Battalion of the U Minh Regiment had overrun Phu Long village and killed the inhabitants.

The ground assault began when the first mortar round exploded on the ARVN fort. The Hoa Luu Battalion and the 309th Battalion attacked in opposite directions, northeast and southwest, and planned to rendezvous in the marketplace in the center of the town. Everything that moved was to be killed and Phu Long put to the torch, especially the new hospital which had become a thorn in the Viet Minh's side. The people valued the hospital and loved Co Linh, the BA CHUA BENH, the healing lady.

Three aspects of the operation troubled Major Tong. Enemy fire support, especially the death ray, and the actions of the ARVN battalion and the 122nd RF Company, the Delta Tigers. In recent days he had lost sleep over the ARVN battalion. If his battalion encountered a strong night patrol, surprise would be lost; if ARVN had established strong defensive positions outside the fort, the attack would stall; if they counterattacked out of the fort in battalion strength, the entire operation would be jeopardized.

"Worry will kill you," Colonel Truc had told him. "Arrangements have been made. I cannot guarantee the death ray will not come because it is controlled by the Americans, but we will conduct diversionary attacks to convince the Americans to send the death ray elsewhere. The ARVN battalion will not leave the fort." Truc emphasized this point. "You will fight no enemy soldiers in Phu Long other than half trained PF rabble. You have been given an additional company which will prevent the 122nd RF Company from reinforcing Phu Long or blocking your escape. The Tigers are weak anyway because of their losses during the Vinh Cheo operation. Kinsman, you will have great success. Remember, my decision is GIET SACH, no survivors. There can be no Christian softheartedness on this operation." He looked hard at Tong.

"Yes, comrade," Tong replied in a loud voice, thinking no Christian softheartedness, no Buddhist softheartedness, no Hoa Hao softheartedness, just no heart for the Vietnamese people. Those with heart, with faith, would die in this war; the survivors would have hearts of stone—a godless people. Colonel Truc will be happy. The state will survive. He shoved these thoughts aside—victory first.

Sergeant Truong was the platoon sergeant of the lead platoon of the lead company from the Hoa Luu District Battalion making the attack up the canal. He had positioned himself with the two lead squads to control the momentum of the attack. One of these squads had killed the American Major almost a year before.

The night had a silvery glow, a full moon. The hour was early. People were talking; children were laughing. There was the sound of music from a wedding or birthday; a dog was barking; the smell of fried fish was in the air; it was a living, vibrant place.

Crump! There was a series of loud explosions. The mortar barrage was hitting the ARVN fort. The two squads immediately moved forward. The lead platoon had bypassed the southern PF outpost. The platoon behind them would destroy the outpost while they were torching dwellings and killing villagers. The untrained PF would experience the terrible shock of night attack, families murdered to their rear, and a frontal assault on their position.

Sergeant Truong deployed his small force, a squad on each side of the road. He entered the first family dwelling. It opened to the road with a cooking fire in front. The family had been alerted by the mortar fire and had started to run for the family shelter. A small boy leading the way was shot in half; just behind him his sister's head exploded. A toddler crying on the hard dirt in front of the hut was smashed with a rifle butt. The pregnant mother leaned over the ruins of her child and was shot to pieces. A howl of primitive rage came from the interior of the hut. A man charged the squad with his ancient German Mauser, held by the barrel like a club. A single shot felled him. They entered the hut; an old couple sat on bamboo matting calmly facing the altar to their ancestors. Sergeant Truong shot them both in the back of the head, execution style. A weak cry came from the shadowy back of the hut. A Viet Minh soldier picked up a small baby by the foot and bashed its head to red jelly against the stone fireplace. "Fire the house!" Sergeant Truong ordered. The house blazed like a funeral pyre stoked by human fuel.

They went to the next house. A small black and white dog ran in front of the squad. With single shot, the dog dragged its paralyzed hindquarters off the road, whining in agony. A bloodlust was on them. They shot, burned, knifed and bludgeoned their way through Phu Long village. The village was burning; the smell of roasting human flesh filled the air. The 2nd Battalion, 3rd Infantry Regiment, 64th ARVN Division remained in its fort, occasionally shooting from protected positions at moving figures that looked like VC.

The Muckers heard the battle erupt in Phu Long. Muffled explosions and small arms fire reverberated the 12 kilometers down the Hoa Luu Canal. Jack frantically grabbed the radio and contacted Capt. Baker, the ARVN Battalion Advisor. There was no attempt at proper radio procedure.

"WHAT THE HELL IS GOING ON?"

"WE'RE UNDER HEAVY MORTAR FIRE, AND THERE ISA GROUND ATTACK ON BOTH SIDES OF THE VILLAGE."

Jack could hear the battle noise over the radio.

"WHAT DO YOUR PEOPLE SAY, THE STAKE OUT PATROLS IN THOSE AREAS?"

There was silence over the radio. Jack turned off the squelch switch. There was a loud rushing sound over the loudspeaker. He pushed the talk button. "ANSWER ME, GODDAMMIT!"

"THERE WERE NO PATROLS." After a pause came, "ORDERS FROM HIGHER."

Jack roared, "YOU MOTHERFUCKER!" He threw the hand mike down, then immediately picked it up again. He looked like he was about to jump through the radio and enter the battle.

"GET YOUR ASSES OUT OF THAT GODDAMNED FORT AND COUNTERATTACK! PEOPLE ARE DYING!"

"NEGATIVE." There was another pause. "ORDERS FROM HIGHER, FROM THE DIVISION SENIOR ADVISOR. WE'RE NOT TO LEAVE OUR POSITION." Capt. Baker's voice was high and cracked.

Jack did not answer. He handed the mike to Cal. "Call Province, get air and Spooky support; we're going to take the Tigers up there."

He whirled and ran to the door almost knocking down Commander Re and Major Tho who had just entered the hut.

"The Tigers are alerted," Commander Re said coolly. "The problem is how to relieve Phu Long. The quickest way is to sampan up the canal, but we're sure to be ambushed. We can stay off the canal and the canal trail and move up through the rice paddies." A series of large explosions echoed down the canal. Commander Re stopped talking.

Major Tho was rapidly shifting from one foot to the other as if he wanted to run to Phu Long. His hand fingered a grenade on his pistol belt. His round face was flushed. The inevitable cigar was clenched tightly in his teeth, this time unlit.

"We go now; we go fast!" He grunted loudly and started to leave the hut.

Commander Re grabbed his arm. "The Tigers will be ambushed. We must skirt the canal and the canal trail."

Major Tho shook off Commander Re's grip, an unusual gesture toward his friend and spiritual mentor.

"The people, the people! Our people!" he shouted through his cigar. "Go now!"

They left the hut. The Tigers were assembling on the parade ground. The Binh Sys were quiet. They could hear the sound of battle up the canal. The sky flickered with light to the northeast as if some crazy fireworks display was taking place. Commander Re held a brief order's group with his platoon leaders. The canal route was out. They would be too vulnerable in sampans. The Tigers would move up the canal trail in a column of platoons. The first platoon would deploy and watch for an ambush. Commander Re shook his head. "Very dangerous," he whispered to Jack. "We should move west of the canal and the canal trail over the rice paddies." Jack didn't hear him. He was between desperation and despair. His life here, the many hard months, the people, all lost. The entire Phu Long enterprise was being blown up in a bloody massacre.

Machinegun fire came to the front. Bright green tracers zoomed erratically down the darkened trail corridor and arced over the canal. The Tigers went to ground. There was small arms fire from the left flank. Commander Re began to position his men to firing positions off the trail. The Tigers were showered by falling palm fronds. Bullets cracked through the blackness. Jack grabbed the hand mike. He was carrying the radio. The team was behind in the District Compound .

"WHERE IS THE AIR SUPPORT?" he transmitted to Cal.

"NONE AVAILABLE," was Cal's terse reply.

There were cries from the lead platoon. "Thieu ta Tho! Thieu ta Tho!" Jack sprinted up the canal trail. Major Tho lay off the trail under the care of a Tiger medic. Jack crashed down beside him. Blood poured from Tho's chest and pooled on the ground. Jack bent over the old Hoa Hao warrior. He was trying to say something.

"Light, light," he breathed to Jack. Incredibly, the Dutchmaster Panatella was still in his mouth. Jack's trembling Zippo lit the cigar. Major Tho briefly inhaled, coughed, then exhaled a mixture of bubbled blood and smoke. "The people, the Hoa Hao," he whispered. The cigar fell from his bloody lips.

Sergeant Truong's two squads reached the marketplace. An evil yellow light from countless fires illuminated the market square. Shadows careened ghostlike across the concrete surface. Facing the market was the new hospital with its brave red and yellow sign. The wooden arch from the opening ceremony still stood, decorated with frayed pieces of crepe paper. The hospital was untouched.

Sergeant Truong placed his men in position around the marketplace. He then stood and stared at the hospital. It seemed to beckon to him. He remembered the warmth of the opening ceremony.

He walked under the arch into the building. It was cool and softly lit. He could smell the newness, the cleanliness. With the sound of combat muted behind him, he felt peace. Somehow, the terror outside was not his world. This was a place where people came to be healed, a sanctuary where all was forgotten except getting well.

There was a flash of white to his left. He whirled and fired the Garand from the hip. With a low groan, more of a sigh, the white disappeared. Sergeant Truong rushed across the room. Co Linh lay on the floor looking up at him, her starched white dress stained bright red across the midriff. "It's the healing lady!" He threw his rifle to the floor, knelt and cradled her in his arms. Co Linh looked into his eyes and raised her hand to touch his cheek. The touch was gentle, like a feather.

HET

THE ENDING

JULY 1967

****** 1 ******

Mother Maria knelt in the rear of the church. It was cool and quiet. Lines of late afternoon sunshine streamed from the windows onto the empty pews. The church had been empty for years. She could remember when all the pews were full. The French time she called it. The French landowners would sit in front in a reserved section, the people in the rear. The languages of reverence were Latin and French. Much of the service she could not understand, but there was a feeling of holiness here, that God was present. The Frenchmen wore light suits, the women brightly colored dresses. The contrast between the French and Vietnamese was stark—style and color against the timeless peasant dress of the Delta.

After the mass, the French would gather and talk on the lawn before returning to their plantations. Many boats were moored to the landing then. The Vietnamese disappeared from the church grounds after the service. The church was a place of worship for the French and Vietnamese. It was also a social gathering place for the French.

There was injustice during the time of the French. They ruled the people in their own land. But those were times of no killing, before the great war. It was right that the French should go. It was right that the Delta people should rule themselves. But what happened now in this terrible war was unforgivable. The killing of innocents for an idea that she didn't understand. Were Colonel Truc and the U Minh Regiment greatly different from the French? She remembered with bittersweet nostalgia the time of the French.

She must pray. Her mind was wandering in this holy place. Perhaps she was too far to the rear. She stared hard at the altar, but the light beams interrupted her weak sight, and the altar was darkened by shadows.

"KINH MUNG MARIA, DAY ON PHUOC, hail Mary, full of grace, " she started. It did not work. Then in French she said, "Je vous salue Marie, pleines de graces." Her thoughts went back to early afternoon. Colonel Truc had come up the river to congratulate Manor Tong on his great victory at Phu Long. Mother Maria had felt pride for Tong, this gallant warrior fighting for his people. Then she had heard the words "GIET SACH." GIET SACH had occurred at Phu Long, even the healing lady had been killed. She could not comprehend that her "son" had led this battle. This was a thing beyond expiation, an affront to God. The killing of the healing lady was like killing a living saint. Mother Maria felt a strong kinship for Co Linh. Her reputation had traveled down the canal to the Vinh Cheo Triangle.

After Colonel Truc departed, Tong had sat on the porch in front of the church looking at the end of the day. She joined him there. For a time they sat in silence, then she spoke, "My son, I cannot believe you have done this terrible thing." He did not answer, only looked at her with deep, black eyes that seemed to look over the abyss, to hell itself. She took his hand, but he gently moved it away. Abruptly he stood and started to walk toward the landing. She rose to go with him.

"No, Mother, I must be alone," he said in a low anguished voice, the only words he spoke to her.

Mother Maria shifted on her aching knees. She felt she must pray, but again, she could not. She fingered her rosary, asking for inspiration but nothing. Finally, she spoke directly to the shadowed altar. "I cannot ask you to forgive him. Though it is a sin, I love Tong as a son. I cannot help myself. Please, give us the understanding, the strength, to stop these terrible sins we commit against ourselves. Please, do not abandon the Delta people." She hesitated and then said, "Amen."

Tong stood on the landing. He watched the sun go down. Night surrounded him, but there was no healing in the darkness. A deadness was inside him as if his soul had died in his living body. He felt the cross around his neck, but it gave him no solace. He could think about mundane things, supply, training, weapon repairs, but he could not face Phu Long. For hours he had tried to grasp the boundaries of this sin. There were no boundaries. He knew why. God had abandoned him. His soul was beyond guilt, beyond redemption. Even the American Major here at this landing had demonstrated compassion for his enemy when he returned the bodies of those he had killed in battle, but not he. He was the executioner, the killer of babies, children, women and old people.

Tong stared into the black night and removed the cross from around his neck. Briefly he looked at the simple cross reflected in the starlight, then he threw it over the canal. It winked through the darkness and disappeared without a sound.

As he parted with the cross, a rush of awareness came to Tong of another time. The time before the cross, before the French. There were other gods then, strong gods who demanded sacrifice.

The night was dying, the horizon graying to the east. He could make out the outline of the church. He walked up the small rise to the church and entered. It was black inside. He could smell the mustiness of the empty pews and hear the echoes of forgotten prayers. From memory he walked up the aisle to the front of the church. He lit one of the candles surrounding the altar. The cross looked down on him with accusation or expectation—which, he couldn't tell. Major Tong, Commander of the Hoa Luu District Battalion, unholstered his pistol.

******2******

It was his last day in Hoa Luu. He stood at attention before an honor guard of the Delta Tigers. General Wells came forward and stood in front of him. He looked into the General's eyes, but the General fixed his eyes on something just over his head. It was a windless hot day. Sweat ran down his back.

"Attention to orders," the narrator started. Jack was to receive three medals: he Bronze Star for Meritorious Service which recognized his one year combat tour, the Bronze Star with V Device for the Vinh Cheo battle, and the Silver Star for the defense of the Hoa Luu compound. The Grey Ghost had recommended him for these battle decorations against pressure from higher headquarters. The Silver Star had been recommended as the Distinguished Service Cross but had been downgraded. Cal Washington was furious over this. "Those bastards don't recognize the Territorial Force War. They don't know we're fighting down here, too. I tell you, Boss, this never would have happened in a U.S. unit."

Jack had replied, "Remember what the Grey Ghost said, 'Professionals are not in this for the medals.'"

"Boss, someday you have to explain to me why we are in 'this.'"

The heart of the problem, Jack thought.

The day before, Commander Re had awarded him the Vietnamese Cross of Gallantry with Gold Star. For the first time since Jack had known him, this warrior and spiritual leader lost his composure. He had trouble reading the citation. After the ceremony Jack had attended his last Hoa Hao party. His head still ached from the effects of Ba Si De whiskey.

The narrator droned on. General Wells was beginning to fidget, Jack noticed. He thought about the last weeks. The terrible night of the Phu Long attack, Major Tho's frantic efforts to rescue his "people," and his final moments with his ever-present cigar. Jack felt his throat contract. He willed Tho's memory away, one of the many things he would think about later. "Later" was becoming a large category. The destruction of the village, the burned corpses, the bloated bodies floating along the canal banks. Even the dogs had been killed. The stench of death, which was with him to this day. Phu Long, a place God forgot. He had physically assaulted Captain Baker, the ARVN Battalion Advisor. The young captain had stood before him at attention.

"Why didn't you leave this fucking fort? Why didn't you attack?" he had screamed. Out of control, he had hit him flush on the jaw. Cal had restrained him.

Jack tried not to think of Co Linh. There was a void deep within him, where a few weeks before, there had been something bright and shining, something pure that replenished his faith. Part of his soul had been lost. For days he drank. His single objective was to remain numb enough not to face his loss. It didn't work. Her memory consumed him and suffocated all other thoughts. He remembered their love, her passion, her stubbornness, and her buoyant dedication to healing the Delta people.

Cal had talked to him. "Boss, this loss will be with you forever. I know because I lost someone close, but, Goddamnit, you must get on with your life. You're a helluva officer. You'll make a great difference to our Army and this war. Put this away for a while. Sometime, when you have returned to the world, think of her again. This sounds impossible, but I know it can be done. Terrible tragedy can destroy you if the memory isn't controlled until a time when you can deal with it." Cal paused. "Jack," for the first and last time Cal called him by his first name. "it's what she would have wanted. If you waste your life, her death will be cheapened."

Cal paused, looking at his friend. "The Grey Ghost and Flip Cochran would be telling you the same thing."

Jack recovered from his destructive grief, but the team noticed a somberness about him, a seriousness that wouldn't leave, like a scar from a terrible battle wound. He never joked or smiled.

The Pacification Task Force concept died in the massacre of Phu Long. Jack wondered if the government agencies would ever work together again toward a pacification goal. The corruption, the prejudice, the bureaucracy, the rank ambition, did the Government have a chance for survival? *ARVN*, he thought, *was the worst problem.* In a civil war where people were the objective, a national Army that didn't relate to the people had no chance. After Phu Long, the people of Hoa Luu would never trust ARVN again.

His own Army? Was the leadership interested in winning or was Vietnam regarded as some sort of war game, a vast ticket punching mechanism designed to advance careers? His view was not fair, he chided himself. He was sure that up north, with the U.S. units, it was different, but where was the overall strategy for victory? There had to be something more than "Win the war in the Central Highlands," the search and destroy strategy of General

Westmoreland. Why wasn't more done in the Southern Delta? Was there a focus on securing the population, or was the American strategy exclusively aimed at fighting battles in the boondocks of Vietnam?

He considered the Sergeant Minh theory and the offensive capability of the VC. In Hoa Luu, the way north was open now. With the departure of the ARVN battalion from Phu Long and the Territorial Forces losses over the past few months, the VC had the capability to stage major offensive operations along the two canals. They were quiet now, but the capability was there. Nobody would listen to this threat. It wasn't "keeping it quiet."

He had fought with heroes. Nobody was braver than the Hoa Hao Binh Sys, the Tigers. There were no finer soldiers than Flip Cochran, the Grey Ghost, and Bob Harris. His team, the Hoa Luu Muckers, were magnificent men: the compassion of Doc Gonzales, the young, steadfast loyalty of Billy Turner, solid Cal Washington, the epitome of the United States Army NCO Corps, and Sergeant Minh, the sad little man who alone had a clear vision for winning this war. Even Don Burns had found himself and had become a valuable member of the team before an enemy mortar round had blown his back open. But what about the senior American leadership? He recalled Bob Harris' words months ago quoting from POGO, 'We have met the enemy and he is us.' The "keep it quiet" tactic wasn't working. The VC were gathering strength at known base areas. He recalled the words of the Grey Ghost, 'There are many Vinh Cheos in Vietnam.' Was there going to be a major attack?

In Hoa Luu something had worked. The objective of winning had bloomed strongly for a time and then withered in the fires of Phu Long. The Hoa Hao had acted as a catalyst. They were strong, moral people. But there was more than that. The Territorial Forces related to the people because they were of the people, almost like colonial militia. They had an immediate stake in winning, and their battle performance reflected this urgency. MACV didn't appreciate their relevance to the war. Leaders like Major Tho and Commander Re demonstrated courageous leadership. Their soldiers would follow them anywhere, and the people knew they cared. For a time, the Pacification Task Force had worked in Phu Long. And, admitted Jack, the advisory effort had been strong. His team and the Vietnamese had been one.

Who were the losers and the winners in the Hoa Luu war? There were no winners. The Delta people were the losers. For a time, some of these people had been given a chance for a better life. This had been lost in the carnage of Phu Long.

A phrase kept repeating itself. These people trusted us; they trusted me.

He was responsible for their deaths, their dashed hopes.

Through his thoughts he caught snatches of the citation. "Heroism in the face of fire," "cool against overwhelming odds," "total disregard for his own safety." And finally, "Reflects great credit on himself and the military service." Cal Washington handed General Wells the Silver Star. He fumbled with the decoration for a second then pinned it on Jack's left breast pocket. Jack felt the tiger claw warm his chest, a brief surge of pride for the Silver Star. At least, here he had been a warrior. But what did these medals really represent? Defeat, victory, or just pieces of metal and ribbon for surviving an impossible situation?

"Congratulations, young man. You've done an outstanding job. Best of luck at Leavenworth. Perhaps we can serve together again in Germany," General Wells said, keeping his eyes fixed on a point above Jack's head.

The helicopter was ticking over on the province road. The crew, as always, was anxious to get out of Indian country. They wanted to pull pitch and reach the safety envelope of 1500 feet. Doc and Billy were doing a heroic job keeping the kids from the aircraft. Today they enjoyed the task. They were next. They would leave the following week. Jack had said his farewell to the team earlier that morning. Doc and Billy waved and shouted above the aircraft noise, "See you in the world, Boss. Remember the Mucker reunion. You promised to provide the booze."

Commander Re, Cal, and Sergeant Minh accompanied him to the helicopter and helped him throw his gear on board. "Whatever happens, Major Travis, you did your best here. I will never forget you," Sergeant Minh said. The beginnings of tears were filling his eyes.

Cal's huge black hand grabbed his. "Boss, professional soldiers never say goodbye. I will always remember this tour. It's been a helluva ride." The two men looked warmly at each other. "We'll serve together again."

"I know," Jack said. They saluted.

Commander Re placed his hand on Jack's shoulder. "We who wear the tiger's claw are together even if oceans and continents separate us." The Commander paused. "The war, my good friend, is not over. Remember that, in Vietnam, there is no moral alternative to victory." Jack tried to talk to this man, the biggest man he would ever meet. Words would not come; he could only nod.

The helicopter lifted off in a cloud of billowing dust and rapidly reached 1500 feet. Jack refused to look out the side window. He had seen enough of this cruel multi-colored land of brown canals, green rice paddies, light blue skies and towering, rain swollen clouds. This beauty was like a matador's cape, hiding fear and sudden death.

With a rush, her memory was with him. He could not keep her locked away in the cobwebbed parts of his mind. Co Linh, Co Linh—her name pealed over and over like the bells of mourning.

EPILOGUE

On the evening of January 31, 1968, six months after Major Travis departed Hoa Luu District, 70,000 enemy soldiers stormed out of base areas such as Vinh Cheo and assaulted over a hundred cities in Vietnam. Thirteen out of sixteen province capitals in the Mekong Delta were hit. The audacity and power of the attack amazed the world. Surprise was complete.

In the South, the doctrine of "keeping it quiet" had failed. The Viet Cong had built up a strong, highly motivated force and had shattered the undeclared treaty of accommodation.

In the North, the twin battle cries of "Search and Destroy" and "Winning the War in the Central Highlands" had become empty slogans. U.S. Forces and ARVN had been tempted out of position to fight in the under populated areas of Vietnam. Napoleonic in concept, the strategic objective of the Viet Minh and North Vietnamese was to deceive U. S. and ARVN Forces to operate away from the objective, and then drive for the unprotected jugular, the population centers of Vietnam.

To prepare for this campaign during the year before Tet '68, battles were conducted throughout Vietnam that varied in scope from the enormous confrontation around Khe Sanh in the North to tiny campaigns in the South such as the Silk Over Steel campaign in Hoa Luu District. These battles were designed to open the way to population centers and denude these areas of security.

Tet '68 worked. Much ink has been spilled on this campaign, which addresses the theoretical questions such as the real nature of the North Vietnamese objectives, and whether or not Tet was a tactical victory for U. S. Forces. These questions are not relevant to his novel, or perhaps even history. The real story of Tet is not the short campaign, but why it was allowed to occur in the first place, and the political aftermath of the battle. Tet '68 was a disaster for our nation of colossal proportions:

— Public opinion accelerated rapidly against the war. People had lost confidence in the national leadership to win in Vietnam. This had a terrible adverse effect on the morale of the American military.

— The presidency of Lyndon B. Johnson drowned in the rains of Tet. He did not run for re-election in November.

215

— General Westmoreland was kicked upstairs to Army Chief of Staff. On a trip to Washington a few months before Tet he had reassured his government that the war was going well.

— The U. S. entered into negotiations with the North Vietnamese that dragged on for five long years and ended with the United States abandoning their South Vietnamese allies.

— The Vietnam hangover shackled American foreign policy for years. Only recently has our nation emerged from this malaise. Even today, the specter of Vietnam provides a sobering backdrop for the War on Terrorism.

The Sampan War is a novel; it is also a serious commentary on a part of the Vietnam War. Perhaps the events surrounding the story and those that have occurred since add pathos and irony to the human tragedy of Hoa Luu District. According to Jack Travis, there were no winners, and the real losers were the people of Phu Long, and, by implication, simple people throughout Vietnam, people who trusted us.

Printed in the United States
68249LVS00005B/1-99